Turn Over the Moon

Saga of the Sorrowless

BOOK I

Ryan Harvey

DREAM TOWER MEDIA

Published by Dream Tower Media.
https://dreamtowermedia.com

Cover art by Zoltan. All rights reserved. To see more work, go to https://zoltanillustration.com. Book Design by Robert Zoltan.

ISBN-13:

OTHER BOOKS FROM DREAM TOWER MEDIA

Rogues of Merth: The Adventures of Dareon and Blue, Book 1

The Long Long Long Long Rescue: A Tale of the Incomparable Quill, Book 1

Betting on the Shadows (Contemporary and Dark Fantasy Tales of Transformation and Redemption)

Tomorrow Girl (and Other Tales of Time Travel, Strange Dimensions, and Alternate Realities)

Sign up for the Dream Tower Media newsletter for information on other releases

https://dreamtowermedia.com/contact/

Listen to Literary Wonder & Adventure Show

https://dreamtowermedia.com/podcast/

For my nephews
Diego and Axel

ACKNOWLEDGMENTS

This whole project may never have started if it weren't for a comment Bill Ward sent to me in an email pointing out that my short story "Farewell to Tyrn" sounded like "a good opening for a novel." Ten days later, I started writing that novel. Thanks for the push I didn't know I needed, Bill!

Throughout creating *Turn Over the Moon* I've enjoyed the support and assistance of numerous people. I would most like to thank Robert Zoltan, Howard Andrew Jones, and John O'Neill for the support that kept me moving ahead against the Sorrow— which very much exists in our world as well as Belde's.

Thank you to all our Kickstarter backers
Suzanne Bacon, Howard Bampton, Chris Beal, Lauren Bennett, Jamie Bisson, Noah Browning, William Carr, Jennifer Choy, Eileen Clark, Storn Cook, William Crawford, The Creative Fund by BackerKit, Patricia D'Orange-Martin, James Enge, Mark James Featherston, Cassandra Freeman, GtheStalker, FredH, Casey Hansen, Corky and Dean Harvey, Cassie Woolrich Harvey, Reed

Harvey, Joseph Hoopman, Barbara Ingram, Eric Jacob, Jennifer, Howard A. Jones, Brandon Juarez, Marianne Kent, Bobbi Knight, Dorothy Kuehnel, James Ladd, John McGuiggan, Armin Martin, Colleen Martin, Kai Martin, Ross Martinson, Matt, Jenny Motzkus, Sandra Mueller, Claire Olsem, Ootagee, Jim Paprocki, Kay Perman, Cheryl Petran, Emilia Pulliainen, Sue Sievers, Shari Elliott Perman Smith, Jim Stavropoulos, Stirring Dragon Games, Robin Sutton, MaryAnn Toner, Chris Torrence, Bill Ward, K. Wilson, Russell Winslow, and Christian Wood.

VEDIL SEA

SHAPER PENINSULA

ATAMI

• Sono

• Katura

• Thulia

Mount
Miurn

OCCILAND
The Gray Lands

• Iyalonda

TEMBLOR
PLAINS

FENCER MOUNTAINS

GLOSS GRASS
PLAINS

Gloser River

Black
Spires

•

• Gaspuh

• Tyrn

• Lodev

BELLINGHAZER
SEA

IDEN

• Rolt

Orkimogg?

AMAN-SAH SEA

ACIVIS
WILDS

BAVTUU LANDS

HADEON MOUNTAINS

Cloudy Top Forests

TAVISH SEA

LAKKAD

Khoromel

CIRRUS MOUNTAINS

Kazee

Urbarg River

Duranji R.

NAJAEL

Lake
Mustok

Karezar

Mirn

LAND of
SCARS

First Scar?

The Summoner?

Dubun-Geb Mts

Donaj River

JALASK PLAINS

Belische?

VATRUSLA

Bljana

Durvill

RAHSS SEA

Turn Over the Moon

Saga of the Sorrowless

Book I

ONE

The Shapers can reach me in my dreams. I escaped their clutches once, but in the blackness of sleep they tear open the walls of my head and slither inside.

In each nightmare they glare down on me as they once glared down on all the land, from the edge of the eastern desert to the dwindling tip of the western peninsula. As they once glared down on my father, bound across his own workbench for their tortures. Even though their eyes are drowned within the dark slits of their masks, I can feel their stares. The robes hiding their bodies flutter around me in a barrier. There is nothing beyond.

The tallest of the wizards, an Artikon draped in black, points a crooked finger at me.

"Sorrowless girl, we shall find you. You cannot flee from us forever."

I try to shout back. These monsters murdered my father and mother. I must answer them. But I can't make a sound. A sorcery of the Shapers, a working of their Art, throttles me.

But then a scream does tear through the dark. It's not mine, but Father's. One of the last sounds I ever heard him make, as the Shapers forced their mind-searing Art on him.

The scream blots away the creatures in masks, and only a gray wisp of them remains. The smoke trail begins to take on a familiar shape, but too soon it drifts away. A voice whispers after it, warm as summer grass, and kindles an ember of hope in me:

I will come for you, little one.

It is the voice of the Woman. Sorrowless ... like me.

TWO

I cried so much the day I escaped from Tyrn that I didn't think I had any tears left. But each time the wagon wheels bumped over a rock and jostled me awake, I felt the wet stain on my cheeks. The Shapers came for me when my eyes were closed, but the world did not look much better when they were open.

I had spent the journey north among Mother's tribesmen hidden under the canvas of a cart filled with spice barrels. It was midsummer and the constant sun made it hard to tell how long the caravan had rolled over the Gloss Grass Plains. A week, maybe. A hundred years, possibly.

The last bump had brought the cart to a halt. The squeaking wheels of the other wagons in the caravan had fallen silent, replaced by the noise of people unloading them. Rain beat on the canvas over my head.

"Rint," I called. The little beak-nose poked his head from around one of the spice barrels and chirped at me.

"We must be there," I said, and made the motion that meant

home to him. Except I made the sign with a limp drop of my hand, because we were not really home. We never would be again.

Rint thrust out his neck and long tail and started weaving among the spice casks. He cracked the hard tip of his beak against each one to make sure there were no devil claws hiding inside. Since we had escaped the Shapers in Tyrn, he had taken on the job of looking out for me with the stout heart of a royal guardian. He knew we were no longer playing games in the streets with other children.

When he came near enough, I grabbed his leafy green body and held him to me. His short forearms gripped my tunic, and his stub of a tongue licked the tears from my face.

"It's just the two of us now," I told him. He tilted his head and looked at me with his emerald eyes. The slit of his pupil expanded as if he understood what I was saying. Maybe he did.

I listened to the voices of the Koltzer men and women around me. Mother had taught me a few words of her language when I was younger. Now I wished she had taught me more. But she never expected her daughter would one day have to seek refuge among these nomads. Mother married a handsome harness-maker of the cities to escape from her people, from their harsh lands and crude ways.

I pushed up an edge of the canvas to get a better look at where we had stopped. The sun had vanished behind storm clouds and the rain made a glistening wall, but I could see the enormous humps of mountains against the sky. A shiver passed through my skin. The Fencer Mountains were tiny smudges of black I used to see on clear summer days when Rint and I played on the roof of Father's workshop. I never imagined I would come so close to them.

A week ago I had never imagined a lot of things.

Rint let go of my tunic and curled into the warmth of my lap. I thought about going to sleep again. If I could dream beyond the Shapers, I might wake up back in my home, with Mother and Father alive and the horrors of that last day nothing more than smoke.

I had closed my eyes for only a moment when there was a tearing noise. A hundred needles of cold rain struck my face.

"Are you the Idenite girl?"

I put my arm across my face to shield it from the downpour, so I couldn't see the owner of the gruff voice.

"Are you deaf? Are you the city girl or not?"

"Y-yes," I answered.

"Time to stop cowering. If you're going to live with Kalzzik's tribe, you work. We don't have a place for bed-sulks, especially little wet-blood girls."

I was so shocked from the rain that I only then realized he was speaking my language. "You know Idenite?"

"What do you think?" he snorted.

"I've never met any Koltzer who knew more than a few words, except my mother."

"So now you know two. Some of us have to volunteer to go into your sewer cities to trade. Now are you going to get your lazy carcass out and help pitch camp, or would you rather drown when the cart fills up?"

I pulled myself over the side and sloshed onto the grass. Rint hopped out and landed beside me. I didn't feel like working at this bully's orders, but I wanted him to see that Belde of Tyrn wasn't a city weakling, and that the Koltzer side of my family made me more than just a "wet-blood." But the rain washed over our faces in waterfalls, and under the blackened sky I couldn't make out much of him aside from his oak-beam bulk.

Whatever he saw of me wasn't impressive. I was shivering in

the rain and the wind gnawed through the thin linen shirt and trousers that were the summer wear for city children.

"Drowned rats look heartier than you," he said. "I'll bet you can't even lift a wagon wheel."

"I can work as good as any boy my age."

"And what's that?"

"Twelve summers."

"A Koltzer woman can hoist a whole cart on her back by eleven summers. I'll bet you city scuts hire slaves to hoist your skirt edges from the mud."

"What's your name?" I asked in Koltzer. I wanted this futch to know I understood some of his language as well.

"Dyzlin, son of Ulgitz. And I know your name. You're Belde, the wet-blood who came crying to the chief for protection. I don't want half-city scuts in our tribe."

"Too bad. Kalzzik made me part of the tribe and doesn't care what you think about it, Dyzlin, son of Ulgitz."

A sheet of white light spilled over both of us. The tribesmen had staked down iron posts holding shielded torches while they worked. The torch-glow was cold and without comfort, but it gave off enough light for Dyzlin and I to see each other clearly at last.

He had the thick, mutton-slab build of the Koltzer, but he was hardly a man. His smooth features showed his real age—maybe only a summer older than me. He had the fair and flinty handsomeness of his people, but everything else about him shouted "brute," like the boys of Tyrn who enjoy chopping off the legs of beak-noses just to hear the yelps they make. He wore the rough clothing the Koltzer favored: a gray hooded tunic and thick hadroskin breeches. It made him seem bigger than he was. Still, he was big.

As Dyzlin looked me over, his surliness started to change. He wasn't seeing a sopping wet rat anymore, but something he couldn't fit neatly into his mind.

"I've heard the stories about you. The Shapers are chasing you because you're one of those sick people who—"

Suddenly, he couldn't stand to meet my gaze. He turned to look at Rint, who shivered at my knees.

"Is this beak-nose your pet?" he asked.

"His name is Rint."

"That's stupid, naming a saurian. They're good for pack animals and mounts. What's the point of naming one?"

"I'll show you." I looked down at Rint, and as I spoke I made a hand-signal to help him interpret my words: "Rint, *mean boy!*"

Rint flew at Dyzlin and grabbed onto his shirt with his forepaws. He snapped his beak at the boy's face—not trying to cut him, only scare him enough so he'd soil his trousers. Dyzlin lurched backwards and splashed into the mud on his rump.

He swatted at the pecking green blur. "Get this thing off me! I'll kill it!"

"I'm sure Rint is terrified."

I clapped my hands. Rint forgot about Dyzlin and hopped back to my side. I reached for the pouch where I kept fern buds as treats for Rint, but they were used up days ago.

Dyzlin struggled back to his feet. Mud coated his back so thickly that if he turned away from us, he'd be invisible against the dark sky. "You'll be sorry for that, city scut! My clan is one of the highest in the tribe, and—"

"And my great-uncle is the chief, so you can go chew grass."

"You'll learn to respect our ways, wet-blood," he shouted, although he kept his distance in case I sicced my horrid, insect-eating, one-foot tall fiend on him again. "It doesn't matter if you're —if you're one of *those* people. I'll make enough Sorrow for you myself."

He gave me a last venomous look, then sloshed off toward where the tribesmen were circling the mounts.

I didn't know if Dyzlin's boasting was only swamp gas or if I had made a serious enemy. But the moment had taken my mind off the life I had left behind.

Glowering in the rain would eventually get me the coughing sickness, so I started toward the center of camp and the massive hide tent the tribe was raising for the chieftain's home. My great-uncle would be in the middle of the flurry. I pulled a blanket from the back of a covered wagon when nobody was looking and draped it over my shoulders. It was made of coarse grass-weave, but it was better than my soggy shirt.

The wind slapped the long grass against my trousers. The thick heaps of green felt strange under my moccasins. Until then, the only grass I had ever walked on was the chubby shoots that grow around Tyrn and along the banks of where the Glosser River flows beside the city.

Of all the cities of Iden, Tyrn lies the nearest to the expanse of the Gloss Grass Plains. I grew up gazing from rooftops at this boundless sward rolling away to the north. I wondered how Mother's people could stand to live in such emptiness. Of course she would want to marry Father and escape from all that open nothing. Life in the city was filled with the babble of market squares, crowded cobbled streets, and massive stone walls that set comforting boundaries. I believed this world was large enough for anyone.

Now I was far from Tyrn and deep in the Gloss Grass Plains where the only walls were the fabric of tents. Here the Koltzer fought tribal wars, grazed herds of sluggish hadrosaurs, and hunted and were hunted by nychs and ravagers and the other killers of the steppes. There was one solid border, however, more titanic than any city wall. A branch of the Fencer Mountains was close enough to block out half the sky. The greatest mountain range in Ahn-Tarqa, these cold peaks split the continent into east and west and flung out arms into the plains on one side and into the forests and deserts on the other.

I preferred the boundaries of city walls. The mountains gave no comfort and made the world too large.

The middle of the camp was a turmoil of men and beasts. The ceratopses that pulled the caravan wagons over the steppes were now helping to hoist tents with ropes lashed around their horns. Leaders of the different clans within the tribe shouted instructions from the backs of their hadrosaurs. Each hadro had war paint on its head crest to show how many enemies its rider had slain. Under the rain and clouds the whole scene was deep with the Sorrow. Only the Koltzer's brash pushing to get the shelters up in time to dry off and eat kept them moving against the Sorrow's flow.

The Sorrow, however, was not my concern.

Rint's forepaws hooked onto my trousers. A crestless hadrosaur, its head far above mine, bellowed in irritation as it loped past us. Rint quivered. He was used to the light riding hadros of city lanes. This draft beast dragging a sledge was twice as tall as anything he'd seen.

The man on the sledge whipping the hadro snarled at us as he passed. "It's okay," I whispered to Rint as I placed him back down in the wake of the sledge. "Everything around here is bigger and dumber. But we'll get used to it."

I spotted my great-uncle among the stir, seated on a wooden chair strapped across the back of a club-tail. Kalzzik was a boulder of a man with a beard that jutted from his chin like a thorn shrub from a cliffside. I couldn't understand much of what he said, but he was yelling at his soaked tribesmen as if they were whiners for slowing down for even a moment in the rain. The only words I understood were a curse he repeated again and again: "You Sorrow-gorged maggots!"

Days before, when I lurched my exhausted body into Kalzzik's tent outside the city walls to beg for shelter, he seemed like the kindest man in all the land. He was Mother's uncle and the only family I had left. Of course he felt like a friendly protector. But the chieftain bellowing orders over thunderclaps was a different man, as unforgiving as the stones of the Fencer Mountains.

I stood under an awning raised on the side of a caravan and thought about whom to approach to ask what I could do to help. I was practicing a few phrases I might try in the Koltzer language when I heard a voice beside me.

"Belde? You are Belde?"

I thought Dyzlin had returned and was ready to make good on his threats. But the boy who had slipped under the awning beside me resembled Dyzlin only in age and his gray clothes.

"You know me?" I spoke in Idenite, not thinking.

He shook his head, and stuttered in a thick accent: "Don't know."

I tried his language: "I, Kalzzik's blood. Yes?"

He nodded, then pointed to himself. "Holzir, son of Iker." He tugged at his ear and then pointed at me.

"You've heard about me," I said in Idenite, and nodded to show I understood.

He pointed to the caravan door. He said something I thought might be "inside," and then started up the steps. I waited for a moment, wondering why a boy who only knew me as a half-blood relation of the chieftain wanted me to enter what was probably the caravan of his clan.

At first I didn't want to go after him. But there was nowhere else to go. I was curious—as well as cold and damp. So I followed the boy named Holzir.

The interior of the caravan was cramped. An oil lamp suspended from a chain on the center beam cast light for me to see two bed slats and a clutter of tools, rope, and pewter pots and pans. The acrid stench of quake-foot blubber from the lamp drenched everything. A clay model of a city stood on a shelf: the craftsmanship was of Vatrusla, a place I knew only from the stories of sailors who docked in Tyrn to trade silks and weird chunks of the Art from distant ports. Next to the model was a half-finished ornament of colored threads crisscrossing a wooden ring. I did not know the pattern, but it must have come from Najael. Anything you don't recognize must come from the deserts of Najael—that's what people say in Tyrn.

In the shadows at the far end of the caravan I saw a quiver of movement. A person lay on an upper bunk, swaddled in a wrap. The cloth rose and fell with shallow breaths, the only hint that what was underneath was alive.

I didn't think more about the sleeping figure, because now I had my first good look at Holzir under the light. Like all the nomad folk of the Gloss Grass Plains, he had pale skin and golden hair. The sturdy build of his shoulders looked like it could stop a falling iron plank. But he was smaller than most Koltzer, and his face was slender with high cheekbones that made sharp shadows across his face under the lamp.

Absently, I touched my own face. I was half-Koltzer. How much of Mother's blood showed? Did my lean frame and darker hair from Father mark me in the tribe's eyes as a "wet-blood"? And there was something else about myself I had learned only recently, and which would be far worse in the eyes of the tribe than being a wet-blood.

However I appeared to this boy, he didn't seem bothered. But his eyes couldn't focus on me. They'd meet my gaze for a moment, then swing away, glancing over my shoulder or down at my feet.

Holzir spoke a word in his language, then made a motion across his face, like he was tugging something over his eyes.

I shook my head. "Don't know," I fumbled in Koltzer.

He repeated the motion. The veins corded along the back of his hand, and his blue eyes drilled straight into mine for a brief moment. Their sheen of sadness explained it all.

The Sorrow. That was what he was saying. The word was different in his language, but in either Koltzer or Idenite it had the echo of a stone plunging down an iron shaft, clanging against the sides until it fades.

I nodded to show I understood. It was his Sorrow keeping Holzir inside instead of helping pitch camp. The Sorrow boils higher on some days than others, although it always simmers. As one crowd of tribesmen labored in the rainfall to set up camp, another crowd huddled inside their caravans, hidden under blankets, while a feeling of hopelessness crushed them. In a few days, the men who now faced the storm would have their time of loneliness in the dark, hiding from life. Back in Tyrn, my friends would sometimes abruptly stop playing in the streets and start to stare at the ground. They'd mutter about needing to go home, and then shuffle off with shoulders stooped and heads crooked as if their parents had punished them. Adults hid their Sorrow better, but there were times when Mother didn't leave the house for days at a time, seeing no one and never answering the door. She and Father spent evening meals inspecting bits of gristle in their stew and only grunting single-word answers when I spoke. They weren't upset at me or at each other. They were upset at life, at having to live. That's what the Sorrow is. Father told me it is everywhere, across all of the lands. Everyone suffers from it.

Almost everyone.

"The Sorrow," I spoke in my language, and copied Holzir's motion across my face.

He tried the word in Idenite, and it came off his tongue with no accent. In any language, the Sorrow is as familiar as your own name.

He forced his eyes to meet mine again for a heartbeat, and he made the motion over his face but stopped halfway. Then he pointed his finger at me.

I understood his meaning: *No Sorrow.*

I nodded. I couldn't explain, and not just because we didn't know each other's language. I scarcely knew what *No Sorrow* meant. Only days ago I had found out it was possible for a person to be without it, and that on Ahn-Tarqa there were those who lived without the feeling life was a waste and that nothing they ever did mattered. Even if I had known it, why would I believe that I was one of those people? "The Sorrowless."

My world crumbled in a single brutal day. My parents were killed, I lost my home, and all I could think of doing was to curl into a ball, holding so tight I would fold in on myself and vanish. To think I was "Sorrowless" sounded like a cruel joke.

But I had reasons to feel sad. The Sorrow needed no reasons. It simply was. And I had the flicker of hope. The whispered promise of another who did not have the Sorrow. The one who had saved my life and sent me to safety with these words:

I will come for you, little one.

I stepped closer to Holzir. He backed away and almost tripped over Rint, who was investigating the bunks to see if any deadly nychs were hiding under them. Rint leaped onto a shelf, knocking over empty glass jars, and hissed at Holzir from eye-level.

"No," I said to Rint, and placed a hand across the ridges running from his neck to his tail. "Friend." I made the sign with my hand to be certain he understood. Although he stopped hissing, he kept skeptical eyes trained on the Koltzer boy.

Holzir swayed back up and found himself only a foot from me.

Now I saw him without shadows. His Sorrow was strong, but he had innocence in his eyes, a quality the Koltzer don't prize.

"Friend," I repeated, and not for Rint this time.

Holzir almost smiled. He turned from me, ducked under a bench, and scrounged through a heap of objects jammed underneath it. Pots and dishes clinked, and then he backed out clutching a wooden object the size of a large book.

Rint inched toward him, his head tilted with curiosity. I followed, and kneeled across from where Holzir sat on the floor. He held the wooden box out toward me. It had a grid of squares painted along both sides and a rusted latch holding it closed.

He laid the box on the caravan floorboards and unfastened the latch. Inside was a set of smooth pebbles. Rint bit at one, but I gently shooed him back and picked up the stone. On one side was a painting of the sun with yellow beams stretching to the edge. I flipped it over. On the reverse side was a crescent moon in gray paint with flecks of silver that sparkled under the lamplight.

I had seen this game played in Tyrn, usually on benches outside taverns. It was called "Sun-or-Moon," and although I had never played it, the rules were familiar.

Holzir started setting up the board. He poured the stones onto the floor and separated them into two piles. The top of the open box created the playing space.

Holzir was intent on trying to explain the rules to me using pantomime. He placed four starting pieces on the board, two showing suns and two showing moons. He pointed to a sun and then to me, and then gestured to the moon and himself. He reached toward one of the pieces in my pile, since Sun had the first move, to show me what to do. But I pushed his hand back and picked up a piece and laid it on the board with the sun looking up. It bracketed a moon piece between another sun, and I turned over the trapped moon so it showed its brighter face.

For a moment, it felt as if I had turned back the Month of the Moon, the dreary days of deep winter when the Sun never peeked over the horizon. Outside now it was the Month of the Sun, but the storm had blotted away the light. The painted suns looking up at me made me smile.

I turned the smile on him. "Your move."

A touch of a grin turned up his mouth—this wet-blood girl *did* know how to play! But he still couldn't look me straight in the face. He placed a moon onto the board to turn over a line of my suns.

He beat me that first game. Harshly. Not a single sun looked up at the end, and I didn't like the sight. I was determined to win next time. Holzir won again, but a few suns beamed up among the victorious moons. Holzir cleared the stones, and we started working on my third loss.

Rint curled up on my lap while Holzir and I played Sun-or-Moon beneath the blubber lamp. The music of the rain on the roof and tribal work songs echoed around us, but we had our own world in the circle of light shining on the board. Playing the game seemed to ease Holzir's Sorrow, and it made me think perhaps I could get used to living among the Koltzer.

For a while, at least. Until the woman disguised behind a Shaper mask and robe fulfilled her promise and came to fetch me. One of the Sorrowless.

THREE

"Beltza!"

That crisp afternoon I didn't feel like answering to the name the tribe had picked for me. And I never felt like answering Bixenta, no matter what name she called me. She had a few nasty ones.

"Can you already smell the dung on her shoes, Rint?"

My friend raised his head from the stone where he was basking in a dollop of sun. Rint was less frisky than he was five years ago and enjoyed more sunlit naps.

The voice shrieked again: "Beltza!"

Rint made a snapping motion with his beak. It was his way of showing he hated something. "I understand," I said. "We'll make the crone burst her heart walking all the way up here."

Rint didn't have the muscles in his face to smile, but the twitch of his eyes and slant of his head was just as good.

From almost the moment he hatched, Rint was a remarkable creature. He could read my hand signals and understand basic commands when he was a month old. After a year he could communicate ideas to me and answer complex requests with his body and chirps and whistles. I had never seen a saurian, even the best-trained hunting mounts, show such intelligence. Father was suspicious of this, especially because of where I had discovered Rint's egg. It wasn't in a beak-nose nest, but inside a small barrel in the cellar of an empty villa. The previous owner, a rich apothecary, had vanished years ago, and the crumbling place had a reputation as haunted—which was why I was poking around it in the first place. Father suspected the apothecary dabbled in a forbidden Art, and it was the cause of his sudden disappearance. Perhaps Rint was the remnant of one of the apothecary's experiments, left forgotten in a corner when dark figures dragged the man away into the night.

Regardless of his suspicions, Father recognized that Rint and I had become close, and I was always a lonely child. He let me keep him.

Rint had grown even smarter during our time in Kalzzik's tribe. To others it seemed as if he could read my mind. He was merely reading my tone and hand signals, but he could interpret these so shrewdly that I'd gotten used to talking to him as if he were listening with human ears. I had become fluent in Koltzer in less than two seasons, but I only spoke to Rint in Idenite so I wouldn't forget my first language. One day, I hoped, I'd have a reason to use it again.

"Beltza!" Bixenta's call was now a shriek. Maybe when she reached me I'd tell her I mistook her yells for the shriek of a dying skinwing. A lie, but not a big one.

Bixenta trudged up through the narrow pass into the gorge. She pulled herself along on a walking stick carved from a nych's leg bone. Her ancient muscles were still spry and she didn't need the walking stick except as a brag trophy. She told a story that her dead husband had throttled the nych with his bare hands. Everybody knew he had scavenged the bone from a carcass, but nobody dared say so around Bixenta. She was the chieftain's older sister, after all.

Bixenta spotted me in my loft. "There you are, you gutter filth!" she said as she jabbed up at me with her bone crutch. She couldn't know what a "gutter" was, since she'd never stepped into a city in her life, but she knew it meant something unclean. "An old lady shouldn't wear out her body hunting for you."

I wondered if I could force her to climb up to get me. I was perched in the cleft of a stone that wind from the gullies of the Fencer Mountains had sculpted into a pillar. I had found a few handholds in it and learned to climb up to the natural chair scooped from its top.

Rint skirled and made a charge at Bixenta, almost causing her to topple. He loved to do this and see her reaction, and she fell for it every time. In her eyes Rint was as fierce as one of the Shapers' trained devil claws.

"Rint, stop," I yelled. I had angered Bixenta enough for one day. If I pushed her any farther she might tell Kalzzik, and he would burden me with chores. I slid down from my pillar and walked to where Bixenta leaned against her staff. Her eyes were on Rint in case he decided to charge again. Rint instead yawned and lay down in another patch of sun.

"What's so important, Aunt Bixenta?" I asked. "We can't be ready to break camp yet. It's the night of the Feast."

"Of course not," she said. "My brother wants to see you in his tent. Important tribe business, he says. But I can't imagine what that would have to do with someone like you."

My chest felt tight. If Kalzzik wanted to see me over affairs of the tribe, it couldn't be good news. Perhaps he had finally cowed to requests from the shamans that a girl from the cities, one who did not have the proper Sorrow, had no place in the tribe—even if she was of Kalzzik's blood.

Sometimes I wished they would hurl me out. I could hate them with hot fury: their murky faces and blank eyes and insistence that ignorance was a virtue. But if they threw me out of the tribe, where could I go? Where else would anyone welcome me?

"Tell Kalzzik I'll come down in a few minutes," I said.

"You think you can tell the chieftain to wait? Do you think you're special because you're a city girl? You're only here because your mother was enough of a vile scut to let a man of the sewers lay with her."

I almost struck her. Bixenta was always serpent-tongued, but this was the first time she'd dared speak of my parents with such unveiled disgust. I wanted to kick away her fake crutch and crack the bone in half to make her feel what it was like to lose an heirloom of someone you loved.

I did the next cruelest thing I could. I gave her my "stare."

The Koltzer couldn't endure looking me straight in the face for more than a few heartbeats before wrenching their eyes away, and I learned early how to make this my weapon. If I fixed my stare on them, forced them to look me eye-to-eye, they recoiled as if I had jaws the size of a ravager's.

They didn't understand the word "Sorrowless." They knew I had a kind of witchery about me, something that made me cut through them like a whetted knife. They knew about the sorcery of the Art and the machines the Shapers and city dwellers made with it. But they didn't understand the hex in my eyes, and it terrified them. The "witch-eyes," some called them. I didn't mind the name.

Bixenta squirmed her gray head away from my stare. "Fine, be a gutter brat! Come when you like, but it had better be before the evening meal or Kalzzik will roast and spice you for dinner!"

"I'd taste better than the offal he gorges himself with," I muttered, but Bixenta had already turned on her bone walking stick and was clomping away.

I waited until she vanished down the hill before I snapped my fingers to wake Rint from his doze. He sprang up and made a motion with his forearms: *Where we go?*

"We have to go see great-uncle Kalzzik. Well, I do." Rint wasn't allowed into Kalzzik's pavilion, but I knew whom I could leave him with.

WHEN I FIRST CAME AMONG the tribe, I waited every day to hear word that a mysterious woman had ridden from the south searching for a refugee from Tyrn. "A girl with strange eyes and a keen-minded saurian pet," the visitor might say.

No one came the first month. Or the month after. Or any month for five years. Waiting for the nameless woman was now a ritual. In each meadow where Kalzzik's tribe camped, I scanned the horizon to catch sight of a solitary figure approaching. On the sandy banks of the Glosser River, I watched for a raft with a single sail steering toward the embankment. Near the trade gates of the stinking cities of the Gray Lands, I stole away from the camp to look for a person signaling to me from the ramparts.

Each year my hopes dimmed. But at least I had hope. Those with the Sorrow had none.

The column above Split-Tongue Gorge was my favorite spy-post to watch for my rescuer. It was a clear day, the clouds all having moved south to leave me with a view of an endless sea of grass. But my vigil had shown only a line of quake-foots passing along the plains. The herd of the long-necked giants let me imagine the Woman was somewhere behind it, waiting for them to pass so she could continue her journey across the long grass to save me as she had promised.

The sight of a quake-foot herd would usually draw out a hunting party of the best warriors from camp. But the Feast of the Falling Moon was that night, and the entire tribe was busy. The celebration marked the point where the march toward the Month of the Sun began. The days would now grow longer than the nights, and the Koltzer could forget about the Sorrow-filled Month of the Moon. The three hundred people of Kalzzik's tribe always camped at Split-Tongue Gorge for the Feast of the Falling Moon and the Spring Equinox Rites. The grass valley was a safe camp-ground, where the arms of the Fencer Mountains provided shelter from wind and enemy tribes, and a nameless river brought fresh water from the hills.

People were already gathered around the bonfire in the middle of camp to start early on the Feast, so I had no trouble avoiding them. The leftover winter wind wafted the first songs of the celebration toward me. The Koltzer tribes cannot read or write, their language has no alphabet, but they have a tradition of songs that could fill up a library. Most of the songs are about the Sorrow, and how people struggle to reach Aman-Sah, a mystery place of white where the dead go to be free from the Sorrow.

Tonight the songs were of praise, although they carried the Sorrow's taint. First the songs lauded the Sky Lords, the Koltzer name for the Lightborn worshipped in Idcn. Then they celebrated the Arrival, when these gods appeared in Ahn-Tarqa in a burst of blinding power. Next came battle songs of the distant time of the Hegemony. This was a red-soaked heroic age when the Shapers conquered almost all of Ahn-Tarqa, and the Koltzer fought from hideouts in the mountains against the devilish Art of the sorcerers. The blessings of the Sky Lords protected them until one day the Shapers wearied of their rule and slunk away.

The Koltzer were the only barbarians I had ever been among, but I imagined that simple folk across the continent who had no writing sang similar epics about the bleak days of the war against the Shapers, each using their own name for the Lightborn as they begged for their aid and blessing in Sorrowful times. They sang of the Arrival in the Valley of the First Scar, where the Lightborn gifted to the people of the land both the Art and the Sorrow. In Iden, we praised the Lightborn for giving us wheat, mill wheels, and medicine. The Koltzer praised the Sky Lords for covering the bare lands with grass and domesticating hadrosaurs for mounts.

As I crossed the camp, the tribe's songs leaped forward hundreds of years to nearer generations. One story, which I had heard more times than there were blades of grass on the plains, told how the young warrior Kalzzik had seized leadership of the tribe when he plotted a fearless attack on an enemy tribe. Kalzzik's "fearless attack" was probably selling a cluster of brides to the other chieftain; my great-uncle was more a schemer than a fighter. The Koltzer thought of these bonfire songs as a way to create an inspiring recent history to defend against the Sorrow. I thought of them as lying.

Rint and I passed one of the wooden pens where Kalzzik kept the finest riding hadros. Rint ran to the posts and stuck his head inside to say "hello" to some of the large animals. He liked to try to make friends with hadros, since there were no beak-noses of any kind kept in the camp and hadros were closest to his breed. But the big beasts, shimmering in camouflage stripes of deep green, had no interest in the tiny thing chirping for their attention.

"No play time today, Rint." I snapped my fingers to hurry him on. He made one more chirp, like sticking his tongue out at the saurians who would not notice him, and skipped after me.

The bragging songs were fading when we reached the small pavilion next to the caravan of Holzir's clan. The tent was lopsided and sagging, as if the family's Sorrow had infected their home. Holzir's clan was one of the runts of the tribe and among the least esteemed.

I held my breath as I pushed open the flap. The inside of the tent always stank of illness. The Sorrow doesn't have its own odor, but it can make the reek of sickness worse. Even after many years, it took a few minutes for me to get used to the air inside the sick tent.

"Belde," Holzir said across the dimness. Using my real name, rather than the respectably ugly name of "Beltza" the tribe had forced on me to hide my mixed blood, meant nobody else was inside. Except the woman on the cot, and she had not heard anything in years.

"Uncle left a few minutes ago," Holzir said as I walked closer. "I hear there's a gathering in Kalzzik's tent."

"I'm supposed to be there. Kalzzik apparently has something important to tell me."

"Then why aren't you there?"

"Whatever the business is, they'll only need me after they've made a decision."

I approached the cot and looked at the woman lying on it. Alzane must have been pretty when she was young. In her shrunken skin was a shadow of girlish beauty. She was the artist who had sculpted the clay city and woven the string-hoop I had seen in the wagon the first night I met Holzir. Her mind, when young, had drifted away from the tribes, and her artwork yearned for the distant regions of Ahn-Tarqa. Holzir thought she may have once met a traveling prophet from the deserts of the east, and she had copied the colors of his robes onto her loom.

That was long ago, before she fell into the Sorrow Sleep, before Holzir had a chance to know his mother as anything other than a woman falling into her own sunset.

23

"How is she today?" I asked

"Same as yesterday. The same as tomorrow." Holzir wiped perspiration off Alzane's forehead. The quiver of her skin was the only sign she was alive.

"I don't think I could play Sun-or-Moon with you today, Belde," Holzir said. "I don't—feel much like it." He avoided using the word "Sorrow" with me, as if it was a sin against the Sky Lords to mention the Sorrow to one who did not have it.

He pointed toward a clay bowl on a folding table. "Could you hand me Mother's supper?"

I passed him the bowl of mashed-up bean paste. "I wouldn't have time for a game, anyway," I said. "I wanted to know if you could watch Rint while I go see what Kalzzik wants."

"Of course, it's no bother." Holzir stirred a spoon in the bowl, scooped up a helping of the paste, and gently opened his mother's mouth. He pushed the spoon in, pressed on her jaw until her mouth shut, and then drew the spoon out through her closed lips. He held her head back against the pillows until she swallowed.

Most people would have left the woman to starve, but Holzir believed that if Alzane could still eat, there must be a cobwebbed place deep within her, trapped among the strands of the Sorrow, that wanted to live.

I watched Holzir take exquisite care spoon-feeding his mother, and felt ashamed that I often thought he was more fortunate than me—even lucky. I didn't have this much of a mother left. I didn't even know how my mother had died.

Holzir handed the bowl back to me, but his eyes were on Alzane's face. "Belde, please don't look at me. I want you to go."

This was how Holzir's Sorrow often spoke. I usually didn't hold it against him when he wanted to be alone, or when he told me he could no longer face the brightness of my eyes.

But right then, anger crawled out of me. "What's the rock in your boot today?"

"You know."

"Maybe I don't. You're not giving me the same Sorrow as usual."

He didn't like it when I used *that* word, but he said nothing about it.

In the pause that lingered after, a song from the bonfires reached us on the wind. A woman's voice, bright as a full winter moon, leaped in forced joy:

> *Kalzzik is dazzling among chiefs!*
> *Kalzzik is magnificent among chiefs!*
> *Before this ravager of the grass,*
> *This iron gate of the mountain pass,*
> *Armies of Iden, the Emperor of Rolt*
> *Cower, cringe, piss, and bolt!*

Holzir snorted at the pompous words and terrible rhymes. "I hate those 'praise songs.' " He said. "I'd rather have a Sorrow-filled one."

"Me too."

Then, suddenly, he decided to sing one. He stroked his mother's cheek as he began. I recognized the song from its first strains: "The Ever-Sorrow of Belische." But I had never listened to the lyrics before, really heard them:

> *Ashes of the Sorrow!*
> *Dust of the Dead!*
> *Who now recalls the City of Seven Rivers:*
> *Vatrusla's gemstone, Belische so proud?*
> *Yet beneath the Shapers she bowed,*

A Sorrow crusted over Sorrow's scab.
"Burn the Sky!" the Shapers cried—
Towers bent and stones melted,
And thus you all, under the Sorrow, did die.
Bones you are now, or less—soil for stones,
Belische's mourners, never leaving
For the late funeral feasts.
Are you worse for this fate in fire
That you could not escape?
Better that you died,
Better they killed you,
And scattered your dust in south winds.
Oh Dust, if I could Raise the Earth,
I'd tell your shades plain:
The Sorrow is mightier than you!
The Sorrow is mightier than life!

Although it was the first time I had opened my ears to the song, I knew the story of Belische. It was in Vatrusla, a misty place of seafarers thousands of leagues away, across the middle barrier of the Fencer Mountains and south of the hills of Dubun-Geb and the Jalask Plains. Somewhere on a river delta once stood a magnificent city called Belische. The Shapers conquered it when they conquered all of Ahn-Tarqa. Then one red day, the city was destroyed in an instant—and every song and tale tells of different villains responsible, different magics that changed Belische into a pit of ash and smoke.

I didn't know if Belische was real or not. But Holzir's voice, a deep, soothing sound, gave me visions of melting towers and a scarred sky. It was a song filled with the Sorrow, but it gave me a bizarre shiver. I'd rarely heard my friend sing, and I wondered how many other people knew he had this skill.

Yet all I could say was, "I wish I could sing."

"Your people have writing. You don't need to sing. If you want to remember your stories, you write them down."

"And why did you sing that song?"

"To remind myself I shouldn't fear. The Sorrow takes us all one day." He put the last spoonful of gruel into his mother's mouth.

"That's not what I feel from the song. It seems angry to me. Why should the people of Belische be killed for no reason? Why accept it and just say 'the Sorrow is better'?"

Holzir shrugged. "Everything looks different to you. You're not like me. Or any of us." He still would not turn to look at me.

"That's not the reason. Think about the story: no matter what your poems say, those people in Belische didn't have to die. They could have left the city before it was destroyed."

"How could they have known to leave?"

"That's not the point, Holzir. If they did know about it, wouldn't they choose to run from it? And if you know about the Sorrow, wouldn't you run from it as well?"

"It sounds so simple for you." He wiped a speckle of gruel from his mother's chin with his tunic sleeve. "I'll be like this one day."

"Not everyone falls into the Sorrow Sleep."

"No, they get ahead of it. They go crazy on a battlefield and get themselves slaughtered. Or they charge into a mad duel they can't win."

That was what happened to Holzir's father, Iker, when Holzir was seven summers old. Iker had taken a challenge in a blood feud over an accusation he had cheated in a quake-riding trial. He died under the edge of his enemy's axe. Iker's death toppled Alzane into the Sorrow Sleep that takes those who live too long— or suffer too much when too young.

Holzir sighed. "Which way will I go, Belde? Don't tell me you haven't thought about it. You look at all of us, me especially, and you wonder how the Sorrow will hack us down."

"I'll die too, someday."

"Not like this." He put his hand on the forehead of the breathing corpse of his mother. "You get to choose, Belde. You only have to feel horrible about your life if you have a reason to. You could have fled from Belische. I don't have that choice."

I was suddenly standing over him, my cheeks flushed red. "Don't tell me about choices, Holzir! I had all my choices ripped away from me five years ago. I didn't ask to be different from you. Do you think I feel wonderful because I can hold up my head around people who scuttle away from me as if I were a walking curse? Do you think 'Sorrowless' means I'm never afraid?"

He looked dwarfish under me, as if I were one of the fabled metal colossuses of the wars with the Shapers and he was a lone warrior standing against it with a toy spear. But he wasn't trying to fight me. He wouldn't even raise his head.

"I know why Kalzzik wants to see you," he said.

The change of subject made me sit back down. "How did you find out?"

"Gechina. She's always the first to bring me gossip."

Gechina was one of my cousins, Bixenta's granddaughter. She warded off the Sorrow in her own vicious way, by spreading every slanderous story she heard and adding her own embellishments. She was closer to the center of the clan than I was, so whatever she had told Holzir was probably near to the truth.

"What did she tell you?"

"I—I can't speak about it. My clan is already low around the fires. If anyone thinks I talked—"

I patted his hand. It was warmer than I expected. His fingers curled. For a short breath it felt like he wanted to seize my arm and keep me sitting there, despite what he had said about wanting me to leave.

I wouldn't force him to tear his thoughts in two. I got up and made a clicking noise to call Rint, who had stood patiently at the tent's entrance. "I'll come back after Kalzzik's done with me. It'll be all right, you'll see."

"Easy for someone like you to say."

I didn't take the bait for a new argument. "I'm sorry we can't play Sun-or-Moon. Tomorrow. Keep an eye on Rint." I moved for the tent flap and out into the daylight before Holzir could say anything more.

"Rint," I whispered before I let the tent flap drop. I pointed to my eyes, and then into the tent. "Keep an eye on him."

Rint clucked that he would.

FOUR

A Koltzer camp is a hideous mess to see either up close or from far away. If you're riding toward one, the lumpy tents resemble clumps of dried hadro dung on the grass, ready to flake away at the next wind. Once you're inside the maze of pavilions and painted wagons, the camp becomes an insect colony that has lost its queen and is scraping by the best it can. And it still smells of hadro dung.

Kalzzik's pavilion was the only one in the camp dyed a different color from the beige of quake-foot hide. He had bathed the canvas in purple dye so it stood out in the camp like an open sore. A pennant stolen from an Idenite scout flapped from the peak, displaying the black and white emblem of the Handless God. The nations of humans worshipped the Lightborn, the givers of the Art and the Sorrow, in one form or another. Only the Shapers and their servants bowed to the unknowable chill of the Handless God. But Kalzzik enjoyed feeling defiant, showing to all the plains that he, at least, was unafraid of the wrath of the Shapers.

Yet every time a rumor came that a column of the masked wizards was passing near, or someone spied one of their flying devices in the sky, Kalzzik immediately struck the pennant and grumbled about "high winds."

The drowsy guards at the pavilion entrance didn't look at me as I walked in. I passed through a small vestibule tent that led to the main one, and endured the side-eyed glances of Kalzzik's personal guard, most of whom were my second or third cousins. I could never keep their names straight, but had no reason to try since they never spoke to me.

I walked into the main tent. My great-uncle was spread over a throne made from piles of cushions, all of them dyed the same pustule purple as the pavilion. A slab of ceratops meat turned on a spit over the fire in front of the gathering, the smoke escaping through a vent hole. Kalzzik's meek second wife Goltka dutifully turned the spit.

I wasn't worried about Kalzzik's fury, since my delay had a purpose aside from avoiding him. If I made Kalzzik wait for me, it would deepen his Sorrow and make him feel useless so that when I finally stood before him, the fire of his anger would only be smoldering embers.

He still had warm coals left in him. When I saw the two men seated next to him, I understood who was stoking his fires. To his right was Ulgitz, leader of the second most powerful clan. To his left was Ulgitz's son. Dyzlin was still a bully after five years, but now he had warrior beads and nych scars to back up the foul wind that blew from both ends of him.

Kalzzik began. "You are late, Beltza, daughter of Kryzin."

"And daughter of Lukan," I added. In my thoughts, I was still "Belde of Tyrn, daughter of Lukan and Kryzin," no matter what anyone else called me.

"Don't speak of your shameful wet-blood ancestry here," Ulgitz said.

I turned my eyes toward him, hoping to use my stare on him, but he wisely chose to look at the lunch waiting for him on the spit instead.

I slipped into tribal-talk: "Great-uncle Kalzzik, I do not understand why you would call me before you to allow another clan to insult me. I am of your blood, and you should not tolerate this behavior from Ulgitz, great a clan head as he is."

"Quiet, Beltza," Kalzzik belched. "This affair concerns Ulgitz's clan. I expect him to speak rudely at times, and later I may shame him at a bonfire tale over it. But he has much to say about this matter."

My great-uncle was playing the plotter again. Ulgitz's clan was a spear point tickling his ribs. They had grown powerful at the bonfires and now had more young warriors than Kalzzik's clan. Poor great-uncle, his bloodline leaned more toward producing girls than boys.

Even worse, the last hunting season had been sparse, food supplies were low, the nych packs were growing bolder in their raids on the hadrosaur pens. Spirits were grim, and Ulgitz's clan was starting to grumble about splitting off.

I lowered my head so my eyes did not meet those of the men sitting like judges before me. I was burning up with the wish to stare down Dyzlin, but thought it best not to press the only advantage I had.

Dyzlin had never forgotten the fright I gave him on the soaking day we met. He bullied and teased me whenever his Sorrow was weak enough to let him. That had lasted for three years. Then he started to act differently toward me, as he was now: he had a stance like a hungry nych, a predator watching a rodent quiver before it shoved it down its gullet. He wanted the greatest revenge on me possible. A man's revenge, not a boy's. He wanted to own me.

The thought was more disgusting to me than eating the rotten ceratops intestines served during the Month of the Moon's Renewal ceremony. Dyzlin was not only a stone-headed brute; he had the sort of angry Sorrow that meant anything he claimed he "loved" would suffer under his fists ... and one day his blade.

"Beltza," Kalzzik said after another rolling belch, "I have received from Ulgitz and his son a generous proposal. His clan has shown great strength and willpower within our mighty tribe—"

Which meant: They're threatening to break off to form their own tribe.

"—and have suggested a way to unify our clans. I have already promised Gechina to the son of Jux, and Ulgitz's oldest son Ixak has married a woman captured in our raid on Tukkik's tribe. But Ulgitz says a most modest marriage will satisfy him."

My great-uncle was selling me off—and thought he was getting a bargain.

"You have passed your seventeenth summer and are already deep into marrying age. Ulgitz's son Dyzlin has shown uncommon interest in you. I'll admit that despite your heritage you have become ... passably attractive. In a thin way. But I despaired that your, uhm, condition and watery blood would keep you from a proper marriage."

Ulgitz slimed in: "We have chosen to overlook common objections to seek peace within the tribe."

Dyzlin had a look of smarmy triumph, although he was too much of a coward to try to lock gazes with me. He was the one who had suggested this "bargain" to my uncle. Ulgitz wouldn't gain much by it, except a way to eventually humiliate Kalzzik. But Dyzlin would get all he had ever wanted from me.

Kalzzik finally spoke the words that were fated from before I stepped into the smoky pavilion: "And so, grandniece Beltza, daughter of Kryzin, daughter of my brother Kylzin, both gone to the Sky Lords in Aman-Sah, I give you in marriage to Dyzlin, son of—"

"No!" I couldn't myself. It was like firing a blackpowder weapon, and my finger kept pulling the trigger. "No! No! *No!*"

When I was done, the only sound in the room was the hiss of fat dripping onto the fire. Goltka had stopped turning the meat. Even the smoke seemed to hover motionless.

"What—did—you say?" Kalzzik growled.

Did he want me to shout it out four more times? I stayed silent.

Ulgitz shifted on his cushion. "If the wet-blood scut wants to insult this honor—"

Dyzlin spoke for the first time: "Nothing a wet-blood screams could insult a true clan of the Koltzer, Father. I'll accept her as she is."

"You're braver in your choice of wives than me," Kalzzik said as if I weren't there. "You may have her, despite—"

"I *won't* marry him, great-uncle," I interrupted. "I said 'no,' and that is exactly what I meant."

Stillness again. And Sorrow. Would the Sorrow win out this moment, and its hopelessness make them retreat?

No, of course not. For the Koltzer, only anger can blot out the Sorrow. It *is* part of the Sorrow for them, a rage against a world that will never let them win. An upstart girl had put up a barricade, and they had to batter it down.

Kalzzik rose to his feet. His calf muscles were still hardy enough to drag up the rolls of fat. "You do not make these decisions, you disrespectful trash of the cities! I took you in when you crawled to me, a scared whelpling running from demons who would have ripped open your head and chewed your brain! What use have you ever been to us but another mouth? No, two mouths.

I forgot about that slinking thing that follows you. What good have you and your—sickness—ever brought to the tribe?"

"I'm not sick!" I shouted. "You are the sick ones! You sit here in hiding spots by the mountains and play warrior games, but all of you are headed to the Sorrow Sleep no matter what your pitiful boasting achieves!"

"I should kill you for this!" Kalzzik shouted. "You are just a woman, like any in this tribe, and women who disrespect their men are staked down in the ravagers' hunting grounds. But—"

He looked at Dyzlin, who still had that horrid smile stuck on his face.

"—this generous offer will actually bring benefit to our tribe. It will also rid me of you. You will be the problem of your husband, and he can do with you as he sees fit."

He waited for my answer, and he would not let his shaking legs drop his steak-stuffed rump down until he had one.

I made a decision. "Yes. I'll do it."

Kalzzik's anger washed away. He seemed satisfied that he hadn't meant his threats seriously, especially now that he'd solved the problem.

Except he hadn't. I had answered "yes" to another proposal, an argument inside my head that none of them heard.

"Very well," Kalzzik said once he settled into his cushions. He patted the back of Ulgitz's hand. "The shamans will conduct the marriage on the Spring Equinox at sunset. A day the Sky Lords approve for unions, wouldn't you agree?"

"Certainly," Dyzlin answered. He had a look of victory, which only required that he raise his eyebrows. The coward still would not meet my eyes and let my stare humiliate him.

The Spring Equinox was three days away. It was enough time to scrape together food and what belongings I had to escape from the tribe.

FIVE

When I was younger, the idea of running away was a mad dream, one easily dismissed the moment I glanced at the terrifying world outside the camp. I could never survive alone on the Gloss Grass Plains, where a ravager might swallow me in one gulp or a nych pack shred me into Sorrowless ribbons. But I was no longer a child. For a half a decade I had lived among the Koltzer and learned the skills that kept them alive. I knew the craft of the plains and mountains, how to handle a knife, dress a hadrosaur kill, nock an arrow. Plus I had a survival drive none of the Koltzer did, one that maybe only a handful of people in all of Ahn-Tarqa possessed.

Yet until now I had never let myself even start to hatch a plan to escape. I clung to a distant promise that rescue was coming from the one person who might understand who I was.

The Woman.

I had thought about making up a name for her. I imagined she was an Idenite, so I tried the prettiest names in my language: Quinella. Isabill. Oulett. None felt right. I tried harsher ones, names that conjured up a hag behind a fruit stand who gives the devil's eye to children who get within a mango-toss of her wormy wares: Urilla. Furnell. Gurstan. Those were far worse. So I gave up, and "The Woman" simply stayed "The Woman" until I met her again.

I had only seen her twice. The first time was when I spied through a hole in the thatch of Father's workshop. Then she was one of the robed and masked shadows, a Shaper in gray taking part in torturing Father. The second time was an hour later, when I opened a door into an alley during my frantic flight across Tyrn and came face-to-mask with a Shaper.

But it was *not* a Shaper. After hearing only a few words hissed through the mask, words that told me the Shapers had killed my parents, I knew a human woman was hidden behind the garments. A woman who was like me, who did not have the Sorrow.

The Woman left me with little—except my life. A pale hand pointed to a route to take, a promise to mislead our hunters so Rint and I could get out of the city. Then came a second promise, the one that haunted me over the next five years: *I will come for you, little one.*

She knew where to search for me. I told her in those few moments in the alley that I'd seek shelter with Mother's people. Whenever I was tempted to flee from the tribe, I stopped myself because I was afraid the Woman would never be able to find me. All she knew was that I was with the Koltzer tribe of Kalzzik, wandering across the northern plains.

Five years passed, and the Woman had not come. Perhaps she was dead. The Shapers could have seen through her disguise and cut out the front of her brain to make her one of their will-less slaves. This waiting could be for nothing, and if I went out to search for her, I would find nothing.

But I would not marry Dyzlin. If I gave in, I would belong to these Sorrow-cursed steppes forever. Worse, I would belong to Dyzlin. He could kill me on my wedding night—he had that right —and Kalzzik would do nothing to stop him. What happened to a girl after her marriage was not her family's affair. And even if a woman with the same bright eyes as mine rode from the plains on the back of a ceratops to demand that Dyzlin hand me over, he would kill me before he let anyone snatch away his little prize.

I had to leave—and finding the Woman was the only goal I had.

I did have something that might be called a "plan" on how to find her. It was dangerous and based on rumors I'd overheard from the Koltzer traders who did business in the cities: slight, hardly believed tales about sanctuaries where people with "witch-eyes" might shelter. Supposedly, these havens were hidden in the cities of the Gray Lands, tucked behind inns and beneath taverns. If I was going to find the Woman on my own, the best place to start was to track down one of these sanctuaries. To reach the Gray Lands required a long, hazardous trek across the Gloss Grass Plains and then the Temblor Plains, where the quake-foot herds were thicker, and so were the ravagers who followed them to pick off strays. The Gray Lands would also put me close to the Shaper dominions and their spies. But where the Shapers lurked, the Woman might also lurk, still disguised as one of them. Maybe when she took off her Shaper mask and robes, she ran one of the shelters that took in people like me.

It was a seedling of hope, but I had to plant something. The Gray Lands it was.

When I returned to the tent to fetch Rint, Holzir was asleep in his cot beside his mother. He already knew about the marriage bargain from Gechina's gossip, but I didn't want to talk about it with him. I might let it slip that I was planning to escape, and he would try to talk me out of it.

I gently roused Rint where he was sleeping beneath the cot and made a "quiet" motion with my finger so he would not chirp happily. We slipped out and headed for the tent where the unmarried girls of Kalzzik's clan stayed. The sun was falling behind the plains and the Gray Lands to the west, and the celebrations of the Feast of the Falling Moon were roaring around the central bonfire. The tents at the edge of the camp were filled only with night air.

"Well, Rint," I said when we reached the empty girl's tent, "if the Woman is slow in coming for us, why not meet her halfway?"

Rint chirped agreement. He sensed adventure, and that was enough for him.

My bed had privacy from the rest of the tent, with a hanging sheet cutting it off in a corner. It wasn't because I deserved a special place, but because the other girls thought I might use my witch-eyes on them. I kept my meager belongings in sacks under the bed, which was a piece of wood on stacked rocks with coarse blankets heaped on top.

Rint cocked his head when I started to stuff a travel pack with my heavy cloak and an extra pair of breeches. He made his signal for *Where we go?* I answered with the sign for *away*, but spoke because I needed to tell myself as well. "We're going to the Gray Lands. If those 'witch-people' sanctuaries are real, we'll find one. We have to trust to fortune and the Lightborn. Although neither has done much for us lately."

I put my hand on the ridges along Rint's back and felt his body suddenly go rigid. He lowered his head below his tail like he was planning to dash away. Somebody was near, and Rint didn't like his scent. I knew who it must be.

I kicked my pack under the cot before turning around. The intruder's shadow crawled up the dividing sheet, wobbling a little.

Dyzlin thought he was being sneaky. He imagined this city girl had dull senses and wouldn't hear his cloddish footsteps.

Dyzlin yanked aside the sheet with a dramatic motion, trying to make me jump with fright. He was disappointed to find me sitting calmly at the edge of the bed waiting for him to make his pathetic appearance.

"Hello, betrothed," he said.

"Men aren't allowed in this tent, Dyzlin."

"Not even a man visiting his bride?" He swayed closer. The reek of berry ale filled up my nose. He'd started early celebrating his upcoming marriage.

I couldn't use my stare against Dyzlin with his eyeballs swimming in ale. My wet palms pressed against the blankets and I thought about reaching for my skinning knife, but it was the first thing I had tossed into my pack and was out of reach.

I spoke measuredly. "Dyzlin, please respect the laws of the tribe and stay away from me until Equinox." The next words almost throttled me to speak. "After that—you can do whatever you want with me."

Dyzlin pitched forward, and his hands clamped onto my shoulders. "You're damn right I'll do whatever I want. There were so many things I wanted to make you suffer when we were younger. But even with your sickness, Kalzzik would protect you." He spit flecks of ale-soaked saliva onto my skin as he shouted. "Now that you're not a girl anymore, I've thought of better things I can do to you. More fun things. And your great-uncle will hand you over with a smile and a war-council seat for me to do them, night after night, any night I want."

Rint hopped on the bed and screeched at Dyzlin, but he knew not to fly at anyone unless I gave him the signal.

"If your stinking pet leaps at me, I'll twist its head off," Dyzlin snarled.

I tried to glance at Rint to tell him with my eyes to remain still, but Dyzlin wouldn't allow even that. "Don't look at the devil thing! As long as I've got you, the little futch stays away."

"You—you won't hold me for long," I managed to get out.

"You better hope I do. Because when I get tired of you, that's when you should really be afraid."

He threw me down in front of the bed. I wanted to scream for help, but Dyzlin had picked the right time to harass me. Everyone was at the feast, eating and drinking and far from hearing my shouts. From where I had fallen I could look under the bed slat for my pack. Maybe I was wrong and the knife was sitting at the top.

The glance was a mistake. Dyzlin sprang and pinned my wrist so I couldn't squirm away. He peered under the cot.

"What's this?" He dragged the pack out.

"It's nothing, I—"

He pressed harder on my wrist and crushed my leg under his knee. "Shut up. I wasn't asking you."

Dyzlin only needed to pull open the drawstrings and see the travel cloak on top to know my plans. He drew the cloak out and shook it in my face. "Where do you think you're going in *this?*"

"Please, let me go," I said. "I promise, I won't run away. It was just—it was panic—"

Wrong choice of word.

"Panic? I make you that sick, city scut?"

He yanked me to my feet. His fingertips pierced like thorns into my upper arms. His teeth grit so hard I heard the enamel scrape. Lost in Sorrow's rage but in a drunkenness that made the Sorrow's restraint weak, he was capable of doing anything to me.

But he was tipsy, and his movements sloppy as he forced my face toward his. I let go of fear for a moment and grabbed anger. This was the petulant, teasing bully from that rainy night when we were children, not a powerful man trying to ravish me. I was better

41

than him, and I'd show him the way I used to show my friend Junius back on the streets of Tyrn every time he tried to brag that a boy could beat a girl at anything.

"Rint, *mean boy!*" I shouted.

Rint couldn't do much, but the words distracted Dyzlin. He turned his head and released his pincher grip on my arms.

"I told you, I'll rip that—"

I pulled a leg hook on him. I wrapped my right foot around the back of his leg, and with my freed hands shoved him backwards. He tripped over my leg, and his sodden body crashed over.

Junius had fallen for the leg hook every time he tried wrestling me. Dyzlin wasn't any smarter.

I expected to buy a few seconds to grab my pack and run for Holzir's tent, where I could hide until Dyzlin sobered up. Shaming him for breaking tribal laws and entering an unmarried girls' tent might keep him away until the wedding.

But Dyzlin crashed down harder than I planned. His head struck the edge of the wood slat of my bed. There was a sharp *crack*. The cot flipped over, Rint went flying off it, and Dyzlin lay still. A dark puddle bloomed on the mat under his head.

My breath was trapped in my chest. If Dyzlin was dead, I was dead as well. Koltzer law was unforgiving to any woman who killed a man from her tribe, no matter what he had done to her. She was staked out naked on the plains for the nychs to feed on.

I ducked to where Dyzlin's body lay bent across the grass mat. I pressed my hand to his chest. There was no movement for a few moments, and my world slipped away. And then ... a shallow rise and fall. I never could have imagined I'd feel overjoyed that Dyzlin was alive.

My plans, however, were dead. I hadn't killed Dyzlin, but I had drawn the blood of another clan. It was provoked, which meant it wasn't a crime. But Dyzlin would claim otherwise and no one would defend me. Dyzlin would tell Kalzzik and his father that I had almost killed him and was planning to run away. Even if they didn't lash me, they'd lock me away in one of the caravans until the wedding. My chances for escape were gone...

Unless I went immediately.

I looked to Rint. "*We go, now.*" I knew he would understand. He hopped up and down and clicked his beak to show that at least one of us thought the idea was fun.

I stuffed the cloak into the pack and threw it over my back. I had a list in my head of the supplies I needed, but I had expected to have at least two days to collect them. Now I'd have to improvise as best I could. Before leaving the tent, I set my bed back on its props and rolled Dyzlin's unconscious body underneath to make him harder to find should anybody go looking for him. I also relished the idea that he might awake suddenly and crack his head on the wooden slat.

The night was warm. A southern gust carried the *squee-squik-squee* of the throat-croaker bugs from the plains to cover the singing around the bonfires. It almost let me forget that the camp was still around me.

No one was near the tent, but I had to chart a path around the other caravans and pavilions to keep away from the people gathered to drink, eat, and sing against the Sorrow. A few folks wandered between the tents, but they only knew me as the witch-girl they should avoid, and they did.

My most important stops were at the larder pits, where hadro and quake-foot meat was buried under layers of salt. Some pits had guards, but the tribe sentries were more concerned with protecting the hadro-pens, which were juicier targets for starving nychs. I passed up two guarded pits, but found a small one left free. I pulled out dried strips of flank, wrapped them in a bit of extra cloth, and packed them away in my bag. Rint and I visited one more pit, then headed to the granary where I picked out fern buds of the mayzok plant—Rint's favorite food—and scavenged up an empty canteen.

Our next stop was an uncertain one I hadn't planned to make when I first decided to run away. Too much risk. But now I had taken enough risks that one more wouldn't hurt. If this were a game of Sun-or-Moon, I was flanked on all sides, and one foolish move would turn over all my suns. Game lost, match lost. I needed every advantage—like the device of the Art closed inside the treasury caravan behind Kalzzik's pavilion.

Rint scouted ahead and chirped to signal the stretch to the treasury was clear. He had figured out we were on a secret mission, and he moved with a stealthy stance, body pressed low to the grass. It almost made me laugh.

"*Guard*," I told him when we reached the caravan on the other side of the tent from the bonfire. Rint flashed into his upright lookout stance, balancing back on his tail. Nobody is better at standing sentry than a beak-nose; Rint could sniff out a fresh fern-bud from inside an iron chest across a meadow of pungent mokkah flowers.

The treasury had its own sentry, but the ancient draft ceratops tethered to the front of the wagon wasn't going to bother us. Its snores shivered the ground, and its single nose horn was so worn down that if it charged, it would be lucky to tickle me. One more lean hunting season and the tribe would chop the poor beast up for winter steaks and carve its frill for shields.

I walked up the steps to the caravan door and pulled the string latch. The door stirred open. Kalzzik had no need to lock his trophy treasury because of the sinister prize inside. It terrified the entire tribe.

But not me. The devices of the Art held no terror for a witch-girl.

My eyes adjusted to the dark interior. Enough nightglow came through the door to show the swords of enemy tribes hanging on the walls, overlapping each other like fish scales. Beside them were shields fashioned in Iden from club-tail hide. The other baubles arranged on the walls were only there to fill space. They might fetch two coppers in a market of Tyrn, half that in the towns of the Gray Lands.

None of these trophies was as exotic or beautiful as the carvings of more distant lands that Holzir's mother had done from only her memory and longings. Here there were no treasures of Najael, no shaking-staffs from the jungles of Lakkad, no mysteries of Vatrusla and its legendary ash city of Belische.

The caravan held one great prize. It was hidden in an oblong wooden case pressed against the far wall as if it had crawled away from the moonlight. What was inside was a common sight in some cities; I had seen them occasionally in Tyrn, always in the hands of servants of the Shapers. To the Koltzer, the object inside was a demon, a breed of evil the Sky Lords had unleashed accidentally and which humans had made even more perverse.

I knelt in front of the case and thumbed open the bronze latch. The blackpowder weapon cradled in the scarlet cushion was a "blastgun." It had two long iron barrels and a stock made from wood so aged it was impossible to tell what kind of tree had been chopped down to make it. But the metal was so polished I could see myself reflected in it.

I picked up the blastgun and tried to imagine the Sorrow others felt burning inside it, and which the Shapers trained their servants to ignore so they could use the weapons. I felt the cold of metal against my hands, but nothing more.

I reached under the cushions and picked up a handful of metal pellets, broke open the gun, and slid two into the barrels. I put the rest of the pellets in the pouch with Rint's fern-buds, and then slipped out of the treasury.

The blastgun had a hemp rope strap so I could carry it over my shoulder, but it was easier to keep it hidden near my tunic with it broken over my arm. I signaled to Rint that we were ready. "I wish I could give you a fern-bud to pay for the guard-duty, old friend," I said, "but we need to save them for later."

Rint nodded—or perhaps it was a trick of the flicker of the bonfire light over the tent-tops. There were many times he acted almost human, or more than human. He was probably a product of the Art himself, as Father had guessed.

We moved under the half-moon to our last stop. It wasn't a dangerous one, but it was the hardest. I thanked the Lightborn, or whatever had taken the burden of watching over me, that Holzir's tent was close to the mountainside edge of the camp.

I stopped outside the front flap. "*Call*," I said to Rint, and he made a trilling that was the signal he used whenever we were separated.

One other person knew that sound. Holzir pulled back the flap moments later to answer it.

I must have been a strange sight, packed for hard travel and with a murderous tool of the Art crooked over my arm. Holzir didn't look surprised.

"You're leaving."

"Yes. You know why."

"Of course. You would never agree to marry a brute like Dyzlin."

The blastgun felt awkward. I shifted it. "It's more than that, Holzir. I can't be among your people any more—"

"*Your people?* You can't stand being around me either?" I couldn't see his eyes well, but the hurt in his voice was acrid.

"N-no," I stuttered. "I'll miss you. You're the only thing about this place I will miss. But I can't let that—I can't allow myself to—" I shuffled in the grass. Dampness was creeping up my legs, or something else was making my limbs feel like they were vanishing.

Holzir's shoulders slumped. "I understand. You're not like any of us. You'd have to go one day. But I hoped you wouldn't run off so soon."

"It can't wait. Rint and I have to get moving, fast." I quickly explained what had happened with Dyzlin.

Even Holzir was astonished. "You drew blood?"

"He might be up at any moment, and then he'll send his whole clan after me. I'll strike for the foothills, and then up beside the falls into the mountains."

"That's smart. If you took a hadro and tried to ride over the plains, they'd catch you for sure."

"The Fencer Mountains will test their Sorrow," I said. "And I'd rather not run into a ravager in the open and get turned into its Feast of the Falling Moon."

"Smart again."

"Beaten you more times at Sun-or-Moon, right?"

"No."

"But it's close."

I wanted to end our farewell there, talking about the game that first brought us together. But Holzir stopped me before I could turn away. "One more thing before you go, Belde. I have a gift for you."

I opened my mouth to tell him I couldn't wait and had no room for extra burdens. But he had already run back into the tent.

Inside was the sound of clinking metal. He wasn't going to ask me to carry along a sword or a war axe? He came back moments later. He had on an earth-brown traveling cloak. The handle of a short sword stuck out from his belt and a pack like mine was strapped over his back. Out of the top of the pack peeked the corner of his Sun-or-Moon board.

"You were right, I was wrong," he said. "The people of Belische would've left if they knew their city would be destroyed. They wouldn't have stayed to die in the Sorrow. Well, I know what's waiting here for me. I won't let the Sorrow Sleep take me that way."

"Holzir, you mean—"

"My gift to you is me."

I had no time to waste arguing. "Holzir, you can't come along. You have to stay with your mother."

"My uncle Dunix will care for her. I asked him before he headed to the bonfires."

"You mean you had already planned to come with me?"

"Of course, nych-brain! Do you think I had time to pack all this just now? I had it ready to go after I talked to you this afternoon. You would never marry Dyzlin, and you couldn't stay if you refused. Then I thought about the song and the city, and mother's carvings and her loom, and I thought about you, and—oh, I had this big speech memorized, but we have to move quickly, right?"

"Yes, we do have to move fast. Me and Rint. Not you." I didn't care if my words hurt this time. I could not let him drag his Sorrow along with me. It was not his fight.

He knew my objections already. "I promise, I won't slow you down. I'll hide my Sorrow. If you do get tired of me, if I'm holding you back or I think I can't make it, then you can go on without me. No regrets. And you need another set of eyes. Somebody who knows the plains and the mountains."

I held up my hand to stop him. I was ready to hurl at him all the reasons he needed to stay back, and how he couldn't help me no matter what promise of "no regrets" he could blabber about while he was still standing by the safety of his own tent.

Then I remembered I had no time for it. There was a simpler, faster way to make him back down.

I put on a smile. It was forced, but he wouldn't see that in the moonlight. "You're a brave Sun-or-Moon player, Holzir, even if it means you risk the whole game each time you put down a stone. But you made the right move." I put my hand on his shoulder. "Come along, my brave traveling companion."

I turned away without giving him a chance to respond with a thank you. He wouldn't last more than an hour on a trek away from the camp. Before I started climbing into the mountains, Holzir would be a cowering, paralyzed wreck terrified at the thought of the journey ahead. Then I could leave him behind. No regrets.

SIX

Our awkward trio of fugitives waited behind the last pavilion before the open steppes. I listened to the south wind, but the only noise came from throat-croakers. Holzir placed his ear to the ground to hear the thumping movement of any nearby ravagers, but there was nothing. Rint clicked to me that he didn't smell any nych packs. We were clear to make a first dash onto the plains.

We reached the nameless river without trouble by following a trail the women use to draw water from the banks. The sun-bright petals of mokkah flowers nodded over the water's edge, their scent a tiny intoxicant that reminded me that people crushed and smoked the pollen in city dens to chase away the Sorrow. I thought the gold color of the flower petals a much better cure for sadness.

"Which crossing is best?" I asked Holzir when I could see the moonlight ripple on the river.

"The uppermost one. The rocks are slippery, but anyone following us won't think to look there first. I hope you and your friend can handle crossing a few slick stones."

"Champion leaper back home," I said. "Well, Rint was. I was second best."

We crawled through the tall reeds along the bank until we reached boulders piled across the current in a row of natural stepping-stones. The crossing was tricky in the meager light, and the blastgun and pack strapped to my back made my balance wobbly. Rint leaped at my heels, humoring me as he skipped along. Holzir moved in front, jumping from rock to rock with a grace I'd never seen in him. His sword occasionally clanged against the rocks. The sound of iron on granite made me wince, even if the noise would never carry over the din of guzzling and gorging back in the camp.

At last I slipped down onto the reeds on the opposite bank. Holzir was tapping his foot waiting for me. "You're slow, city girl."

"Watch how you speak to me. I've got a weapon of the Art."

He scrunched up his face. He didn't like that I was carrying the blastgun. It frightened him the way it would anybody from the superstitious tribes of the plains. Still, he was handling this better than I expected.

The crossing dropped us into a sward that led to the tiers of the waterfall feeding the nameless river. The short grass crunched under our moccasins as we dashed across the open patch. A small path climbed into a crevice beside the falls and up through the foothills. The chill wind of the mountains that flowed down it made me want to stop to draw out my traveling cloak, but there was no time.

I knew my way up to the second step of the falls. Past that all I had to go on were my memories of maps.

"Where do you expect to go once you're in the peaks?" Holzir asked.

Telling him that I was making for the Gray Lands might have terrified him into turning back right there. But I didn't want him to start pelting me with more questions, so I lied. "I don't know. I just want to get us out of the reach of the tribe. They won't follow far, I hope."

He nodded. "Too much Sorrow for them. That's why you think we can get away?"

"That's the move. Doesn't it feel like too much Sorrow for you already?"

"I've felt worse."

Yes, he had. He was coping too well for my plans.

"I also have Rint to find out small paths," I said as I patted the beak-nose's head. The journey felt like a game to Rint. I might be the Sorrowless one, but he had the calmest head of our trio.

We started the ascent. The dark sky above hardly stood out from the brooding mountainside, but it was somewhere up there that many races believed lay Aman-Sah, the paradise where the Lightborn would gather the dead and take the Sorrow from them, as the Lightborn had once given the Sorrow to humans after the Arrival, somewhere in the morning of time.

I was nowhere near Aman-Sah. I wasn't rising into an airy paradise but into the heartless Fencer Mountains, with only a frightened young man and a small saurian as my companions. If there was an Aman-Sah, if the Lightborn were real and not legends invented to explain the Sorrow and the Art, I was as far from them as I could imagine I would ever be.

But with each pull of my body up the trail, I was a few feet farther out of the pit that had almost filled in over my head.

We had gone about a hundred feet up the ravine, attacking the gradual slope with a steady climb, when Holzir stopped. "We're being followed."

"A hunting party?"

"I think it's only one person. I saw a shape jumping across the stones."

I turned around, but my eyes weren't as sharp as Holzir's. I couldn't see anything on the rocks. However, I had brought along a second set of senses. "Rint," I said to the saurian, "*track*." I made a motion behind me so he knew which way to look.

He scampered down the ravine, whipping along so fast that I felt bad he had to slow himself down to keep pace with my awkward human climbing.

I could still see his leafy-green color at the bottom of the trail when he started chirping and clicking with the hard tips of his snout. "Rint's caught the scent," I said. "One person. Male."

"He could tell you all that?"

"You would never believe the sort of things Rint has learned to say in clicks." Hunting and tracking are instinctual for a beak-nose, and teaching Rint to give out signals for "how many" and "what kind" were the easiest tricks I taught him.

Holzir said, "If it's one person, I think I can guess who it is."

"I'm thinking the same thing. For somebody with a bashed head, that pisser Dyzlin is moving fast. So we'll have to move faster."

Rint enjoyed the new pace. Holzir and I didn't. The climb steepened, solid grips were scarce, and gravel slipped under my hands and moccasins. *Gloves*, that was one thing I had forgotten to bring. I knew I'd soon have a long list of forgotten items. Holzir had thought out my escape better than I had: he had on a pair of hadrosaur-hide gloves.

Spray misted over our backs, and the roar of the waterfall kept us from hearing our pursuer. I looked behind me whenever I felt it was safe, but the steep way caused my stomach to drop. Rint would give an alert if he felt we were in immediate danger, but he would have to rely on his nose rather than his ears.

We reached an outcrop over the foaming pool of the second step in the falls. My moccasins didn't like the slick granite, so I clung to the rear wall. Holzir held onto my arm, and we steadied each other.

Rint gave a shriek I didn't like at all.

"Dyzlin's getting closer," I said.

"The crack you laid on his head must not have hurt him enough."

I dared to look down the way we'd come. A figure slunk in the shadows of the ravine. The moon-glitter on the mist made it hard to see, but it had to be Dyzlin. No one else would go out to chase me alone. Had he alerted anyone else? Or was he trying to drag me back on his own, or even kill me in a Sorrow-rage?

"The next climb is easier. Maybe we can put some distance between us." Holzir didn't sound hopeful.

The grips dried as the ravine snaked away from the waterfall. The moon poured helpful light straight down on us, although its half-shape reminded me of a mocking sneer tipped on its side. Rint was in the lead; the shimmer of his bright skin was a guide we could follow.

Rint vanished above, and Holzir after him. "There's another ledge up here," he shouted. His voice was getting wheezy, and the burning in my muscles was begging me to stop. I had not realized how exhausted I was until I reached the ledge. My feet hit level ground, and then I toppled over. Holzir caught me before I bruised anything.

"We've got to rest," he said. "Even someone like you has to stop to take a few breaths."

"All right," I gasped.

After I got enough air into my lungs, I could see the ledge was larger than I'd first thought. It was a wide fissure torn into the mountainside, and the stones above formed a half-cave of shelter.

Before Rint went on guard to sniff out the blood that was still staining Dyzlin's hair, we heard a shout below. Too close below.

"You can't keep climbing forever, witch!"

The taunt stung, because he was right. I needed a few minutes before trying the next cliff face, and the climb looked treacherous, almost sheer without any stone fences to shield us.

Holzir opened his mouth to shout back, but I grabbed his leg. "Don't let him know we're here. Don't give him a target."

"We can at least throw something at him," Holzir said. It wasn't a plan, just desperation. He was losing hope fast. Rage could drive Dyzlin for hours, but Holzir wouldn't last much longer. He was looking for something to keep his mind from slipping deep into the Sorrow, where it would be hard to struggle back up. This ledge was probably where his travels with me would end. They might be where *my* travels would end.

Holzir lugged up a rock as large as his head from the fissure floor and looked over the edge. He hurled the stone, but there wasn't a shout from below, only the crunch of the rock as it shattered.

He grabbed another stone, larger this time. He was stronger than I had guessed, or else despair was driving his muscles. He rolled the stone off the ledge, but again there was only the sound of it breaking.

"I don't know if those hit," Holzir said. "I can't see him."

"He can spot you. Every time you lean over, he'll swing to the side."

"I'll wait until he gets closer, then push him off as he comes up."

I shook my head. "Dyzlin's dumb but he's also a trained hunter. If he knows where we are, he won't blunder straight into us."

"Then what do we do? If we climb, he'll catch us on the mountainside. And we can't wait for him to come grab us here."

"Yes we can." I pushed myself upright and drew the blastgun from my back.

Holzir's eyes bulged. "You can't use that Shaper crud. It's—it's devil-work."

I broke the gun open to check the pellets. "The Art is older than the Shapers. Or don't you believe in the Sky Lords?"

"Of course, but—"

"Well I do too. But in Iden we call them 'the Lightborn.' Maybe we did the wrong thing with the Art they gave us, and that's where the Sorrow comes from. But now—" I snapped the gun shut. "—I know the *right* thing to do with the Art."

Holzir was afraid to approach the weapon in my arms, but he was curious. "How does it work? What magic makes it run?"

"It's simple," I said. "When I pull this lever, a hammer on the back of the gun shoots the metal out, more forceful than any arrow."

Holzir looked away and eyed another rock. "I should try again. Maybe he'll be careless now—"

But we were the careless ones. Rint was guarding the wrong direction, looking over the ledge. He didn't know what was happening until it was too late. I had a moment of warning, but not enough to do anything except open my mouth to shout. By then the shadow climbing on the overhang of the fissure had hurled itself down onto Holzir. Dyzlin must have climbed up the almost straight cliff side next to the ravine to get above us.

Holzir crumpled as Dyzlin's weight dropped onto him. Dyzlin started beating at Holzir with his meat-lump fists. Holzir fought, but his opponent was larger, so the best Holzir could do was block the blows trying to batter him unconscious.

Rint sprinted to join the fray, but I shouted, "*Stop!*" It wasn't only a call to Rint, but to the other two in the fissure.

It worked. The three froze in a tableau under the moonlight. Holzir was on his knees, ready to fend off more blows. Rint stood with his legs bent for a leap. Dyzlin was in the center, looking like a devil from a bonfire-story with his face red with wrath and blood streaming down his blonde hair. His mad eyes were fixed on the blastgun I was pointing at him.

"So, the city witch finally uses her witch-weapons," Dyzlin said. "And on top of betraying the chieftain, she's also a thief."

"You're scared," I answered. "Don't pretend. You know what this is. A twitch of my finger, you die."

Something like a laugh, but closer to stones grinding, came from Dyzlin's chest. "You don't know how to work the magic."

"I'm a city witch, or are you too dull to remember what you just said?" I wiggled my finger on the trigger, but my talk was seasoned with bluff. I'd never fired a blackpowder weapon. I didn't even know if this one would work when I squeezed the trigger. I could only trust what I had seen in the streets of my childhood, and the memories of men firing at Rint and me as we fled from the Shapers in Tyrn.

Dyzlin sensed my doubt. He started forward. "Put down the Shaper poison and perhaps I won't beat you as a man should beat his slattern wife."

"I'm not your wife." I prodded the gun barrels at him.

He slowed, but didn't stop. "Put it down, return to the camp, and I won't tell anyone you ran off."

So nobody else knew I was gone yet. One piece of good news.

"I *will* use this." I forced my hands to hold the gun steady. Dyzlin hesitated. The Sorrow was pressing on him, brought on by the terror of the strange Art aimed at him. But madness and pain danced in his eyes. Sorrow and rage are a deadly mixture that can overwhelm a mind. If Dyzlin lost all his senses, he might be crazed enough to overpower me.

We were so enrapt in our face-off that neither of us noticed Holzir. He came out of his crouch suddenly and lunged at Dyzlin's back. His arm wrapped around the bigger man's neck. "Don't touch her, you hadro-humping futch!"

"Holzir, get out of the way!" He didn't hear me. He was too busy trying to stop Dyzlin from breaking his hold. Holzir wasn't strong enough to overpower Dyzlin. Once Dyzlin got over the surprise, he ducked and easily tossed Holzir over his shoulder and onto the ground. Dyzlin's hand went immediately for the axe dangling from his belt.

Dyzlin's axe flashed up into the air, ready to cleave through Holzir's skull.

I clamped down on the trigger.

The burst of magic from the blastgun slammed me into the wall as the flash of Art turned the fissure to daylight. Dyzlin's axe clattered to the ground. Dyzlin fell after it. At first he dropped silently, crumpling onto a leg that was ripped into red tatters. But as he pitched over onto his back, the scream he made was something I never imagined I'd hear from a warrior's throat. Even through the ringing in my ears from the blastgun's explosion I could hear Dyzlin's shriek.

I had the second pellet ready to fire, but didn't need it. Dyzlin's right leg was a ruin of blood and bone. I had never seen a blastgun hit anything, and now I understood why people cringed from them. Dyzlin's howl mixed real hurt and superstitious terror. A sword slash was pain, but to him the Art was venom.

Rint pressed against my leg. The noise had terrified him, and he had jumped to my side, even though I was the one who had created the thunderbolt. I slung the gun across my back and tugged at Holzir where he lay. He was in a state of shock himself. Blood from Dyzlin's leg wound was splattered across his face.

"You—you did it," Holzir stuttered. "You killed him."

I wiped the blood off him with my sleeve. "He'll live. But he won't be climbing after us."

Dyzlin's screams turned into curses, the ripest and nastiest ever heard around the bonfires with older warriors. I had never learned these words of the Koltzer language and was glad.

I pulled Holzir to his feet. He was on the verge of drowning in a stupor. I gave him a rough shake that managed to get his eyes to focus enough to concentrate on my words: "Follow me. Think of nothing else. *Follow*."

At first the power of the Art had shocked me, but now it flamed raw energy through my limbs. It had pushed the crippled Dyzlin inches from madness, but I felt as if my insides were on fire and I had to unleash it. If I needed any proof I was Sorrowless, this was it.

The climb was still a nightmare. Holzir moved like one of the bronze and steel colossuses of the legends of the Hegemony: he moved only because I moved, and had no other will than that. I forgot about my plan of trying to lose him for the moment. I just needed to get him to safety. I climbed slowly enough that he could keep me within reach; he had to touch my leg now and then, or he might fade entirely and stop for hours until his Sorrow eased.

Wind huffed down the mountainside, and the moon vanished as clouds swept over it. It was the warning signs of a "striker," the terror-storms that plunge from the Fencer Mountains and can change a summer day into a flood in a heartbeat.

We reached a level pass that snaked between the lowest peaks. I slung Holzir onto the ground, trying to be gentle but losing my grip at the end. He dropped against the rock wall and stared up at the sky. "A striker is coming," he muttered as he listened to the wind's howl. At least he was aware of something.

I heard another noise that at first I thought was the approaching storm. Then it turned into a skirl like the call of a skinwing, the flying beasts that were the only saurians who lived in the bare rocks.

Then at last I recognized what it was. It was words in my native language, which I had not heard for years except from my own mouth.

Mother and Father calling to me, looking down from Aman-Sah. The Woman, calling my name as she found me at last. The sounds of Tyrn's street sellers and my friends and I hooting to each other as we dodged between carts in our summer play days. The sound brought all this to my mind—but it was none of those things.

It was Dyzlin. He had changed from Koltzer curses, asking the Sky Lords to shrivel my womb, to curses in Idenite. He had not deigned to speak my own tongue to me since I had mastered his, but now he wanted me to hear him clearer than anything he had ever said.

"Belde—I'll get you—find you! Make you suffer, Belde! I'll feed you to the Shapers!"

My hand constricted around the weapon resting across my knees. I didn't notice how tight I was gripping it until Holzir touched my hand. "What is it, Belde? What's he shouting?"

"Nothing. Nothing." It had to be nothing. Dyzlin's threats had no power. I was away from the Koltzer, except for the downcast one sitting across from me. I wasn't safe, but I was safe from Dyzlin. He was going anywhere today, and he would never find me again.

I set the blastgun and my pack down beside me and settled against the rock wall. I had to consider the next part of the journey, the one beyond the reach of the tribe, beyond the reach of my knowledge.

But that was tomorrow. When the sun was up and I could see the range and the valleys open to me, I'd decide where to move next.

The striker hit with the speed of its name. The clouds flew

over us like hunting skinwings and dropped rain. We jumped up and dashed a stretch down the pass until we came to a depression in the rocks that might be called a cave by desperate people. We huddled together to squeeze back from the sheets of water, and Rint curled around my neck.

We sat side by side for a few minutes, staring at the shimmering wall of water. Then Holzir spoke:

"Well, I outmaneuvered you again, Belde. All moons."

"What are you talking about?" I said.

"You said 'yes' too quickly when I told you I was coming along. You're more stubborn than that. You were planning to ditch me as soon I slowed down, maybe abandon me at the foot of the mountains. But I knew I could outlast the Sorrow just long enough. And now you're stuck with me."

I turned to look at him, but he still had to draw his eyes away from my gaze. The Sorrow was there, but he was right—he'd gotten far enough along I could never send him back. What had happened with Dyzlin made it impossible for him to return. Not only that, he'd helped me cross the river, make the climb, watch out for ravagers, and defeat Dyzlin.

"You—you damn pisser!" I shouted. Then I sunk my head into my arms and felt the oddest emotion of all that strange day wash over me. Relief.

SEVEN

Each time Holzir complained we were lost, I reminded him it was impossible for us to be "lost" since we knew where we needed to go. "We just have to push west," I said. "We've got the perfect guidepost for that." I pointed toward Ravager Fang, the highest peak of the local range, which did have the appearance of the serrated tooth of a giant carnosaur. "If anyone's on our trail, they won't think of going that direction."

"Of course they won't," Holzir said. "It's a cursed place. Which is why we shouldn't go there either."

I sighed and kept moving over the stone trail. Koltzer superstitions meant nothing to me, but they needled Holzir. Trying to explain to him that it was strategy to head that direction did no good. To him, Ravager Fang was a place forbidden by the Sky Lords and guarded by "cloud-wights," flying creatures neither man nor skinwing that drunk bonfire singers probably invented.

But even with his unease, Holzir had followed me for two days and nights while I tried every dell or gap in the mountains to cut a way to Ravager Fang. Abrupt cliffs, gorges, and rapids blocked us at many spots, but Rint's knack for finding new paths kept us on the move. Yet for all of our work, the toothy peak still loomed far away.

On the third day of toiling through the western spur of the Fencer Mountains, I grudgingly accepted that, yes, we were lost.

We didn't dare move at night, when the monotony of rotting limestone around us turned into a jagged nightmare and the temperature plunged to where we wondered why the water in our canteens didn't freeze. We had no firewood or fuel. I cursed my carelessness, but how could I have lugged chips of dried hadro dung along with me into the Fencer Mountains? At least during the day the air was crisp and light; it was almost exciting after years on the grass. The peaks appeared to have no life at all, and the naked stones were enough to scare away anything that thought about growing. It meant no extra food, but also no saurians stalking us.

"Can we eat?" Holzir said.

"Not unless more jerky has grown in your pack since the last time you asked." We had food for at least five days if we kept down to a single daily ration. Water was plentiful from the streams trickling down in the spring melt.

Holzir didn't need more food than me. He liked to stop and eat because it usually meant we'd play a game of Sun-or-Moon. A bit of home to cheer him.

An hour later, as the sun reached its summit, we came to a round granite plateau. I couldn't see a way down, and Rint couldn't scout out anything either. We would have to backtrack through the crevice and find another path. It was a good time to stop and chew on salted jerky and swallow spring water.

Even before I had the food pulled from my pack, Holzir had the Sun-or-Moon board set down and was portioning out the stones for the game. I settled in, deciding I would let him win to boost his spirits.

But he played well, and I soon stopped giving up easy moves. He took aggressive outer positions, captured two corners, and then launched an attack from the sides. If I had any chance of winning, I had to play a cautious middle game and flip over as many of his moons as possible in a strike at the end.

I was clinging by my fingernails to hold the center of the board when he finally spoke. "Belde, where are we going? Tell me the truth."

"I don't know." I played a foolish move as I said it, but he didn't notice and made a minor play that flipped over only one of my suns.

"I know you don't know *where* in the Fencer Mountains. I mean, once we get out of the mountains."

"I don't know that either." Another stupid move, and he caught it this time. I lost a full rank of suns.

"Do you Sorrowless always lie?" He looked me in the eyes for as long as he could stand before turning back to the game to wait for my move.

"Holzir, I don't know what the other 'Sorrowless' are like, or even how many there are. I've only met one other person like me."

"You never told me that. Who was he?"

"She."

"She. Why did you never tell me about her?" He tapped the board to insist I make my move.

I held the stone between my thumb and forefinger, flipping it around so I could see both the sun and moon side. "She has something to do with where I'm going. But it's hardly a plan. Only an idea. It seems so far off, there's no reason to talk about it."

I put the piece down, facing the wrong side up, and had to flip it over. It was one of only two moves I could make, but it was the better one. Holzir slapped down his piece and flipped over a full row. I had no chance now.

"There is a reason to talk about it, Belde. You didn't want me along, but I'm here. So I want to know about this Sorrowless woman and this 'idea.' It has to do with—*that* day, right?"

I played my last move, which flipped over two of his moons and left him open to fill in the last square and win. Three-quarters of the board was filled with his shimmering moons.

"Yes, *that* day." I reached out to clear the stones, but he pulled the board away from me.

"You think I can't stand to hear about it? Up here everything is Sorrow, Belde. A bit more won't hurt me much."

I had never told anyone in Kalzzik's tribe about the day Rint and I escaped from Tyrn. Most of them didn't care where I came from. They knew an Idenite man, a harness-maker whose real name they never learned ("Lukan," I reminded them, and then they forgot again) had stolen the heart of pretty Kryzin, daughter of the chief's youngest brother, and lured her to a foul city. They would rather have Kryzin back than her daughter, and who or what this "Beltza" was wasn't their affair. Always incurious, the Koltzer. It was a way to shield themselves against the arrows of the Sorrow.

But it was fine that they didn't want to hear my story, because it hurt me even to think about it. I looked down at the board, almost all turned to moons. That day was the opposite, filled with the unsetting summer sun. But the memory wasn't of the light of joy. It was the haunted light of the afternoon, when the day tells you it's dying and you've wasted it.

"The Shapers came to my house that morning," I said, still looking down at the board.

"You saw a Shaper up close?"

I nodded. The nearest most Koltzer ever come to these wizards is when they spot black caravans heading into the Gray Lands on their way to the Shapers' spired cities on the western peninsula. The black and white banners of the Handless God are enough to make the Koltzer flee the other way across the plains. They don't need to see the huffing machines of the Art or armies of devil claws to frighten them. To them, the Shapers and all they command are the pinnacle the Sorrow.

"What are the Shapers like?" Holzir asked.

"They didn't seem as horrible as the stories. At least, not on the outside. I only saw four of them, and I found out later one wasn't a real Shaper. I couldn't see what sort of bodies they had because they wore enormous robes. Their masks are simple, with nothing on them except eye slits. The most important of them, the one the servants called an 'Artikon,' had many prongs along the edge of his mask, while the other masks had smooth edges. They rode into the city in one of those carriages that don't need a harness team to pull it. Their Idenite servants pretended they had business with Father as a harness maker. But—"

Rint pecked at my hand, as if he did not want to hear the rest. He had lived it as well. He was perched at my side when I stared down through a hiding space behind the straw over Father's workshop.

"Then the Shapers entered the house. They strapped Father down to his workbench and tortured him with a bright globe that shot a kind of wizard-power into his body. It made him shriek until he almost tore out his lungs."

Holzir looked shocked. "You didn't do anything about it?"

"What could I do? Charge down there and tell them to leave my father alone? They'd only truss me up in the corner, next to where they had stuffed Mother, and keep on torturing him."

"But what did they want with him? Did they—did they ki—"

"Yes, they *killed* him, Holzir! And Mother. I didn't see it happen. If I had, I'd be dead too, and you wouldn't have your little story."

He backed away as if I had tried to slap him. But my body had curled inward, with my arms crossed over my chest so tight I could've stopped myself from breathing.

He didn't need to hear the next part. He wouldn't understand it and only ask more annoying questions. Besides, I didn't fully understand it. What had the Shapers wanted? I could only guess that there was something inside their glowing orb only the Sorrowless could stand to see, and the Shapers wanted to know what it was. Flashes of it crawled into my brain as I watched Father drop into madness. There were hints of a sprawling story that happened long before I was born, before the days when the Shapers ruled Ahn-Tarqa, maybe before the Lightborn appeared in the Valley of the First Scar.

I unwrapped myself when I felt I could go on. "Father stopped screaming long enough to say something to the Shapers. It made them realize they were torturing the wrong person. They were looking for someone without the Sorrow. They had spied on our house for months, and thought it was Father. But he said something—"

Please, please don't hurt her.

Those words betrayed me. But Father wasn't in control of himself, and they betrayed him as well. Condemned him.

"I didn't know until then that I was Sorrowless. I had heard Mother and Father talking when they didn't think I could hear that there was something 'different' about me, and it worried them. They didn't want anyone else to know I wasn't like the other children. But when Father cried out, the Shapers realized it was *me* they were searching for, the harness-maker's daughter. I knew then what I was, and I had to run. Rint and I had to run."

I put my hand onto Rint's back. He chirped and licked my

fingers with his tiny tongue. That stopped my tears from coming back. I hadn't let myself cry about that day for years.

Holzir waited a moment, trying to pack into his head all I had said. "I still don't see what this has to do with that person you met."

"I told you that one of the Shapers wasn't actually a Shaper. She was a human living among them in secret."

"A spy?"

"I think so. I know almost nothing about her, except that she was like me. Sorrowless. She helped me escape, sent the Idenite servants in the wrong direction, so Rint and I were able to slip out of the city and get to Kalzzik's caravan.

"The woman in the mask said only a few things to me, but one of them was a promise. She said she would come back to find me ... one day."

I started to turn over the stones on the board, one by one. I wanted to see the welcoming face of the sun staring up at me.

"Do you think she meant it? That she would come back for you?"

"I've depended on it every day of my life. I stayed in the tribe at first because I had nowhere else to go. Later I stayed because I thought it was the only place where she knew to look for me. If it weren't for her, I'd have left long ago."

Holzir's face darkened. "I wasn't a friend enough to make you stay?"

I hit the Sun-or-Moon board so hard that pieces flew up and clattered onto the ground. "This isn't about you, Holzir! Didn't you hear anything I said?"

"Sorry, sorry." He couldn't look at me, and started to clean up the scattered game stones.

"No—you weren't enough, all right? The Koltzer aren't my people, even with Mother's blood. Nobody in Ahn-Tarqa is my people except a woman I met for a few moments. Whose face I don't know, whose name I don't know. You asked to come along with me, and I said 'yes,' but don't for a moment imagine any of this is about an ignorant grass-chewer like you!"

I wasn't thinking and suddenly seized the game board. I cocked my arm back, ready to hurl it off the edge of the plateau.

I don't know if I really would have done it or not. But suddenly Holzir's arm clamped around my wrist, the hold like a death-grip on a sword handle.

"No! No! No!" he screamed.

Then I understood. "Your mother—?"

"She carved it. Please put it down, Belde."

He let go, and I carefully placed the board down. But my anger was still burning. I wouldn't say "sorry." Once I let go of the game board and Holzir had stopped his shallow breathing, I turned my back on him. In the thick silence I already regretted losing my temper. It would only drive Holzir into a corner of the Sorrow and slow us down more. And some of what I said I didn't mean. But he was so slow about understanding that I couldn't hold back. Why didn't he see what I had sacrificed? All he'd ever given up in life was a family member he had lost years ago. All he needed to remember her was a game board. I was always alone, and the only hope I ever had of changing that was a vague pledge made through a mask in an alley.

Holzir didn't speak again. He collected the stones, and I heard him set them back inside the case. Each stone clinked into place in exact rows. It was a silly ritual, since the moment the case moved the stones inside would slide out of their stacks. It was a routine he followed whenever the Sorrow lay heavy on him.

I waited until I heard the latch click shut, and I then turned around but did not give him a look. Instead I marched toward the way we had entered the plateau. I snapped my fingers and Rint came to my side, although with unusual hesitancy. If Holzir still wanted to follow me, he could, but there was no invitation.

We were about a hundred paces back along the trail before I heard Holzir walking up behind us. He was singing, the first time he had let the mountain walls hear this sound. It was "The Ever-Sorrow of Belische," but he was changing the words:

> *Oh Dust, if I could Raise the Earth,*
> *I'd tell your shades plain:*
> *The Sorrowless are mightier than you!*
> *The Sorrowless are mightier than Life!*

I didn't acknowledge him, but my heart felt lighter even though the embers of rage were scalding the rest of me.

OUR CAMP that night was like the marriage of a Sorrowful old couple who can't stand the sight of each other but have no strength to get away. Holzir and I sat on opposite sides of a gravel ditch and said nothing. I thought of ways to apologize, then decided that if Holzir had begged to come along and cause trouble, he needed to apologize to me for being selfish. Then I started to think about apologizing again.

Rint stood beside my knees, which I had pulled toward my chest to put an extra barrier between Holzir and me. Rint could read bodies as well as I could read words, and he knew that Holzir and I were angry at each other. He made a chirp that could mean a few things, but was probably *Why?*

"Because that futch is a selfish, Sorrow-bitten pus sack," I said, soft enough that Holzir wouldn't hear. "I wish he'd never asked to come along."

Rint bent his neck to scratch his mouth, the sign for *hungry*.

"Change the subject, huh?" I said. "All right, a late snack, but only this once."

I reached into my pack and rummaged through the lighter clothing and the cold touch of the knife until I found the bundle of fern buds. I lifted out a medium-sized one and held it toward Rint.

His beak snapped forward, but he only caught the morsel between the hard ends of his jaws instead of gulping it down. He leaped over my knees and scampered across the gully.

Holzir stirred when Rint scratched one of his forepaws against his leg. I watched silently, wondering what Rint was trying to do. He rarely approached another person unless I asked him to.

Rint raised his head up to eye-level so Holzir had to look at him. Holzir blinked, then said, "What is it Rint? She won't talk to you either?"

"Pus sack," I said into my sleeve.

Rint stretched his head forward; the fern bud hung loose in his beak. Holzir understood what Rint was trying to do, and put out his palm. Rint laid the fern bud into Holzir's hand as gently as if he were rolling an egg into a nest. He then chirped up at the boy's face and turned around and chirped at me.

"Your tag-along thinks we should talk more," Holzir said.

I might have smiled, but I still had my mouth covered.

"Like you always tell me, he's smarter than most people," Holzir continued.

"He is. He is."

Rint came back to me, and made a dipping signal with his tail: *I do good?*

"Good. The best," I said.

We still didn't speak for the short time we stayed awake. Rint had said enough.

EIGHT

"It's hard to tell anything. I can't see the plains in any direction," Holzir called down. He had climbed up to a promontory to spy out possible routes. We had circled Ravager Fang all day, arriving at the same distance from it march after march.

"It can't be that impossible to reach," I shouted up.

"Maybe we should try another landmark?"

"There's nothing taller for us to see than Ravager Fang. And I still think it's our best chance. Water must flow down the north side and into the Lazzun Marshes. If we get to Ravager Fang, we can follow the streams."

"Following them from this side hasn't gotten us far," he said. The brooks and springs ducked under the rocks and through tunnels to lose us, almost as if they did it on purpose.

"Do you have better ideas?" I called. "Aside from picking another rock that's harder to see?"

"It would help if you told me where you want to go."

Rint's nighttime peacemaking session was enough to hold Holzir and I together for the morning, but hunger and getting re-lost every hour were straining the truce. I needed to tell him the truth now, whatever the immediate consequences.

"We're heading toward the nearest city in the Gray Lands."

I didn't look up to see his reaction. He didn't say anything.

"Go ahead, Holzir. Tell me I'm crazy."

"You're crazy, Belde. But I already knew that."

He backed off; he didn't want to start another fight either. But he wouldn't walk with me into the Gray Lands easily. I might have to take him up on his promise that he would let me go on alone if he broke apart. But "no regrets"? That was impossible now that we'd gotten this far.

"Well, that gives me some idea," Holzir said. "We have to come down on the north side." He pointed toward a long butte perhaps a league off. "Let's see if there's a way over there. The sides look climbable, and the top might give us a view of the Temblor Plains on the north."

It wasn't likely. But I had no better direction to offer. Rint seemed out of ideas as well. He was turning in circles, sniffing the thin air as if he thought another animal might be near. I ignored him, since we hadn't seen anything alive for the past few days. The little beak-nose was just getting restless.

We managed to get to the foot of the butte by early afternoon, although the trek took us through a crawlway beneath a boulder that almost tore holes in our breeches. As we neared the butte, the sloped sides gave me a peculiar feeling. They looked too much like the walls of a fortress. It had to be my imagination. What kind of people could survive in this lifeless place? Yet the sense that some hand—human or other—had molded the slopes made me understand why the Koltzer believed the region around Ravager Fang was cursed.

We climbed down a boulder face and into a trench that formed a dry moat for the butte. Holzir's remark earlier that it looked climbable now seemed like a joke when we stared up the sides. "This doesn't look like an easy climbing job, even for you," I told him.

He chewed his lower lip as he looked at the few pockmarks that might serve as grips on the fifty-span high wall. "It's tall enough that if I do make it, I'll have a perfect view of how to get over to Ravager Fang."

"And it's tall enough that if you don't make it, you'll be a heap of broken bones."

As Holzir considered the dangerous climb and his chances, I noticed Rint wasn't moving around my feet. I was so used to seeing a spot of green slinking and weaving through my legs whenever we stopped that a prickle of fear ran over my skin.

"Rint!" I called.

I got an immediate answer, and not the one I expected. Rint gave out his *happy happy* squeal. He was perched on an outcrop over a shoot of green that matched his own skin.

Rint snapped at the plant peeking through the rocks, but didn't chew on it. He was hungry but smart enough to know he shouldn't munch on anything he saw growing. He kept doing his *happy* squeal, hoping I would tell him it was okay to gobble down the plant.

"How could anything grow up here?" Holzir said when we reached Rint's find.

"If anything could grow in these dead lands, it would be this." The plant looked sickly. Coming closer, I saw the green wasn't the healthy shade of the lush ferns and cycad fronds that hadros feed on. It was streaked with rot, and the leaves drooped as if simply trying to grow was too much effort to be worth it.

I waved "*no*" at Rint, and his head sagged in imitation of the plant. He had been eager to try a new kind of food. But I wouldn't garnish the soup of a futch like Dyzlin with a sprig of this diseased thing.

Rint started to push his beak into the small stones at the base of the plant, trying to burrow at something underneath it. I reached out and touched a leaf of the plant. Short prickles rubbed the ridges on my thumb. "It feels almost like—like skin."

Holzir drew a breath and yanked my hand away as if the plant were about to send crawling vines around my arm. "I know what this is," Holzir said. "Flesh-weed."

"Is it poison?" I wiped my hand against my breeches.

"No, but I think Rint has the right idea."

He joined the beak nose in moving away the rubble around the weed. "Flesh-weed doesn't grow from dirt."

As he pulled away the biggest stone, a death stench struck my nose. Even Rint recoiled from what was revealed as Holzir pushed away the rest of the stone pile.

"It grows from corpses."

The body had decayed slowly in the thin air, but it had gone far enough that it was hard to tell what sort of animal it once was—and I didn't want a closer look. The weed had wormed through the remains of muscle and skin, making the shape of the bones difficult to see. It looked the right size for nych or juvenile hadrosaur. Or a person.

Holzir had the stomach to get nearer. His full Koltzer blood had less distaste for the reek of dead flesh. "Whatever it is didn't die here of pox or starvation. Something's been chewing it. No ... *pecking* at it—"

That was enough warning to make our senses flare up. And barely enough to flatten ourselves to the ground as the shadow of enormous wings swooped over us.

"Skinwing!" Holzir shouted as we hit the stones.

Rint crowded under my arm. He felt the movement in the air

before we did and leaped down. I'd scold him later about paying so much attention to a stupid weed that he missed a skinwing diving down at us.

I raised my head, too Sorrowless-curious for my own good. I had only seen skinwings from a distance, when they snatched up hatchlings from hadrosaur herds that had wandered too close to the Fencer Mountains. This one looked large enough to haul off a grown man: the outstretched wings could fill up Kalzzik's tent, and its tapering beak was longer than a battle sword. Ribs poked through the shrunken flesh of its torso. The skinwing hadn't eaten since catching whatever it had buried under the stones. It must have perched on the top of the butte, watching us to see if we were going to steal its preserved morsel.

The skinwing reached the end of the trench, banked sharply to fly up and turn around to start another run at us. For an enormous saurian, it could whip around far too quickly.

"Run!" Holzir shouted. He grabbed my arm and we got up from the ground to make a dash to the shelter of the butte. The skinwing would find it tricky to drop down on us if we were pressed against the steep wall.

The skinwing kicked up rock dust as it fluttered it to a landing on top of the corpse. It was about ten strides away from where the three of us, Rint now clinging onto my pack, were huddled in the lee of the butte. It stretched out its naked wings and made an ear-shredding caw. The way it jerked around its crested head made it look like a string puppet with tangled lines.

"Does it want us, or that dead thing?" Holzir asked.

"Maybe it doesn't know. I think it's sick, like that weed." Saurians could get strange diseases that made them crazed. Eating the wrong fungus could make a quake-foot go on a rampage, and bites from other sick animals caused a death fever that drove saurians so wild they broke their own necks in their thrashings.

Something similar had seized this skinwing and driven it into the peaks to die with its last kill.

"Can we slip away from it?" I whispered.

"The only fast way out is back over the boulders. Want to try that, Sorrowless girl?"

No time to get angry at his sneering. "Well, do *you* have any ideas?"

"What about the witch-weapon?"

In the panic I had forgotten about the blastgun over my back. I had tried not to think about it during the past few days; it seemed to serve no purpose in the dead hills, and I didn't want Holzir reminded of it.

I reached to unsling the twine strap from my shoulders. But the moment I moved, the skinwing started to hop up and down on its rotted prize.

"Move slower." Holzir had his fingers around his sword hilt. "If it charges, I'll try to hack at its neck. You concentrate on using that —*thing*."

When Holzir started to draw the iron blade from his belt, the skinwing jerked its head toward him. While it was distracted, I slipped the strap over my head and inched the blackpowder weapon into my hands.

Rint jumped from my pack onto the ground, and the skinwing followed him with feverish eyes. "*Rint, stay!*" I hissed. He was trying to make his own diversion, but he was the easiest of the three of us for the skinwing to pluck up. Luckily, the beak-nose obeyed me and stayed in place at my feet.

There was still a pellet inside the blastgun, so all I had to do was brace the weapon against my shoulder and aim. But I grabbed the gun by the barrel instead of the stock, and when I clumsily tried to bring it around, it broke open in the middle. The metal pellet slipped out. I tried to grab it before it fell, but I fumbled the gun onto the rocks, where it landed with a loud *clunk*.

The skinwing jolted as if I really had shot it. With two flaps of its wings, it lifted from its perch and hurtled toward us.

"Go right, I'll go left!" Holzir yelled. I snatched up the empty gun and did as he said, Rint running behind me.

I almost stumbled from the awkward position of the blastgun in my hands. I was trying to flee and load new pellets into the weapon at the same time. If the skinwing came after me, it would have an easy time knocking me to the ground.

But Holzir yelled at it and waved his sword so it glinted in the sun. That caught the crazed mind of the skinwing, and it started to flap toward him. It was too close to the ground to maneuver, and that saved Holzir from losing his head to a snap of the enormous beak. The skinwing moved clumsily in the trench, and when Holzir swung the sword at it, it made a side lunge that scraped a wing against the butte. It dropped onto its feet to get its balance.

I pulled my eyes from the fight to concentrate on getting two pellets from the pouch wedged into the blastgun barrels. My hands shook and the pounding of my heart made every action seem as if it were under the control of someone other than Belde of Tyrn.

As the second pellet clicked into place, I glanced back up. Holzir was hidden behind the wingspan of the creature, which was flapping a few feet off the ground. Holzir's sword rang against rock—he must be swinging wildly to keep it back.

The gun snicked shut. I braced the wooden stock against my shoulder to take aim.

The skinwing skittered around madly, and its head snapped at the boy whom I still couldn't see. Where was I supposed to aim? A shot through the wings might hit Holzir. I raised the metal tip at the end of the barrel so it was near the crest on the back of the skinwing's head, but with all the practice I had it would need the Lightborn's guiding hands for me to hit anything. Perhaps the noise of the weapon would scare the thing away from Holzir.

Before I could squeeze the trigger, a sound like an explosion filled my ears. Dust blew into the air, and Holzir and the skinwing vanished.

It happened so fast that at first I thought panic had tricked my eyes. Then I remembered seeing the ground beneath the skinwing starting to crack. The creature must have knocked apart a thin cover over a crevasse and fallen in—and Holzir went with it.

I ran toward the pit that had opened at the base of the ridge, the loaded blastgun still at the ready. Rint dashed before me, as if to remind me to slow down and not risk ripping open another hole.

Rocks were still teetering at the edge and crumbling into the pit. I slowed down and started yelling: "Holzir! Holzir! Are you all right?" I was scared I would get the worst answer possible: none.

First the only noise was the slither of settling pebbles and my pounding heart. Then from below: "I'm fine, but the flying pisser isn't doing so well."

It was such a relief to hear Holzir's voice that I almost fumbled the blastgun from my fingers again. I wondered why I felt such a lift in my spirits, when yesterday I had tried to make Holzir leave me alone forever.

I leaned over—cautiously—to peer into the pit. It dropped twenty spans below the butte, still far enough to kill or cripple Holzir. But he was on his feet, looking quite satisfied with himself. The skinwing had fallen first and must have broken Holzir's fall. It would never be getting up: Holzir had moved fast to take advantage of the shock, and the skinwing's head lay a foot away from the bloody stump of its neck.

"We don't need your witch-weapons, see?" He swung the red-stained sword. "The Sorrow of the Koltzer is the Sorrow of its foes!"

I had never heard Holzir shout the tribe's battle cry. He had gone on hunts and raids, but unlike the windbags in Dyzlin's clan, he never told about them afterwards, not even in song. I wondered if he had ever killed in battle. It didn't seem he could—he was too gentle for his own people. Hadn't he left his tribe behind to travel unknown paths with a witch-girl?

"You're sure you're not hurt?" Rint made an empathetic squeak to echo my question.

"Some bruises. Nothing worse."

I examined the pit closer. The walls were sheer and impossible for anyone to climb. "How am I going to get you out?"

"Oh, it's about *you* again?" But he laughed as he said it. The killing of the skinwing had lifted his spirits higher than I'd seen since our escape. "You didn't remember to bring rope, did you?"

Add that to the list of items I had forgotten. How long before my forgetfulness got us killed?

"It doesn't matter," he said before I could answer. "I've got a coil in my pack. I'll tie the end around a rock and hurl it up to you. Then you can climb down."

"What are you talking about? You're climbing up, nych-brain!"

He shook his head, and the grin on his face showed he was proud to know something I didn't. "You'll try to jump down here when I tell you what I've found. There's a tunnel going right under the butte."

I couldn't see anything from above, but Holzir pointed toward a dark side of the pit. "It might lead nowhere," I said. "Maybe just trap us when it sinks into an underground stream."

"Not this one. I can see light on the other side. And—it's not a natural tunnel. Someone cut it out of the stones."

He was right. I almost jumped down to him.

NINE

I ran my palm over the inside of the tunnel that bored underneath the butte. "It's smooth. Like it was sanded and polished." Rint had already found this out, and was making a game of dashing up and sliding down the slick stone.

Holzir stood alone on the far side of the pit, wary of the tunnel mouth. His early enthusiasm started to ebb while I made the descent on the rope. By the time I reached the bottom and my excitement to look at his discovery was almost exploding me open, his Sorrow was trying to clamp him shut.

"Do you think that the—the Shapers dug this?" he asked.

"No, I don't think so. This is something, uhm, weirder." The Shapers used the sorcerer's ash from blackpowder weapons to blast apart stones. The glossy sides of this passage looked as if a magical bolt had seared a hole from one side to the other in a single burst. From what I knew of the Shapers, they had no tools for work so elegant.

"If this goes all the way under the rock, it'll put us right at Ravager Fang's gum-line," Holizr said.

My eyes moved over the mystery corridor punched clean through a mountain. "Somebody wanted to get there desperately."

"Or they wanted to get out. Maybe it's part of Ravager Fang's curse."

But there was no other path, and Holzir knew it as well as I did. I straightened my pack. "We'd better move if we want to see what's on the other side before sunset."

Holzir acted as if he had changed into a stalagmite at the bottom of the pit. I reached out and took his hand. His feet started to shuffle forward. "Brave Holzir," I crooned in the tone of a bonfire storyteller speaking to children, "slayer of the sky-hunter, strode at the side of the witch-girl toward the brooding mystery of Ravager Fang."

He said nothing, but his feet moved faster. His gloved hand tightened around mine. His other hand gripped the sword, still coated in the gore of the skinwing.

We moved at a slow gait through the tunnel, since the floor was so slick it was like walking on oiled glass. It cut off the sounds of the mountains, and when we reached the middle it seemed the rest of the world had fallen asleep.

Holzir started to sing. The smooth walls were like an open-air theater, and for a moment the man next to me wasn't scared Holzir, Sorrowful Holzir, but truly was "Holzir the Brave":

> *Two striders across the hills,*
> *Laugh at riders in the dust.*
> *They walk blind toward the Art,*
> *But the Sky Lords they trust.*
> *Sorrowful and Sorrowless*
> *Fear neither Moon nor Sun,*
> *Side by side, they flip the stones*

Until both can claim they won.

"I don't know that song," I said when he stopped.

"Neither did I, until now. I made it up."

"I wish you had shared more of your song-writing talent before, Holzir. It might have made life with your tribe a bit easier."

"I'm less afraid to share my songs when I'm afraid of almost everything else."

It was dusk when we reached the other end of the tunnel. We dropped a few feet from the opening onto a flat surface of black rock. The falling sun showed the walls of an enormous shallow well, and I thought we had walked into a dead end. Whatever had burrowed through the stones had done so to escape from a pit with no other way out.

But how had they gotten into the pit in the first place? That question made my heart beat faster. So did the next one: Who were "they"?

We moved from the shadow of the wall. The tunnel had not brought us to the foot of Ravager Fang as Holzir had guessed; the mountain's roots were a short walk away. Between it and us lay a pasture of stone, a place burned out of the mountain like a heated sword had plunged from the sky and sliced the rock open. The walls were as smooth as the tunnel, but instead of the polished silver sheen, they were roasted charcoal black. This place had been scorched.

The limestone face of Ravager Fang glowered over the pit like a mourner at an open grave. But Ravager Fang wasn't a fire-mountain; there were none in the Fencer Mountains. No natural fire had done this. This was the Art on a scale that shouldn't exist—not in the control of anything living. If the Shapers wielded this power in their pale hands, they could re-conquer all the lands and start a second Hegemony in less than a year.

Holzir didn't collapse on the ground and start shivering in fear at the awesome sight, which I would expect from most Koltzer and even Idenites. Only servants of the Shapers could be prepared for this. Or someone without the Sorrow. Yet Holzir held my hand and stayed steady as we stared at the inscrutable majesty of the place.

I scanned the ridge of the well, which formed a circle except where the toe of Ravager Fang wedged into it. That granite peak was also blackened, and the most amazing sight of all jutted out from it. It made me forget anything else had seemed strange at all.

Three fingers pointed straight from the rock face. They were too thin to be made of stone, and their gray colors weren't the granite of the Fencer Mountains, but of steel stressed by rain and wind. The three metal sheets widened until they reached a base beneath the rubble. The stones about it bulged, hinting at a globular giant trapped beneath. Something tremendous was just under the rock covering.

"Is it a fortress?" Holzir asked.

"I don't know. I've never seen anything like it. Whatever is beneath those—" I had no idea what the metal spires were, so my mind settled on a word. "—*fins* must be enormous."

"Why would anybody build something like that up here? It has to come from the Shapers, Belde! No one else would build an evil thing so far from the rest of the world."

I started to walk across the blackened ground toward the buried object. "How do we know it's evil? Not all Art is bad. You're forgetting how I saved us from Dyzlin."

He didn't have an answer for that.

"Besides," I continued, "I don't think anybody built this here. Look at the burned walls. And the tunnel leading away. It fell here. When it hit, it blew out this pit, and whoever was inside bored their way out."

"Nothing so large could stay in the air," Holzir said. "Even the Shapers can't build something larger than a skinwing that can fly."

This was true. And there was only one people who might have made a flying machine so massive that its fall would rip open a mountainside and leave a permanent pit. For the moment, I didn't dream farther than that. The ideas crowding my mind were too fantastic.

"Your tribe has songs about great sky machines, doesn't it? I remember one about people from the Cirrus Mountains, Sky Lords who—"

"Most of our songs are just stories, Belde. Like Belische. Who knows if that ever happened?"

"If this happened," I made a circle with my arm to take in the pit, "then the Art could certainly wipe out a city."

Holzir dropped his gaze to the scorched ground. I had pressed too far and his Sorrow was rising. I turned back to examine the wreck.

A doorway into the machine was at the level of the floor of the pit, slanted at an angle like it opened into a house that had tilted over. The rocks around it were slick. Someone had used the same power that created the tunnel to cut an escape from the door.

I felt a tingling elation, the same kind as when I thought of the Woman's promise to find me. I wanted to dash to the strange door, fling it open, and find the secrets of the lost days of Ahn-Tarqa. Common sense kept hold and made me walk toward the opening cautiously.

Holzir didn't come along, and even Rint stayed back. The beak-nose kept his head tilted to the sky. He had no interest in the Art or the mysterious craft; he wanted to know if there were more skinwings in the area looking to have him for dinner.

I had my eyes on the door as I walked, so I didn't pay attention to what was happening overhead. Rint and Holzir sounded out warnings at the same time, and I looked up without knowing what they were trying to tell me. I guessed that the skinwing had a mate, because the sunlight was muted through huge flaps of skin on the wings of a creature diving toward the ground.

This time I was ready and raised the blastgun. But I didn't shoot, because something about the movement of the animal looked strange. It wasn't flying straight for me, but flapping toward an empty patch before the doorway. For a moment in the light, I noticed hair bristling from the top of the creature's head. Many saurians have feathers, but never hair like a person or fur like a rodent.

The winged thing dropped to the ground and onto its knees. I had the gun aimed at it, but my finger was off the trigger.

It made no move except to turn its head my way. "Are you the messenger? Have you come at the last, to arrive at sunset of the longest day?"

The language was Idenite, although in a style from an old parchment. Dusty and dead "schoolbook" language from centuries past.

"What is that, Belde?" Holzir asked from behind me.

I stared at the flying creature. It was human in shape except for the flaps of skin that stretched from its hands and connected at the ankles. The arms looked twice as long as they should be, and the body was as bony as a starved beggar. Yet it was a man, or had once been.

"Are you not the messenger?" the winged man asked when I simply stared.

How could I answer? The man did not seem dangerous: he carried no weapon, and his stance looked more exhausted than tensed for a fight.

"Do you have speech?" the winged man asked. "Are you the messenger?"

"I—I don't know what you mean," I choked out in Idenite.

Silver irises flashed, but the face was obscured in the shadows of dusk.

"You have come armed, as to a battle," he said.

I lowered the blastgun. "I thought you might be a skinwing."

The winged man tilted his head. "They still come here, although scant food is left. But the folk of the peaks have not come in ages. When I first looked upon you, I thought you had come to take my place. But you have no wings. You are of the folk of the earth. And of them, only the messenger would come to me."

I looked back to Holzir. He had not moved, but gazed in wonder and recognition. "That must be a cloud-wight," he said. "From the songs. Don't you remember, Belde?"

I did. Holzir had mentioned cloud-wights a few times when he warned me against coming near Ravager Fang. One of the reasons the Koltzer tribes feared the western arm of the Fencer Mountains was because they believed a violent race with the power of skin-wings laired there and caught anyone they found to sacrifice to their cloud gods. But this "cloud-wight" did not look ready to slay us. It looked ready to die.

I turned back to the creature, who seemed content to wait until the moon rose for me to answer.

I chose: "I am the messenger."

"That is best." He sat down and crossed his arms so the coppery skin flaps folded under him and vanished. He changed from a bizarre apparition to a scrawny caricature of an old man. I felt safe enough to start walking toward him.

He spoke, although not to any specific listener: "When the others elected me as the guardian, the chieftain addressed me and said, 'Vhal-Far, you must protect the Shrine of Forgotten Memory. But it may happen that none shall come to relieve you. There are no newborns, no one younger to take the sacred burden when your time ends.' But I told the chieftain I would not shy from the sacred duty entrusted to the folk of the peaks. So I have remained, feasting on rats and roots, until you came to end my task."

The winged man who called himself Vhal-Far let his head droop so that it almost vanished within his folded arms. I knelt, setting the blackpowder weapon out of sight behind me. Vhal-Far had shown no interest in it. He seemed to not even see me after I lied that I was this "messenger" his people had spent years, decades, maybe centuries waiting for.

Then Vhal-Far remembered my presence and raised his head. The cloud-wight's flesh was filled with craters and cracks, and the hair I had glanced in the sunlight was only a few white strands clinging to his skull. The pupils in a tarnished silver setting were shrunk almost to nothing. If Vhal-Far had been the youngest of his folk when they chose him to guard this place, the others must have died long ago.

"Vhal-Far, tell unto me why you guard this place ... the shrine." It was a weak attempt to speak his ancient dialect, but he understood me.

"You are the messenger. You must know why you placed the burden upon us."

I didn't want him to discover I was lying, so I tried a different approach. "Vhal-Far, how many seasons have passed since the burden was placed upon you?"

He hunched his shoulders. "What does time mean? Only the folk of the earth concern themselves with time. We do not, for time never touches us while we live in the air. Yet—yet now all are dead in the ground. I am the last."

He spoke with disbelief; he could not understand *how* time had touched his people and let them die off, leaving him waiting in solitude on a task that might never end.

I felt like placing my hand on his decrepit shoulder and telling him I understood. I had waited years for someone to come ease my life, someone who belonged to "my people," whom I barely knew as anything except a voice behind a mask and rumors of others hidden like black rice grains in the white rice pile of Ahn-Tarqa.

Holzir padded up behind me, certain now the pathetic figure wouldn't harm us. "What language are you speaking?"

"It's a kind of very old Idenite." Holzir had learned a few phrases of Idenite during the time that he taught me Koltzer, but he had no hope of understanding anything in Vhal-Far's antique speech. "He says he's the last guardian of this place he calls 'The Shrine of Forgotten Memory.' The others of his race have all died."

"That explains why nobody I know, even the biggest braggart, claims he's seen a cloud-wight." Holzir rubbed his chin. "But what's 'The Shrine of Forgotten Memory'? How can something be a memory if it's forgotten?"

"Somebody forgot the place. Maybe if I plead forgetting, I'll find out who."

I looked back to the cloud-wight, who had studied and then lost interest in Holzir. "Vhal-Far, those who have sent me have forgotten much. Such is the curse of the shrine, is that not true? Time eats away at the memory of those on the ground, like, uhm, flies eating rotten meat. Tell me what I have forgotten." My stabs at the old manner of speech wouldn't have won me a herald's job in the ancient kingdoms, but Vhal-Far didn't mind. He appeared glad to spend a bit more time with the messenger now that his only task was done.

"I know pieces only. We of the peaks understand not the letters of the People of the Light."

Every spot of my skin tingled. "People of the Light? You mean the Lightborn?"

The cloud-wight cocked his head. "Do you now title yourself the 'Lightborn' and not the old name?"

"Yes, yes," I said, trying to hold back the thrill. He didn't know the name 'Lightborn,' but 'People of the Light' was close enough. It was what I had dared to think when I saw the metal giant in the rocks. The Lightborn were real, and this crashed flying device was their making! But where had they gone, and why had they left the Sorrow and the Art behind them, as the stories said they did?

"The People of the Light," I continued, "they have forgotten. Tell me, why did they leave your folk as sentries of the shrine?"

Vhal-Far shrugged his wings. "I cannot read their letters. They commanded the folk of the peaks to remain behind when they sought other lands. We would await them, and keep this place safe from the Elder."

Elder. That word also caused a jolt. It sounded similar to another name almost never spoken. *Eldru* ... the name the Shapers called themselves.

"What lies inside the shrine? What must I retrieve so we may be safe from the Elder?"

Vhal-Far looked at me with a glance so exhausted that I wondered why he didn't simply lie down and stop living. "I only guard, Messenger. I cannot enter. That is your task."

He stood up and raised his wings as if meaning to fly away. But his limbs trembled with fatigue, and I wondered if he had any strength left to climb to a perch and glide on the air again. Life had seemed to bleed from him since I arrived. His task was almost finished.

He held out a finger toward the doorway. I started for it.

Holzir's hand dropped onto my shoulder. "Do you want me to go with you?"

I tried to see in his eyes if he believed he could do what he said. Of course he couldn't return my gaze. "It's a machine of Art beneath those rocks, Holzir. Maybe the greatest one in Ahn-Tarqa. Do you think you can tolerate it?"

He shook his head. "It wouldn't be right of me not to offer, would it?" He reached down and picked up the blastgun from where I had left it. It took all his focus to allow him to touch it. "You'll need your witch-weapon."

I pushed his hand back. "There's nothing inside there that would be frightened by a creaky piece of the Art. You keep watch on it."

I approached the canted doorway, leaving Holzir and Rint behind. The beak-nose knew without me signing that he couldn't come either. Vhal-Far stayed as well, showing no interest in what was inside the place he had guarded for so many years.

I pushed open the metal portal. It squeaked at being disturbed from centuries of stillness. But what lay on the other side wasn't still. The hair on my neck prickled. Something powerful, like an approaching storm, flowed outward.

I wasn't the messenger the cloud-wight had expected, but once I passed inside, I would have all the responsibilities that long-dead person was meant to take on. Everything would change.

I stepped across the threshold.

TEN

I had to feel my way by touch beyond the first turn in the corridor. The metal of the walls was so smooth it seemed impossible a blacksmith could have forged it. Steel is a precious commodity in Iden, imported from smelters of the cities of Vatrusla, but this was too precise and hard for even the finest Vatruslan steel.

I stepped on a piece of the grooved metal floor that gave beneath my weight. A glare sprang up in front of my eyes. It was light from a glow globe, the simple lamps powered by the Art used in the cities during deep winter. But I had never seen any that flared so brightly and without flickering as the red and blue lines of light that spread along the passageway.

Along with the lights came a humming sound. The rocks that trapped the machine quivered and my teeth chattered. The machine of the Art was coming to life. The lines of red and blue beckoned me toward its beating heart.

I followed the curve of the passage, taking my way warily along the tilted corridor. The slant made me dizzy as my head kept telling me that I was teetering over and about to fall.

The passage ended at a door without a latch. Block writing crossed the middle of it. The language was a garble, even though I recognized the letters. But a sign with a picture of a hand pressing against a black square was all the instruction I needed. I put my hand against the square beneath the picture and pushed.

The door sighed open, pulling into a pocket. A series of three tones sounded. The chamber beyond was dark, but the wheeze of air and the purr of the Art told me that the door opened onto a cavernous space.

The globes on the ceiling snapped to life with a frigid glow, and I stared inside the core of the behemoth called "The Shrine of Forgotten Memory."

Holzir's doubts made sense: How could anyone forget this?

The domed chamber slanted like the rest of the corridors, so at first I could not get a sense what the place was used for. I had seen sailing ships on the Glosser River, and if this were a kind of "airship," it might have parts similar to watercraft. But the rudimentary machines of the Art that I knew looked like fleas on the back of a quake-foot compared what was crowded here.

The airship pulsed with power, but only a few of the devices were working. Shards of gears were strewn over the floor. A tower of wires had toppled and smashed a bank of machinery. Walkways crossed in a web over my head. Machines lined the walls; I'd never seen anything like them before, even when I had entered the Cruncher that powered the Art of Tyrn on the frightful day I escaped from the Shapers.

I started across the chamber, thankful the builders had made the floor from ridged rubber that kept me from slipping. I passed what looked like a row of closets, each with a door made from a clear material that didn't reflect light the way glass should. Each had space to fit a single person, standing upright. Above each door was a simple drawing of a man with wings. Were these the cells where the cloud-wights were kept? Were they prisoners, pets, or slaves?

Nearby was a table covered with glass shards and metal stands that must have once held containers. Among the smashed glass were a few objects that looked like sewing needles attached to the ends of plungers.

The opposite end of the dome bulged into an area reachable by a set of stairs. The machines here still flickered. I didn't understand the use of any of them. Even a Shaper might find them baffling. Above the benches of switches and knobs was a row of glass panes that glowed with a curious pattern. It looked like a swarm of insects flying in front of a light.

A helm. I finally made a connection between this airship and a familiar sailing ship. This raised deck of machines looked like the spot where a captain would stand to look over the prow at a flowing river.

One of the fizzling glass panes changed. The insect swarm stopped, and the rectangle glowed a soothing blue. Letters scrolled across the glass, although I still couldn't read them. I tried to commit some to memory to figure out later, but the words marched past so speedily that I had no hope of getting anything from them.

The letters stopped, and a picture replaced them. I recognized the shape: it resembled maps of Ahn-Tarqa I had seen in the stalls of merchants who hocked them to sailors. None looked exactly like the others, but all had a similar outline showing the sickle curve of the peninsula to the west, and the thick bulge of the rest of the continent to the east. There was also a second mass of land, another continent, attached to the east with only a narrow ribbon of ocean between it and Ahn-Tarqa.

This map had no names or features on it that I knew from the days when a little girl and her beak-nose pet had pestered merchants to let them look at their maps. I saw a few mountains, but the rest was solid white—as if the person drawing the map had forgotten to fill it in.

But then, an invisible hand went to work at that task. The shape of the continent stretched and pulled as the hand painted life onto it. The strange second continent broke away and moved to the north. Mountain chains rose to make the fences that split and separated the land. The deserts of the Najael filled in the east coast with burning gold. Green forests sprouted to create the Acivis Wilds along the north of Lakkad and the jungles of the Bavtuus. Finally, the great plains rolling toward Iden spread in amber across the west with the blue veins of rivers trickling through them. Past the plains, the sickle of the Shapers' peninsula remained empty.

There were no names on the map, but two features stood out. There was a flashing red dot, marking where the airship had crashed. The location looked about right. The second was a green dot in the middle of the continent, in peaks I knew must be the Cirrus Mountains. Was this where the ship had come from? Were the Koltzer songs right about the Sky Lords of the Cirrus and their flying ships?

Words popped up beside the red dot, perhaps detailing the crash location. I had no chance to understand what they said, if they were trying to say anything to me at all. I wasn't the intended messenger. The ship was preaching to someone who did not even know its language.

Then I did recognize a word. It flashed over the map in large letters. It touched the same familiar region of my thoughts the map had. It was "Ahn-Tarqa," but the letters were redrawn. I knew this was important, so I stared at the word and burned it into my memory. If I took no other knowledge back with me, I would at least have this strange way of writing "Ahn-Tarqa."

The way the Lightborn had written it.

The Lightborn. It was in my thoughts now without hesitation or fear. All this was the work of the Lightborn. The "Sky Lords" of the Koltzer. The "Torch People" of the Bavtuu. The Shapers built wicked machines, but they could never craft anything as intricate as these glowing picture-glass panes that created images from nothing. The Shapers built chariots that flew on flapping wings, but they could not lift into the air something the size of three sailing galleys. Only the Lightborn, who had given the world the Sorrow and the Art, could achieve such miracles.

But the messenger wasn't supposed to come to this shrine and just read a few words off a picture-glass. The Lightborn who had crashed here and tunneled to freedom had meant to return to retrieve something important. What? How could someone thousands of years removed solve the riddle? I couldn't even read their language. Asking Vhal-Far would be no help. He had never entered the shrine, and the cloud-wight's language had changed over the centuries as well.

The light on the picture-glass started to grow weaker. I blinked, and then noticed all the glow globes inside the dome were dimming. The whirring noise ebbed. Whatever the shrine had to show me was finished, and it was closing itself down to seal me in the dark with no way out.

The veins in my head pulsed. I felt dizzy. I sat down in the failing light, trying to clear my mind. Nausea flooded over me, as if the airship was flipping upside down. I shut my eyes, trying to stop from throwing up. After a few deep breaths, the sickness started to ease, but my head buzzed like a gnat swarm was trapped inside. I opened my eyes at last ... and saw a woman dressed in silver walking around the airship's deck.

She was beautiful and pale. She drifted through the wreckage, acting like everything was normal and working exquisitely. She passed cold and lightless benches of machines and nodded at them in approval.

A ghost? Or my imagination losing control?

I sat still and watched the figure move about her tasks. Her single-piece uniform looked metallic, as if a silversmith had found a way to weave the metal of his profession into cloth. The woman looked around at cabinets that must have once stood over the broken machines. The cabinets were no more ... as was she. She was a phantom in my head, going about chores that had no meaning after thousands of years.

Why was I imagining her at all? She searched the non-existent lockers as if she knew exactly where everything was. This was precision I couldn't invent, especially if I were delirious.

No, she wasn't my imagination. A power inside the Shrine of Forgotten Memory was making me remember her. It was pushing thoughts into my head.

I might have shut my eyes and told myself I was crazy. But I had seen this happen before: in the shining globe—the "vision orb" as its wielders called it—that the Shapers forced Father to gaze into. They used it to test if he were Sorrowless, because only someone without the Sorrow could look into what was inside the orb without going mad.

From my hiding spot in the rafters on that terrible day, I had glanced into the vision orb's light ... and waking dreams attacked me. I saw ice, and people in bulging orange outfits with shields over their eyes, and a black and white beast that resembled the sigil of the Shapers' Handless God.

This ghost-woman making preparations on dead machines must come from the same power as the vision orb. It was sending images into my head. It was a gentler vision, not a rush of power, but it still dazzled me.

The silver woman noticed something. Not me. She turned to face the center of the dome, where a circle was painted, and started to talk to it. I could barely hear her, but her motions were like someone making an introduction. The messenger was supposed to stand on that circle to receive instructions. I got up, still wobbly from the rush of the power burrowing into my head, and walked to the circle. I stood on it and faced the woman. As I did, her body became more solid, and her words crystallized.

I didn't expect to understand anything the silver woman was saying. The language of the Lightborn that appeared on the picture-glass was a garble to me. Why should their spoken words mean anything more?

But the moment the memory of her speech entered my head, I almost toppled over. *I understood her.* Not everything. But snatches of words and phrases. Even the words I didn't understand had a rhythm I recognized.

She was speaking my native language. An even more archaic version than what the cloud-wight spoke, going back so many generations that the meaning of it was lost. But it was the beginning of the language I had learned from my parents.

The language of the Lightborn had changed into Idenite.

My head was like a jug with water from a waterfall pouring into it, splashing out as more gushed in. If I had the Sorrow, I would have gone utterly mad that instant. I still teetered toward it.

Because I was facing a truth I had suspected from when the cloud-wight first mentioned "The People of the Light."

The similarity of language must mean the Lightborn had stayed on Ahn-Tarqa, at least long enough to spread their language to its people. Maybe they had stayed longer. *Maybe they were still among us.*

I couldn't keep that thought in my mind for a moment without feeling like I would faint. *Focus, keep focused, Belde.*

I picked out the silver woman's words, trying to piece them together: *Cure failed. Records. Escape.* Over and over the name *Elder*, and its sinister similarity to *Eldru.*

I steadied myself and stared into the woman's eyes, which were the same argent color as her uniform. So much was entering my head, but what could I do with it? How could I carry any of it away and make use of it? I didn't even know what it meant, or if this were what "the messenger" was supposed to achieve.

The woman continued her speech, not caring that her listener was struggling to keep pace. The memory-voice became more urgent, the motions of the woman's hands more animated. *Elder*, again and again. *Return fails. Time. Not the answer. Cure.* She pointed toward the table with the needle-plunger, and made a motion like she was sticking one into herself, and then repeated strongly: *Failure.* She tapped her head. *New illness.*

None of it made sense. I shrugged as if I could tell a memory thousands of years old that I didn't understand.

At last the silver woman finished what instructions she had to give, concluding with a gesture of finality and a bow of her head. Now she would disappear, and I would be as confused as before, left with knowledge of the Lightborn but not a single notion of what a seventeen-year-old runaway could do with it.

But the silver woman had one final task. She gestured to a cube on the floor a few feet away. I had ignored it until then, thinking it was another piece of debris. But when I looked closer, I saw it was fixed to the deck.

The silver woman bent over the cube and looked as if she were pressing a latch on its side. The ritual was supposed to mean something to the messenger, telling him or her where to look. The woman stood up again, and placed her hand to her head like a salute before she vanished. She then spoke the only full sentence understood I completely: "To save humanity."

I copied the salute and echoed: "To save humanity." It seemed the respectful thing to do, whatever else had been planned. I had become the messenger.

My head cleared, and I noticed the lights inside the shrine were almost dark. The scant power the airship had preserved for the messenger's return was draining away.

I ran to the cube, which was the size of a child's kickball. There were two buttons on the side, impossible to see unless you knew to look for them. I pressed both at once. The top of the cube flipped open, and a radiance I remembered from years ago glowed inside.

I knew to shield my eyes as I reached inside the cube. My hand rested on the warm curve of a globe. I scooped up the round treasure, keeping my eyes sealed so no glance of the memories stored inside could enter my head. I had suffered enough of that for one day. I reached for my pack and stuffed the orb inside, down deep so my clothes swallowed it and dimmed the light.

As the glow from the globe faded in my pack, the lights in the chamber finished dying. By the time I stepped into the passage to find my way out, the ship had finished sliding into its last sleep. It had waited so long to come to life once again so it could die forever. I carried its last life spark with me—whatever it was.

VHAL-FAR'S BRONZE body was folded over his knees in a prayer toward the evening sky of the west, where long ago the masters of the buried ship had gone in search of help. I started to understand their story, and why the cloud-wights had come to name this place "The Shrine of Forgotten Memory." I had that "memory" inside my pack. In the ancient past, someone had forgotten that the orb and its knowledge were waiting in the abandoned ship. The people of the airship hadn't taken the vision orb with them when they escaped from the site where they had crashed, choosing to return for it later and leave its protection to the winged creatures aboard the ship. They must have feared an enemy would catch them with the orb and seize its precious memories, so they let it remain in this hidden mountain fastness with a few watchful flying eyes as guards.

The task "to save humanity" was forgotten. And now the last flying eye had shut.

Rint stood a few feet away, holding himself with a stillness that matched the cloud-wight's. Holzir stood over the bent figure. He did not look at me; his tribal superstition made him frightened to see what I might have brought back from the buried metal machine. It was easier to look at the empty shell of Vhal-Far.

"How long ago did he die?" I asked.

"He said a few words to me after you went inside. I think he was talking to me, but it was hard to tell. Then he walked this far, sat down, and started humming. It was like this—" Holzir made a noise from the back of his throat.

"The sound of the airship," I said. "It made a noise like that when I entered. He must have felt it."

"He kept humming for a few minutes, then the hum sounded like the wheels of a cart slowing down on a steep road. Then he was silent. I knew he was gone."

"His job was finished. His body was only waiting to catch up with the choice he had made to die."

"Waiting for the *messenger*." Holzir looked at me, caught between doubt and wonder.

"I was the best he would get, Holzir. The people who crashed that ship—" I decided not to call them by their powerful name yet. "—are long gone. The real messenger died with them. Could you, or any of your tribesmen, have gone in there?"

"Could any of your city folk?"

I conceded with a shrug. "No. Neither could the sailors of Vatrusla, or the nomads of Najael. Not even the Shapers. The ... ghosts ... inside would be too much even for them."

Holzir stepped around the kneeling body. "What did those ghosts tell Belde the Sorrowless?" It wasn't doubt or wonder in his voice now, but defiance. "Is it too much even for Holzir the Brave, slayer of the sky-hunter? You forget that I've managed to hold your witch-weapon all this time."

The gun was still in his arms. I hadn't noticed until then.

I didn't dare mention the Lightborn. It would be too much for him. That I may have learned the Lightborn's bloodline was still on Ahn-Tarqa was almost too much for me to handle. "I found the thing the Shapers used on my father. One just like it. The Shapers want to know what's inside of it, but they can't look at it themselves or it makes their Sorrow destroy them. Only the Sorrowless can look into one."

"So what's inside?"

"I haven't looked. Not yet."

Last night I had accused Holzir of selfishness. Now I understood I was guilty of it as well. I wanted to find the woman who had promised to come for me because I wanted shelter. I wanted a new place to belong to replace the one the Shapers had stolen from me. I wanted to find a place with people who thought as I did.

Now my escape was no longer just about me. I had picked up a task. Whatever hid inside the orb was something the Shapers would kill to obtain. They had already killed: Mother and Father and unknown others who stood across their path. My family's home couldn't have been the first one the Shapers visited with their murderous tools on their quest.

I still had to find the Woman, but not just for myself. I had a gift to deliver to her, something that might be a gift to all of Ahn-Tarqa. "To save humanity."

As my mind danced with plans, Holzir studied something on the ground. He hunched down with the blastgun over his knees. "When the winged man was humming, I saw him moving his fingers over the dirt. I didn't think it was anything, and I didn't want to disturb him. But, look here—" He pointed to scratches in the rock dust. "It's a map. A simple one, but see: this circle and the line coming from it must be the pit we're in. And here's a trail, through these peaks." Holzir pointed toward two dwarf copies of Ravager Fang that peeked over the ridge to the east. They were dark enough to stand out against the purple evening. "He must have known about these from his flights. He could see a way out of here that we never could. If I'm reading it right, this path over the shoulder of Ravager Fang—"

"—will drop us on the north side of the mountains," I finished.

Holzir stood up. "So, is it time for us to come down from the hills?"

I nodded. "Getting to Ravager Fang showed us the way down after all."

"And are we still heading for the Gray Lands?" He paused to remember, then said: "Those hideouts I've heard about from the traders. You think those rumors are true?"

"Hear a rumor often enough, it probably has some bit of truth. And if we want to find the Woman, that's where to start."

"That woman, she can help with—whatever you've found?"

"It's either ask her or ask the Shapers. They're the only two I can think of."

"I'll take the first choice then. We'd better get in a short march before it's blacker than a nych's winter burrow." He turned around and moved toward the shoulder of the mountain.

As he walked away from me, I realized something the dusk

and my own dizzy head had missed until then. *Holzir had looked me in the eyes and not once turned his gaze away.*

Did he even know he had done it? As I watched him walk toward the secret trail, a blackpowder gun resting in his arms, I wondered—could the Sorrow be erased? Could it be wiped away, spot by spot, like a splotch of grease scrubbed from a workshop floor?

The orb in my pack tugged at my thoughts as Rint and I followed Holzir. Maybe the orb could answer these questions. Or perhaps it merely offered a glance into an impossible paradise, the kind that might exist only in a past that had been extinguished long before the lamps in the Shrine of Forgotten Memory.

ELEVEN

The path Vhal-Far had scratched for us in the dust led along streambeds cut deep into the rocks. These were the unlucky meltwaters of the Fencer Mountains. The fortunate snowmelt flowed down the south face of the peaks, where it joined the exuberant waters of the Glosser River and found its way to the freedom of the sea. The streams that guided us down the north face of the mountains were headed for a different fate: a burial ground called the Lazzun Marshes.

When the last of the mossy foothills ended, Holzir and I stared over wetlands that sprawled with no end in sight. Somewhere at the north edge were the Temblor Plains, but how long we might have to slosh through the marshes to reach open land was impossible to guess. But neither of us hesitated to march onward. Our food would run out in a day, and the marshes teemed with fish and rodents that could serve as disgusting meals when we needed them. We trudged into the slough, seeking spots of hard land where we could, wading through the murk when we couldn't.

I had met the Lazzun Marshes before, but with the safety of a league of grass between us. During the first autumn I lived among the Koltzer, Kalzzik's tribe had pursued a quake-foot herd across the Temblor Plains and staked out a prime hunting ground close to the edges of the marshes. Each day, Kalzzik sent out hunters to haul back enough quake-foot meat to keep bellies full for the summer.

Seen from a camp on the plains, the Lazzun Marshes looked like a blot of mud and reeds. The only animals were slithering venomous things, scurrying rats, and flocks of long-legged birds whose flesh was oily and indigestible. Quake-foots fed on the thick swamp grass along the edges, although they were not stupid enough to wander into the noisome muck and sink.

Now that I was actually in the marshes, I found the whole place was noxious. The stink was wretched, especially when my feet slipped off the hummocks and caused a bubble of gas to burst in my face. But the squishy heaps of decay weren't the worst part. It was the hot, humid air. After the thin mountain air, this phlegmy soup made me hate breathing. The damp heat made Holzir strip off his tunic and go bare-chested. Modesty wouldn't let me go that far, so I suffered with the fabric glued to my skin.

During the first day's march, we found a strip of semi-solid ground made from the roots of black cypress. The tree branches sagged into the water as if crying over having to grow in such a nightmare place. I welcomed the trees, however, because the mountains had made me accustomed to having cover. The thought of the orb inside my pack, which gave off a light that might signal anyone or anything roaming the plains, made me more aware of needing places to hide.

The airship had raised my spirits, but the sludge seeping into my moccasins tried to drag them under and drown them. Holzir seemed to march slower the farther we waded into the marshes. I was afraid that any progress he had made with his Sorrow would die in this miasma.

Rint was in a better mood. He was almost jolly. He had a new world over his head filled with juicy insects to leap at and snap down his gullet. The bloated swamp-needles buzzing over the brackish water had become his new favorite delicacy.

We stepped cautiously to avoid the serpents writhing around, but the life of the swamp seemed to want to stay clear of us. The only exception was the blood-sucker flies, some of which were as long as my thumb, and which swarmed around us constantly.

A gas bubble as big as a wagon wheel bulged at my feet, and if I hadn't leaned back at the last moment, the burst would have geysered ooze across my face. "The marsh phantoms must have lost their noses long ago if they lived here," I tried to joke. It was the first time I had mentioned the most famous legend of the Lazzun Marshes.

"No such thing as marsh phantoms," Holzir said, but his shoulders tightened. He wasn't as certain as he wished he was. In the middle of this suffocating mist, where any creature could be hiding a foot away and eyeing us, I wasn't certain either.

Tales of the marsh phantoms did the most to keep the Koltzer away from the Lazzun Marshes. I knew the stories from my first autumn with the tribe, when I often listened to singers around the bonfires. I was struggling to learn the language; Holzir did most of my tutoring, because Bixenta hadn't the patience to deal with my "sickness." I sat near the evening gatherings to practice listening. I stayed outside the circle, close to the dark so the others would not notice me. The singers' rhymes and phrases that repeated like a wheel clicking over cobbled pavement were easier to understand than the jabber I usually heard around me.

That was how I heard about the Phantoms of the Lazzun Marshes, who had their own corner of spook stories. They were neither human nor saurian, but terrors that flitted between both. They were white as bleached bones and could move across the top of the heavy air. The phantoms ensured that anyone who journeyed into the marsh mists would never return to the clean light. They even snatched away those who came too close to the edge of their domain. "The dead, some say. The never-dead, say others," a singer at a bonfire would chant, weaving the kind of nonsense their poems loved. "White shapes, red lusts, always hating—"

On and on the singers rolled their verses, bringing listeners into a fear that might take away their own Sorrow as they quivered thinking about these impossible demons of the marshes.

Two warriors of Kalzzik's tribe had ventured toward the marshes while we were camped there; they hoped to raise their clan's standing with their courage. Neither returned before Kalzzik pulled up stakes a week later. No one went to search for them, and the marsh phantoms were the whispered reason.

A juicy crunching sound pulled me from the memory. Rint was chomping on a hard-shelled swamp-needle. Its wing twitched from his mouth. I wished my beak-nose friend would stop enjoying himself so much. And stop looking so well fed. "We can't eat bugs like you, Rint. Find us something warm and furry." I made a crawling hand motion that my friend knew meant *rodent*. He might be able to hoist one of the tinier critters in his mouth, but my stomach wasn't empty enough yet for me to consider filling it with raw rat.

Our first half-day march seemed to get us no closer to the green of the Temblor Plains that peeked occasionally through the murk. In a few spots we had to wade through brown swirls of water that rose up to our knees, and when we reached the next moss-coated hummock we sat down and stripped off our moccasins and wrung the water from the legs of our breeches to keep from getting rashes.

After a few sloppy crossings, I noticed something strange about my shoes and the bottoms of my breeches. The color was bleeding out of them and turning white. It was happening to Holzir's clothes, and the pale stain even spread to Rint as well. I noticed as he hopped up at the first lamp-bug of the evening that his feet had changed to white, as if he had slipped stockings over his feet.

"There's something in the water," Holzir said. "Don't drink it."

I'd never considered it. Fortunately, the springs of the mountains left us with full canteens.

"We'll all be tooth-white before we get out of here." I almost added, "like phantoms," but thought better of it. Night was coming, and the stories about the marsh phantoms were alive again.

We camped in the bowl formed from the roots of a cypress tree. Rint brought up a few rodents he had caught by their whip-tails, but Holzir and I instead chewed the last of the salted hadro flank from our packs. Nobody suggested taking wood from the tree to make a fire to cook Rint's gifts. It wasn't only that we weren't hungry for a swamp rat feast. We felt the curious eyes of the marshes searching for us. Whether it was phantoms, or only snakes slithering through the reeds, the Lazzun Marshes seemed to think and spy, and we wanted to hide from them for as long as possible.

The blood-sucker flies disappeared at dark, and a swarm of lamp-bugs substituted for a starry sky. I lay back on my travel cloak and watched their hypnotic dance against the fog ceiling. My legs felt as heavy as a quake-foot's, and I soon floated toward sleep while Holzir kept watch.

"Do you think those lights are the marsh phantoms?" he asked, dragging me from my drowse. He was looking at the witch-lanterns hanging like a string of torches at the edge of sight.

"No. It's a kind of natural magic in the bog. The gas that bubbles up makes a glow. You can't see it until night. Maybe that's all the marsh phantoms are—people spooked by a few night fires." I looked down at the white of my breeches. "The same taint that makes the witch-lanterns is probably what's turning *us* into ghosts. Maybe it will look fashionable in the cities."

"I still don't like the lights," Holzir said. He had his sword on his lap and turned it over nervously. I tapped the blastgun beside me so he knew it was ready. Since meeting the skinwing, I made sure two pellets were loaded in it at all times.

I settled back to let the lamp-bugs dance me to sleep, but Holzir interrupted again.

"Belde, have you ever seen Aman-Sah?"

I groaned. "Of course not, silly. I'm still alive. Who knows if there even is such a thing."

"No. I don't mean after you die. I mean the big water. The place where the Glosser River ends."

"Oh, the Aman-Sah Sea. No, I've never seen it. I used to love to sit on the docks when I was a girl and watch the ships sailing on the river, coming from distant places. Blue sails for Vatrusla. Great ribbons of color streaming off the masts of the far eastern traders from Najael..." I felt myself drifting back to sleep with the warmth of those memories; a clean warmth leagues away from the stuffy cooker where I was now.

"Did you ever want to ride one of those ships down to the sea?"

I yawned. "I dreamed of it. But I loved my parents, my home. I never thought I would leave. But if I did—it would be toward the sea, not north like this. There's the Vedil Sea farther north, but it's smaller. At least what I've seen on maps."

I heard Holzir shifting his sword across his lap. "I always thought the Aman-Sah Sea would take away the Sorrow. Something that big would make all your troubles seem like nothing.

Watching the flicking tails of mosasaurs, the necks of the water serpents rising out of the waves ... it must be the most beautiful sight in Ahn-Tarqa."

"If you've written a song about it—"

"I've been thinking about one."

"—now is not the time to sing it." I yawned loudly to make the point. I didn't care if it bothered him.

"I just wanted to know if you've seen it. Or—"

The stop in his voice was strange. My mind stirred up from the lure of sleep for a moment. "Or what?"

"The orb, Belde. Why don't you look at it now?"

I kept my eyes closed. "Why the sudden interest in that?"

"Maybe—maybe it will tell us where we need to go."

"It doesn't have that sort of thing to tell me. I don't remember much from the first one—"

"First one?"

I opened one eye. "The orb they forced my father to look into. It wasn't orders like, 'go here, do this.' Besides, the light from it is so strong that if there really are marsh phantoms, the orb would draw them to us like nychs scenting quake-foot blood."

"I was just—" He fiddled with the sword. "—curious, that's all."

Holzir, son of Iker, was changing. That he wanted to come on this mad adventure was a start, but I hadn't expected he would show interest in the Art, or that the darker part of my search would intrigue him. Maybe he was just trying to act less selfish to convince me he was worth keeping along.

But the sea. He had never told me he thought about the sea.

I almost opened my mouth to apologize for insulting him that day when I nearly hurled away his Sun-or-Moon board. But he wouldn't know what I was apologizing about, and if I started to explain, the apology wouldn't feel real to me. Another time.

TWELVE

The discovery came a soggy, blood-sucker-filled march from camp the next morning. A breeze from the mountains had spread the mist thin so the plains were visible ahead. The trees had also thinned, but that meant fewer roots to walk on and keep us out of the water. We'd soon have to give up wringing out our clothes and accept the wet rubbing blistering our skin.

Rint jumped in front of me and started hissing at a black object sticking up from the water. "What is it?" I asked. He was so busy making threatening noises at the corner of black that he missed my hand signals.

"I'll check it," Holzir said. "Keep watch to the left. I thought I saw something moving in the reeds."

The object sticking from the mud was probably the floating nest of a swamp bird, but I kept the gun cradled in my arm while Holzir went to see what had made Rint so anxious. He took hold of the corner and pulled it from the muck. Almost immediately, he dropped it.

"What is it?" I asked.

"I don't know. I—I can't get near it."

Holzir's body was trembling. It was like the first time he had seen me aiming the blastgun, but four times as strong. What could have that power?

I had to squish my hand deep into the black broth to grab the thing. It felt pebbly, like saurian skin. I dragged it to the surface and let the mud drip off it until its eyes stared into mine.

I didn't blanch or drop it. But the breath stopped in my throat and my heart almost stopped as well.

It was nothing more than a wedge-shaped mask with two slanted eyeholes. But I had seen it before, and it could belong to only one race.

"*Shapers.*" The word made the air thicker.

Holzir was still shivering. "Those monsters are here. They must be the marsh phantoms, carrying off people to twist with their Art."

Seeing the mask had plunged an icicle into my heart. But it was absurd to imagine Shapers wandering around a bog. They almost never left the black towers on their haunted peninsula. When they did travel to human cities, they cloistered themselves inside metal carriages and sent servants out to do their bloody work.

The mask had no business lying in the middle of this marsh. Which was the worst thought of all.

"It looks like it's been here for years," I said.

"But it hasn't turned white."

"Maybe the way the hide is treated keeps it from bleaching." I rubbed more slime from the mask, and found a slash torn from one edge to the other. A claw mark, maybe from a nych. Again, baffling. It would mean a Shaper had gone off on its own into the marshes and fell to an attack from a nych. Nothing in the stories about Shapers spoke of them having that sort of courage, or stupidity. They plotted, schemed, and wove the Art from within the shelter of their towers and barriers and made slaves shoulder the danger.

While I gazed into the slits of the mask, wondering if it would speak its secrets to me if I stared long enough, Rint found another piece of the puzzle.

Holzir didn't try to pick up this mystery object. He only pointed so I could see where it was half sunk in a clump of mud around the reeds. I followed Rint to the object and hoisted it out. I held it up so Holzir could get a better look.

"I think it's a helmet," Holzir said. He came closer and tapped the surface. "If it's a battle helm, it's made of very weak metal."

It was broken in half, so neither of us could identify it with any tribe or nation we knew. It had lain in the swamp for years: layers of corrosion crusted over it, and if I bent it even a bit it might shatter apart.

"The marsh phantoms must have gotten whoever wore that helmet," Holzir said. "Maybe he had taken the Shaper captive, and—"

I was only half-listening; Rint had grabbed my attention. He had put himself in a triangle stance, with his stiff tail pushing down into the water to hold his head up. A stranger was moving nearby, and Rint was trying to spy it out.

I leaped back onto the moss mound nearest to us and beckoned Holzir to follow me up to the harder footing. "Something is out there," I whispered.

I had the blastgun ready. Holzir had his sword drawn. Rint joined us, but kept his head pointed toward the noise so we knew where to look.

Holzir gestured with the tip of the sword: "I think I can see it. A white smudge behind the weeds."

The mist thickened, teasing us for trying to look deeper into it, so I couldn't see what Holzir had. But it was still out there. Rint laid his neck and tail parallel to the grass, his "point-pose." The white specter was watching us from the camouflage of the reeds.

"Maybe it's a tribe of Koltzer outcasts," Holzir spoke softly. "They might have lived here for years."

"Do you think any people could live in this muck?"

"It sounds better to me than the marsh phantoms."

This time we both saw the cloudy shape leap from the grass. The mist curled open as it appeared, then snicked shut again as it vanished. Distance was tricky to tell in the fog, but I thought it was crouched less than twenty strides from us.

Holzir had a shaky grip on his sword handle. "I hope the Art of your weapon can hurt ghosts."

"That's no ghost." I had an idea, a terrible one, of what it was. I'd rather face a ghost. "It's bleached white from living in the waters. It's whatever is behind the stories of the Marsh Phantoms —but it *isn't* a ghost."

"Then wh—"

The thing lunged, uncoiling from the reeds in a white bolt. Holzir was nearest to it, but the attacking blur aimed for me.

Rint screeched as I squeezed the trigger on the blastgun. The recoil made me slip on the damp moss, but the fall saved me from getting skewered on the spear in the phantom's grip. My shot went wild, but I had another pellet left.

Holzir jumped at my attacker. In the flash of exploding powder, he had seen a breathing creature: a ghostly blur, but made of bones and muscles. It was covered with a shabby coat of feathers and had a pronounced snout and large red eyes. Holzir struck from behind with his blade before the phantom could turn around and use its spear.

Blood spurted from the creature's shoulder and stained its pale feathers red. The phantom screeched and jabbed with its weapon at the man who had driven a sword-point into its back.

I couldn't risk a wild shot; my eyes could barely make out the phantom against the sky except for the crimson gushing down its back. I grabbed the barrel of the blastgun and swung the wooden end at where the thing's legs should be.

The phantom stumbled, and the spear in the grip of its spindly hands punctured the hummock instead of the man on ground. Holzir followed through with an accurate sword cut at the creature's neck. It screeched, then flattened onto the grass. A swarm of blood-sucker flies immediately descended to feast on the spurting wounds.

"It's a nych!" Holzir gasped now that he could get a good look. "You were right, Belde. The water bled it white."

Although the dead thing had a nych's toothy snout and sickle-talons on its feet, it was as tall as Holzir and it gripped the spear with hands no natural saurian could have. The nychs of the forests and plains never grow so large and straight-limbed, and they have neither the minds nor the hands to use any kind of weapon.

The true marker of where this nightmare came from was the only spot on it not stained white or red. A helmet of verdigris-covered metal clung to its head, the same kind of helm we had found. When I reached out to touch it, I felt brass under the tarnish. I lifted the edge of the cap. Copper wires ran from the underside of the helmt and burrowed through the feathers into the animal's braincase.

"Devil claw," I said.

Holzir swallowed hard. "Then Shapers must be near. I told you, the mask—"

"It wasn't under anyone's control," I said. Devil claws were occasional sights during the Month of the Moon when Shaper caravans steamed through the cities. While the masked sorcerers remained shut inside their metal wagons, columns of devil claws protected them. Each specially bred saurian was controlled through a magic in the helmets that forced the wills of their masters into their minds. Devil claws were perfect, mindless killing devices for the Shapers' armies. This devil claw, however, had only part of its helmet, and the wires were loose and slashed.

As I pried the spear from its talons, I tried to explain to Holzir my guess about what had occurred. "The Shapers passed through the swamp with a phalanx of devil claws. Maybe the marsh phantom legend already existed because of the witch-lights, and the Shapers wanted to discover if it was a power they could catch, tame, and deform. But something happened, some failure of their Art, and they lost control of the devil claws. The nychs broke free and killed their masters."

Holzir's eyes were darting all around, looking into the mist curtains. "A pack of these things, loose and hunting the marsh?"

"And smarter than any saurian you've ever seen. Except for Rint, of course." I reached out and patted Rint on the back. He was jabbing at the dead devil claw with his beak.

"We'll have to run for it," Holzir said. "There could be an army of these phantoms out there."

I tucked the blastgun under one arm and held onto the spear. "Some of the devil claws must have died out. But they killed two of your tribesmen a few years ago, so there are still enough left."

Holzir looked down at Rint. "Does your friend have a sharp enough nose to sniff out a route around them?"

I hoped so. Rint needed only basic hand signs to know what to do. He didn't want to encounter devil claws any more than we did. He took off through the reeds and we followed. Pushing through the water wouldn't matter any more, even if it meant we caught a coughing sickness. We had to reach the hard turf of the Temblor

Plains and take the chance that the devil claws wouldn't stray from their swamp home.

Holzir and I ran side by side, each looking a different direction into the fog walls. I shouldered the blastgun and kept the spear ready. There were only a few blackpowder pellets left in my pouch, and if we had to make a sprint over the plains I would need all those shots to scare off any devil claws snapping at our feet.

The screeches started soon after we began running. It was the same noise the first devil claw had made when it attacked us. "They're onto us," Holzir said.

So far Rint had guided us so that we hadn't run into any more of the things. I risked a glance behind as we crested a hillock of dried peat. There was a white shape and the dull shine of a helmet, but it vanished before I turned my head so I wouldn't trumble face down into the water.

"One's behind us," I shouted.

"Definitely two to our right," Holzir answered. "They're keeping pace, not attacking."

Now I saw a white shape leaping in and out of the grass to our left. It carried a scythe-shaped weapon and matched our speed.

They were trying to corral us, like Koltzer herders forcing a stampede of hadros into a canyon trap. It was up to Rint to get us past wherever the devil claws were trying to snare us. His nose would do better than our eyes to get us through the mist. The plains must be drawing closer, but the devil claws might be cunning enough to station a guard at the edge of the marshes.

Rint gave his warning shriek—*danger!*—but didn't slow down.

A devil claw stood in our path, a piece of cruel metal grasped in its talons. It was leaning back on its hind legs, ready to strike.

We didn't have time to turn away or dodge around it. I tightened my grip around the spear, and Holzir and I charged.

Rint knew what he was doing; he hadn't led us this way by

mistake. He charged for the mound where the devil claw was poised and ran between its legs. The devil claw was smarter than most saurians, but it couldn't fight the instinct to look down and snap at whatever nuisance had dashed under it.

That instinct killed it. Holzir sprang onto the mushy grass and slashed at the devil claw's head. It parried with the iron rod it was using as a weapon, but it was off-balance. I seized the opening and struck from below. The spearhead punched through feathers and into its belly.

We didn't stop to check if it was dead. It wasn't going to pester us any more. Holzir hollered the war cry, "The Sorrow of the Koltzer is the Sorrow of its foes!" It was only the second time I'd heard him say it.

"Are you starting to enjoy this?" I asked as we began running again.

"My uncle never thought I would make much of a warrior. But need makes many warriors."

"We don't need a warrior right now as much as a runner."

"I can do that too!" He sprinted on, dashing so fast across the swamp water that he looked like a skinwing skimming over a lake to catch fish.

A strange time for high spirits. But that was the Sorrow, especially for the Koltzer. Near-death was better than near-life. I had real fears to make me run fast as the rapids of the Glosser River, and for the first time the Sorrow was outpacing me.

Our pale enemies were unhappy we had broken their blockade. The devil claws to the left and right pressed closer. But Rint had guessed the terrain and leaped onto a tangle of roots spread from a behemoth cypress. The pursuers to the sides lost their way, but the scrape of the claws over the roots behind us showed that the rear-guard forcing us forward hadn't slowed.

My lungs hated the thick air, and now they hated me. My

whole body was splattered with mud, and if I came through this I might end up half-ghost myself.

One of the phantoms lunged from my left. It carried no weapon, but devil claws never lack for the natural ripping hooks on their feet. I flattened myself into the sludge, which gushed into my nose. The claw of the phantom hooked the threads of my cloak. If I were a span higher, the claw would have ripped open the back of my neck.

Holzir pivoted when he heard me fall. But I moved faster. The devil claw had dropped into the mud and flipped back around. The muck around it was thick enough to give me the extra second I needed. The blastgun shot into my hand. There wasn't any need to aim from so close. I pulled the trigger. The pale head splattered. Feathers launched into the air among a red mist.

Holzir looked in astonishment at the twitching headless corpse.

"Don't think about it," I said. "No more Sorrow for you today."

I tossed the spear away and pressed the stock of the blastgun against my shoulder. If the devil claws were making runs from the side, we must be close to escaping. It was the last sprint, and I would need all the blackpowder pellets left if we were to reach the end alive.

This was the third time I had loaded the weapon. I was getting skilled at it. I hardly had to break stride to snap the next two shots into the barrel. Holzir ran ahead of me, trailing Rint. I had the back. Our herders were closing the gap behind me.

Holzir hollered: "Belde! The plains, they're just ahead!"

I should have been relieved, but now the rest of the marsh phantoms would close in and finish us off. If they were toying with their prey before, now they would get serious about losing their supper of soft human flesh.

I turned and fired a shot into a devil claw that thought it had caught me. It was another close shot that needed no aim. The nych smashed back into the fog, leaving a blood spray behind.

"Run, Holzir! Don't think of anything else!"

The ghosts wavered, surprised at the sudden killing of one of their flock. I took up the slack and in moments my feet were pounding across flat grass. Beautiful solid earth. I took advantage of every step on the springy soil.

I almost bumped into Holzir, who was standing still where the mist barrier ended along with the Lazzun Marshes. He was staring across the open Temblor Plains at another marvel—and obstacle.

The ground shook, but we hadn't noticed it in the madness of the last few minutes. The thundering came from thousands of footfalls of a herd of perhaps fifty quake-foots stomping across the plain. They were less than a half a league away. Maybe closer. It was hard to tell the distance on a flat plain against a gray sky.

Holzir grabbed my arm and locked eyes with me in a way he shouldn't be able to. "Belde, do you trust me?"

"Of course, but—"

"Then follow me. You and Rint. I'll lead." He sprinted straight for the herd.

I signed to Rint to keep to my side. We dashed after our Koltzer friend.

I looked over my shoulder as I ran, wet fingers curled around the blastgun's trigger. I couldn't risk trying to shoot the devil claws until they got nearer, but that wouldn't take long. The marsh phantoms burst through the mist walls, not held back as I had hoped. In the open with nothing to block their sight, they lowered their bodies and broke into demon-sprints. No woman or man, or even a beak-nose, could outrun a sprinting devil claw.

The quake-foot herd was moving at an angle toward the edge of the marshes. These were the armor-back kind, tinier than the thunder beasts of the south, but to us each one was a mountain on legs thick as pine trunks. Quake-foots have no care for humans. A single one can crush a man on a hadrosaur in its way without its nut-sized mind wondering about the bump on the grass.

And Holzir had us dashing straight toward them.

Maybe he thought getting flattened was a better death than getting flayed. Or perhaps he hoped our pursuers would shy away from the herd. But I didn't ask Holzir what he was doing. I had said I trusted him, and amazingly I meant it.

I unloaded a shot into a devil claw at the front of the pack. I almost missed the head-shot from slippery footing, but shattering its shoulder was enough to stop it. Two more devil claws jumped over the carcass. I only had one pellet loaded. I stopped running to aim and shoot the front nych in the leg. It whipped over and blocked the one that followed it. That bought me a time to reload while on the run.

The quake-foots were making good on their name. The ground flounced as if it were about to rip apart beneath us. My fingers quivered as I slipped the next pellet into place. Two more after this, and that was it.

Holzir wasn't looking back when I gunned down our pursuer. He had his eyes on the herd closing with us. He had picked the right approach to get us there fast—and probably flattened faster.

I had the last pellets in the gun, but at least five devil claws remained. They carried spears, and I thanked my tiny bit of luck that they didn't have the right kind of muscles to hurl them.

The shadow of the quake-foot herd passed overhead. Holzir started to run alongside the smallest bull.

Then I realized what he was trying to do. He was going to "quake ride."

Quake riding is the highest test of manhood among the tribes of the Koltzer. It's a challenge few take up, because it is so Sorrow-bitten dangerous. Holzir's father Iker had done it, but a charge of lying about it was what sparked the blood-duel that ended in Iker's death.

I hoped that what Holzir wanted us to do now—climb the tail of a moving quake-foot and ride on its back—wasn't a suicidal attempt to vindicate his father. But there was no other choice. The devil claws were closing, I had two shots left, and running through the trampling herd would turn us into flatbread in moments.

"*Rint, up!*" I shouted. The beak-nose jumped onto my leg and then hopped to grab onto my pack so we would stay together.

"It'll be just like those jumps at home," I told him. We were champion jumpers back in Tyrn among our friends. Now we were going for the biggest jumping contest of all.

The quake-foot that Holzir was running toward had a tail that stretched out a few spans from the ground at its tip, low enough for Holzir to leap and grab it. If he slipped, he'd have only a moment to move before the next beast crushed him.

I took my last chance to even the odds. I pivoted, dropped to one knee. The blastgun stock was wedged against my shoulder. I squeezed the trigger twice and emptied the barrels. Two more devil claws, only a stride away from slicing a city girl into halves, hurtled back in crimson explosions. Three more were running up. The useless weapon could only slow me down now, so I hurled it at them and ran.

Holzir passed behind the rear leg of the quake-foot and under its tail. Beyond was a blur of moving limbs that looked as if an entire forest of oaks was on the march.

Holzir leaped at the tail, and on the first try hooked his arm around the thinnest part. The rigid tail, which balanced the immense length and neck of the body, held under him. He pulled and got onto the ridge along the quake-foot's back.

I raced along the same path as Holzir, but the fall of one of the animal's great feet threw me off balance. One step in the wrong direction and I would have been pulped. The shrieks of the devil claws were close, but they were frustrated, uncertain how to get around the quake-foots to drag off their prey.

Holzir leaned over the tail as if he were a kid hanging across the high branch of a tree. "Belde, grab my hand!"

I needed the help. My pack weighed more than I expected. Another woman would've dropped it and leaped to save her life. But not only was Rint clinging to the pack, the vision orb was in there as well. I couldn't lose that any more than I would sacrifice Rint.

I missed on the first try and had to sprint harder to keep up. This put me running straight toward a devil claw that had worked its way through the stomping legs. The devil claw charged me as I dashed for Holzir's dangling hand.

I made the running jump. My bare skin grabbed Holzir's wrist. The motion swung me, and I pulled my legs up as the devil claw snapped. The jaws snicked close a finger's width beneath me.

I started to swing back, still gripping Holzir's wrist. But the devil claw did not have a second chance at me. The quake-foot behind us dropped down its foot and pulped the white-feathered killer into the plains.

"Grab something else, Belde! I can barely hold you!" My arm muscles were burning, so the strain on Holzir must have been about to break his back. I grabbed at the knobby skin with my other hand and held on. Rint hopped from my back and onto the tail, which took off some weight. Holzir pulled and I reached farther up with my other hand until I got to the ridge along the top of the tail.

I folded my body in half over the tail. It was a risky perch, but it felt like I had washed up from the swells of a river and onto a solid slab of rock.

"I thought ... this was ... supposed to ... be tough," I wheezed.

"My father rode one twice this size," Holzir crowed. "But we can't stay on this part. If the herd turns, the tail will fling us off."

We climbed the rest of the tail, like fleas with poor balance, toward the two plates of chitinous armor across the quake-foot's back. I told myself it was no different than the games I played as a girl where my friends and I would try to cross wooden planks between barrels without slipping. The only difference was that the entire world was shaking at the same time. Rint made it easily, and watching him move along the crest as the tail widened helped focus my mind on pushing forward.

The armor plate was smooth and had a flat stretch in the center. We collapsed on it as if it were the safest sanctuary on Ahn-Tarqa. We were on the back of a swift-moving saurian in the middle of the Temblor Plains, with no idea where we were going, yet we felt we could pitch a tent and live happily here for the rest of our lives.

"My father rode a larger one," Holzir repeated.

"He'd think you were just as brave." I reached from where I was lying and put my hand on his shoulder. "Holzir the Brave. If you want to sing that song about the sea, you could now."

"I'd rather just concentrate on not slipping. Later. I promise."

I closed my eyes. I wouldn't sleep, not on the rocking back of the quake-foot, but I wanted the world blotted away for a few hours. Then I would see where the rivers of our strange journey had swept us.

THIRTEEN

Holzir and I clung to the back of our oblivious wagon the whole night. In the morning, the herd reached a small lake where the plains slanted toward hills of dry grass and scrub brush. Our mount kneeled down to rest, and we took the chance to slide off and sneak between the stationary legs of the other quake-foots while they waited their turn to sip from the lake's edge. We didn't relax or even speak until we were packed into a shallow canyon narrow enough that even the smallest of the herd couldn't stumble into it.

A freshwater lake might mean there was a settlement nearby. When we looked out from the ravine and across the hills, we saw a smudge of soiled clouds that could only come from the smoke of hundreds of chimneys.

The herd had carried us far west, covering in a single night what would've taken us a week to cross on foot. The Temblor Plains were ending, and before us were the moors of Occiland. The Gray Lands.

We had seen this city before: Iyalonda. Kalzzik's tribe had

camped near it one winter. Koltzer tribes reluctantly stop at Iyalonda when food supplies are low or when they have extra hadro mounts to trade for the finer weapons of a city blacksmith. But only tribesmen who know the coarse Idenite of the cities go inside to conduct trading. Dyzlin had learned Idenite so he could take on this job—and he probably pocketed most of the money made on the trades for himself. Neither Holzir nor I knew anything about what was inside Iyalonda's walls aside from its reputation. And the cities of the Gray Lands have reputations that do no good for anyone forced to live in them.

The Gray Lands are wedged in a triangle below the Vedil Sea, with the Temblor Plains to the east and the taboo lands of the Shapers' peninsula to the west. Although the true name of the region is Occiland, the title "The Gray Lands" stuck to it centuries before because the smoke from the cities mixed with the clouds drifting south from the sea to create a permanent bleak shroud over the land. Plants, grass, and shrubs grow here, but they never seem to show any color. A loose confederation of cramped city-states survives on trade from Iden and shady deals with the Shapers' agents. But the Shapers never recruit willing servants from the Gray Lands; even those soulless sorcerers have no tolerance for the hardscrabble liars and robbers who live in these sewers.

I had grown to hate living among the Sorrow-filled and ignorant Koltzer, but the cleanliness of the plains was fresh spring water compared to what must fester in the shanties of Iyalonda. The acrid stench from the fire towers reached us even at this distance. The city did not use glow globes to brighten the streets and instead depended on subterranean coal furnaces that lit enormous torch towers. The largest city of Occiland, Gaspuh, had earned the nickname "Gasper" because of its belching towers. Iyalonda seemed to be racing to catch up.

"From one swamp to another," Holzir sighed as he watched the crawl of smoke over the steeples and roofs.

"At least they'll have food better than swamp rat. No offense, Rint." But the beak-nose was already asleep at my feet.

"I think I'd rather live in the marshes," Holzir sighed.

"It won't be that awful. I spent the first years of my life running around in town alleys and gutters, remember?"

"This is no place like Tyrn."

No, and the street knowledge of the daughter of a prosperous tradesman wouldn't get us far in a cesspool like Iyalonda. But I had meant to come to the Gray Lands, and inside one of these towns might be a sanctuary for the Sorrowless. Maybe there was even a system of couriers and underground messengers. Anything to let the Woman know I was looking for her.

"We need food, no matter what," I said. "I'm not sure how we'll get it without money, though."

"Every day we find out something else *you* forgot to bring." Holzir reached into his pack, scrounged in the bottom, and pulled out a fistful of copper coins. "If life is cheap in the Gray Lands, maybe this will buy us a meal or cot for the night."

"Or a knife in the back. Better keep it hidden."

He promptly buried the coins. Our money troubles were fixed, but we still had our strange clothing to draw attention. The marsh trek had stained them into a patchwork of white. The pattern on the front of Holzir's shirt looked like a ravager's open maw.

I pointed at it. "You might have a sign of one of the guilds on your chest. The Legion of the Silent Throat-Slitters or some such thing." I meant it as a joke, but Iyalonda probably did have a guild dedicated to such a gory trade. "Look for sackcloth once we get into town. We can cut them into beggars' shawls and go in disguise that way."

Holzir wasn't listening. He was studying the curls of smoke

from the torch towers as if they were new marsh phantoms. I prodded him with my moccasin. "Did you hear anything I just said?"

"Do we really need to go into that stink pit?"

"Oh, not this again." But I didn't push. His Sorrow was wrestling with him. I felt more at ease looking at Iyalonda because I grew up in a city, but I understood his fears. Barren mountains and a bog stuffed with slimy but honest life was more appealing to a Koltzer man. A few days ago I would have shouted at him, reminded him I was the one who allowed him to come along. Not any more. No matter how he grumbled, Holzir knew what we had to do, and he'd do it to whatever end.

I laid a hand on his pack. "You haven't seen if the stain got to your game board."

Holzir's thoughts flashed to his beloved object. "I forgot about that!" He rummaged through the pack, tugged out the Sun-or-Moon case, and inspected it with the precision eyes of a jeweler. "A few white flecks, but the stones will be fine since they were locked inside."

"Why don't you check to make sure?"

He laid down the board and flipped it open to examine each stone. As he did, I started to lay the stones on the board in the opening formation. Once he finished, I placed down one more stone, sun-up, as a starting move.

I smiled. "Your turn."

We played until nightfall, and then continued under a three-quarter moon in the warmest night yet of spring. The herd moved on, and after Holzir beat me four times in a row, we were ready for a last sleep before taking the road to Iyalonda.

. . .

THE TRADERS with pack animals and wagon teams shuffling along the dirt road paid no mind to the two people in splotched white rags and their beak-nose companion. Most traders had swords and axes clanking from their belts under their serge robes, so the blade pushed through Holzir's sash drew no attention. A few looked from under their hoods at Rint hopping by my side: saurians that are not used as draft animals or for meat are rare in the Gray Lands. But the onlookers creaked back to their own Sorrowful thoughts and ignored Rint. Just to be safe, I had Rint hop up to ride on my pack, where he would get less notice.

Each city of Occiland has a prince or mayor or king or whatever title the top man chooses to scribble on the slate swinging over his wormwood palace. Control really belongs to the thief guilds and the sects of believers in feuding gods, most of which were invented in the city and appear in temples nowhere else in Ahn-Tarqa. Some of the towns use the Art for meager works such as glow globes and air messages to other towns, while others kill on sight anyone who shows the slightest sorcerer's power.

My blastgun was gone, and I had buried the orb deep in my pack, wrapping it with the travel cloak I no longer needed in the warm weather. If Iyalonda was one of the Gray Land cities with laws against the Art, I could avoid a fast beheading.

A weak clay wall surrounded Iyalonda, and fang-birds perched in an unbroken line of black and red feathers across its merlons. I always wondered if Tyrn used some power of the Art in its walls to keep these toothy-pests from nesting on them. If it was true, Iyalonda didn't believe in using the same power. I would have to look out for Rint to make sure these tiny flying nychs didn't snatch him up.

Holizr and I squeezed into a line that passed a two-story shack guarding the eastern gate. Sentries in brown tabards with city livery stitched on them leaned against the posts to discourage travelers from trying to get past anywhere but the guardhouse road. From the porch of the shack, a bent willow of a man pestered the wagons as they rolled past. The tin medallion around his neck gave him official permission to pester. The sound of belching from inside the shack warned everyone that men who were far more dangerous to irritate were only steps away in case of trouble.

"What are you children peddling?" the gate warden asked in Idenite when it was our turn for review. "Your packs don't look heavy enough to make our city worth the stop."

"We're foot-sore travelers," I said. "We've little to sell. We're only looking for a bed for the night."

"Humph." Watery eyes stared at our clothing. Then he spoke in a stunted but understandable Koltzer. "I know this cloth you wear. You from tribes. Where your people?"

Holzir answered, relieved to hear his own tongue. "Dead in a blood feud. We seek refuge."

The warden stared at the odd stains on our clothes. "Your foes have white blood?" But this weed of a man had already lost interest in us. He slipped back to Idenite: "Go on, but you grass-chewers won't find much welcome. There are strange goings-on up the northwest road, I hear."

A chill spread from my heart to my fingertips. "What's happening on the road?"

"Mind your lip, scut. Don't stay long, if you're smart. The Sorrow is heavy this season."

I wanted to ask more; it might lead me to a sanctuary. But Holzir pushed me onward. "Whatever you wanted to ask, you can ask in the city," he said once the gate warden started questioning the man behind us riding an exhausted club-tail. "That twisted futch doesn't know anything. He thinks we're children, and it's best he keeps thinking we're harmless so nobody else hears about us."

I was annoyed because I wanted to know right away if I was on the right track. But I had to grudgingly admit Holzir's caution was smarter.

Iyalonda and its squalor swelled around us. Rint chose to hide on my back rather than run through the mush on the streets. Only a few steps inside, and two fang-birds swooped down at us and cackled. They looked so unnervingly like nychs, only smaller with more feathers, that for a moment I thought to reach for my lost gun. Holzir pulled out his sword and swatted at them. The fang-birds flew off, but the crowd turned to stare at us. "Keep that sheathed. You're in a city," I said through the side of my mouth. "Just be as invisible as you can. These aren't the open plains."

"I know that," he snapped. But he put away the sword and stayed close and quiet after that, remembering his own advice about looking like harmless nobodies.

The narrow ways between the mud-brick buildings pressed even narrower from shop awnings and the traffic of club-tails and ceratopses. The beasts were small compared to the wild herd animals, and their owners had filed down their horns and side spikes so they wouldn't impale the crowds, but Holzir almost got the horn of one ceratops rammed through his chest. The owner, face hidden under a fall of tin trinkets, snarled something in a language neither of us understood. Holzir danced out the way, shaken, but he'd soon find that these near-misses happened every few minutes.

I was hurting with hunger, and the last of our dried meat was gone. Holzir was also famished, but the stench of the streets made it easier not to think about food. Our noses got used to the gutters and piles of saurian dung, but it was harder to get used to the babble of speech all around us. Iyalonda is smaller than Tyrn, but Tyrn spreads its arms wide to give people room. Iyalonda gathers in its mud-crusted arms to crush everyone together.

As Holzir and I wove through the sticky mob, we brushed past people in every degree of rags and tatters. Even the people dressed in finery had the air of wickedness and desperation. None of the traders looked wealthy, and the ornaments that decked their clothes and pierced the frills of their ceratopses and head crests of their hadros were corroded. Traders with valuable wares and saurian-tamers who breed strong bloodlines travel south to Iden. Only those with little to offer came to Iyalonda, too near to the lands of the Shapers.

When I was a girl, I'd seen many people from distant lands visiting Tyrn, and I loved to ask them where they had come from and hear any stories their Sorrow might allow them to tell. I saw many folk from those same nations wandering Iyalonda's streets, but if I opened my mouth to any of these dregs, I might get robbed or beaten.

There was a dark giant of the Bavtuu tribes with two swords strapped at his hips. Lakkadians with olive skin counted money in hovels, probably counterfeit coins they would dribble onto the streets. A dark-eyed Vatruslan woman with stark white skin perched on a stoop outside a house with a swath of red paint on its lintel—a sign, as in Tyrn, that men could buy pleasure for a few gold pieces inside. Walking past her, apparently holding out to find a prettier woman for his coin, was an Idenite with a soldier's tunic under a coat of stitched feathers. An army deserter: I'd seen many since we'd passed the gates.

The red-painted harlots' houses made Holzir nervous. He would grip onto my wrist and drag me to the other side of the street whenever one of the doxies on the doorsteps looked our way. They would eye him first, then decide he was too poor to be worth their time. Their gazes would then go to me. Holzir knew exactly what went on behind their looks.

"If we don't step carefully, they'll snatch you off the pavement and put you to work," he said. "They need fresh meat with the speed the men in this dung hole must use up whores."

"You think of me as *meat?*" I asked.

"No—I didn't mean ... They probably don't often see a bright-faced pretty girl in Iyalonda. If I were a whoremaster, I'd want—"

He decided it was better to be quiet. I wasn't thinking about what he had left unsaid, but what he had said. It was the first time Holzir had called me "pretty." I never thought of the word connected to me. "Pretty" is petite. I was rough and damaged. A pretty girl could wear a filmy dress, a colorful muslin over her breasts, and bat eyelashes at admirers. I had never worn a dress, and never had any admirers except a Koltzer brute whose affection I returned by shooting him in the leg.

But Holzir was right that any girl, pretty or not, could turn into another commodity traded in Iyalonda like cheap silk. We stayed on the other side of the street from the red-paint houses, even if it put us near a violent alehouse.

The flow of people pushed us into a snickleway. We avoided getting crushed when a club-tail smashed through the alley. It battered over stands and caused the merchants selling boiled rodents and rotting vegetables to pull the rider from the club-tail's back and pummel him. Men wearing the livery of the city guard watched and yawned.

We crawled along the tiny street until we found an overturned wagon spilling grain and weevils from torn sacks. The wagon team was nothing more than an old woman dragging it along with a rope over her shoulder, but she was flat on the ground, cold as the stones.

Holzir pulled out his sword. "You said something about burlap?"

I felt a tinge of disgust taking from a dead woman. But Holzir was already sawing away the cloth from the sacks, and I joined in with my knife. If I stopped to feel pity for everyone who suffered in Iyalonda, I might never move again.

We shook the weevils from the sacks and thrust our heads through the holes. Rint hopped down from my shoulder and had some playtime snapping up the insects among the grain. As I had many times on the journey, I envied my green-skinned friend. Sorrowful and Sorrowless meant nothing to him as long as he could run at my side and get a feast of juicy gnats and beetles.

"Well, don't we look like regular sacks of meal," I said when we had our new tunics on. "We'll be lucky if a Gray Lander doesn't grab us and pack us into his cart."

Holzir wasn't feeling humorous. "This was your idea. And is there a 'next' in your plan?"

"Let's find a market square and an inn. I hope your money will pay for the night." I thought about searching the dead woman's clothes to see if she had any coins, but that I considered it for even a moment revolted me. We weren't that downtrodden yet; Holzir's coppers could get us through a day, and by then I might have some idea where to look for safety.

As we trudged back onto the main streets, fear of discovery was dulled under Iyalonda's poverty and smoke-filled sky. The gate warden had said the Sorrow was heavy this season, and I could almost see it in the air. Whatever strange things were happening up the road, they had infected the city. Its Sorrow swirled about me, but at least I had only my own fears to worry about. Holzir had to shoulder the city's Sorrow along with his own ... and his shoulders might as well have scraped along the ground now.

Once I had told myself I had no care for the rest of the sorry people of Ahn-Tarqa and only wanted to find my own kind and stay in their safety. But I had tossed that away. The world did not have to be this way, and thousands of years ago someone had tried to solve it. The Lightborn "brought the Art and the Sorrow"—but maybe the second only came from a mistake, and they had tried to fix it. "To save humanity."

The Sorrow had drowned whatever solution they had. Or they simply forgot it, as they had forgotten the airship. All Ahn-Tarqa might turn into Iyalonda one day, if the Shapers didn't re-conquer it first.

The orb was tingling against my skin through the pack. Soon, I'd look into it to find the answers. Or the beginnings of answers.

FOURTEEN

A sign nailed to a bell tower told us we had reached Six-Crossing, where six streets collided in a crowded market. The largest torch tower in the city belched at the north side of the market, and the air was so sooty that maybe we didn't need to disguise our white-stained clothes. The air would turn them black in minutes.

I had my ears open, trying to pluck up anything in the languages I knew. There was a jabber of Idenite all around, a pidgin version for buying and selling, so I might pick out news about the fears the gate warden had mentioned. The weight of the Sorrow in Iyalonda spoke of something very wrong; I had to know what it was before I decided where to go next.

On the other side of Six-Crossing was a bright orange awning and a flag that marked it as a caravansary catering to merchants from Iden. It was the first one I had seen in Iyalonda.

"Holzir, I'm heading over there." I pointed out the awning.

"What's there?"

"People from the south. I might hear news about what's going on outside the city."

"How will you find me again?"

"Stand at the foot of the torch tower," I said. "But first go buy a few pieces of fruit from one of the stands."

He nodded, which took as much energy as he could muster. "It might take all my coppers to buy anything we can stomach."

"Then get something we can't stomach. We'll hold our noses." I laughed, but the joke clanked against the iron wall of Holzir's Sorrow. If only we had room to sit down and play Sun-or-Moon, it might cheer him.

The caravansary was beneath a stone building. The orange awning was the only spot of color. Riding hadros with small sail-crests munched from feeding troughs at the edge of the cara-vansary, and I slipped between them instead of walking through the bead curtain of the front archway. I couldn't expect an easy welcome from melancholy traders just because I came from the same country. Spying was my first order of business, and Rint was the best spy-helper anybody could want.

He knew exactly what I was trying to do without any signals. He hopped off my pack and slunk through the hadros' feet. I followed him toward a wood wall that marked off the stalls for the ceratopses. Rint wedged his beak into a weak spot between the boards, next to the stall of a sleepy ceratops rubbing its horn against a post. I peeked between the slats and had a wide view of the porch.

"Smart boy," I said to Rint. He rubbed his head against my leg.

I overheard the chatter of merchants sitting around a hearth and roasting spears of meat over the flames. I couldn't tell what kind of animal they were cooking, but the smell made my mouth water. The men looked like pureblood Idenites, but their thread-bare cloaks had seen their best times ten years ago. They were muttering about local brew-houses and which brothels had the best wares. After a few minutes cramped beside the stall listening to their prattle, I was ready to give up and try to sneak to another spot. Then I heard one of them grumble the word *Shaper*.

I was alert then.

"I don't get what they're playing at out there," said a man with a pockmarked face. "They usually travel during the Month of the Moon and bang on people's doors and carry them off. But this puking camp has been squatting there for a week."

"What's the difference?" grunted a man through a mouth half-full of meat. "Not like I wanted to go up the northwest road. The towns out there aren't worth a ravager's fart for trade, and it's too close to those wizard lands."

"Still don't like them hovering so blasted near," the first man said. "The more they stay close, the worse the Sorrow gets in this town. And Sorrow-bitten people don't like buying."

The youngest merchant, who had the look of the hardest Sorrow of the group, said: "I hear they're out hunting for someone. Not new servants or slaves or any of the usual sort. There's supposed to be a band of queer folk roaming about, and the Shapers want them."

My gasp almost gave me away. A snort from the ceratops in the stall covered the noise.

The younger man continued: "The Shapers've been peering more into the cities, looking for these queer ones. This camp they've made—they're doing something unnatural in it. Using the Art to make new sorcery. Might be they're planning to conquer all the lands again, like they once did."

"Nych piss to that," said the pockmarked man. "Yeah, they're hunting for somebody. They're always hunting. But I hear it's nothing more than bandits on the south road down to Iden. Common thieves, but the Shapers will do for them quick. Snatch them and scoop out their brains."

"Why would those masked futches care a turd about bandits?" the younger man asked. "No, they're after those folk I've heard about. There's something weird about them. The Shapers love whatever is weird. They *eat* it."

"None of it makes sense to me," said a man I couldn't see through the flames. "I'd just rather the Shapers move off and let us get back to feeling rotten the right and natural way. I can't take their Sorrow."

That closed down the talk, and the merchants went back to the business of chewing with an occasional belch. Few people could speak about the Shapers for long without silence dropping over them.

But I had learned enough. *Shapers were camped nearby.* Somewhere on the northwest road. And they were looking for "weird people." That meant one thing: the Sorrowless. If what I had heard was true, a band of the Sorrowless might be hiding to the south.

But why would any Sorrowless be wandering outside the city, if there were supposed to be sanctuaries for them inside? Had the Shapers camped here to seek out these Sorrowless? Maybe it was the other way around, and the Sorrowless were here to spy on the Shapers.

Either way, the news was troubling. I had to decide tonight if we risked staying in the city or tried to hire onto a caravan to get out. I waved at Rint, and we squeezed through the tight spot beside the stables.

I raced back into the crowd of Six-Crossings to the foot of the torch tower. Holzir wasn't there. Maybe I had come too soon, and he was still haggling to get us a few morsels to eat. But my racing thoughts kept coming up with worse possibilities. I picked up Rint and set him on my pack, then started searching among the crowd to spot the fair-haired Koltzer in sackcloth. I didn't dare shout his name and bring attention to myself, and he would never hear me over the marketplace din unless he were right next to—

A hand landed on my shoulder and I snapped around. Holzir was behind me, a pleased look on his face.

I came close to dropping as dead as the woman we had left on the street. "Where were you?"

"I had to take a quick trip into an alley to add to the piss smell. But I've got good news."

"I've got bad news, but tell me yours first. Did you get food?"

"Better. I found an inn that will put us up and give us a meal for the night. For nothing."

I shook my head. "Who would do that?"

"You don't believe there can be good-hearted people in Iyalonda?"

"It's strange hearing that from you."

"Aren't these the sort of people you were looking for?"

He might be right. But it seemed a ludicrous stroke of luck out of a children's story that we might stumble onto a sanctuary so fast.

He tugged at my sleeve. "Come on, the landlady is waiting for us."

I followed him down one of the wide streets leading from Six-Crossings. While we walked, I told him the gossip from the caravansary. "We have to decide if we stay and keep searching for a safe spot in the city, or if we slip out," I said. "If the Sorrowless are on the road, maybe we can meet up with them. They'll know how to use the globe."

"I'm more worried about hearing there are Shapers so close by."

"That's why staying here might be smarter. If the Shapers are hunting for these Sorrowless people out on the road, they're likely to catch me—us—if we try to leave."

"I don't want to hear any more about Shapers and other nonsense tonight. Not when we've got shelter and food."

He brought me to the front porch of an inn nestled in a sharp turn in the street. It had no name over its doorway, but candles glowed from the upper windows and its simple wood and clay front was unsoiled. It was the most inviting place I'd seen yet in Iyalonda.

The woman on the steps might have walked in from a dream of my old world. She had on a clean white overdress of the southern style, like Mother often wore. Soft gray hair peeked from under her woven cap. Her cheeks were blushed pink like the tanzen flowers boys give to girls in courtship. Her smile wasn't something I expected in the grimy city.

"Is this the girl you told me about, Holzir?" She spoke accented but perfect Koltzer, and she said Holzir's name like a sweet aunt who spoils her nephews.

"Belde, this is Menteus. She owns the inn."

An Idenite name. I felt more at ease. I gave the bow that youth of Tyrn give to all the elderly.

"Such a polite girl. You two are fortunate you didn't go into any of the other inns. The men here are nothing more than ravagers wearing breeches. They'd have done horrible things to a pretty one like you. But my place has clean rooms, and you'll be safe here."

Caution edged into my thoughts. "Why would you take us in without money?"

Menteus waved at us to approach her. "Come into the parlor and we'll talk. The street is never safe."

We walked through the door at her invitation. Menteus even grinned at Rint as he hopped over the threshold. That stirred my suspicions. Innkeepers usually ask to have any animals placed in the stables. Something was amiss here, and I hoped it was because the inn was a front for hiding the Sorrowless.

Coziness enfolded us when we entered what Menteus called the parlor. The walls were smooth red clay, the stone floor freshly swept. A wooden table stood in the middle of the room, and a cook fire warmed a pot suspended from an iron hook. A few other people were gathered around the fire. They looked wealthier than the other visitors to the city we had seen, dressed in floor-length robes of finely woven cloth.

"Have a seat and I'll pour you something warm to drink." Menteus bustled us into chairs. Rint tried to hop onto the tabletop, but I wouldn't let him test our hostess' hospitality that far, so I clicked my fingers and pointed at him to keep to the floor. He gave me a resentful twist of the neck, but obeyed.

The other guests in the parlor paid no attention to us and sipped contentedly from mugs of steaming tea that smelled of jaspizzik leaves. Menteus brought us clay mugs with the hot liquid, and then returned with a basket of dark bread. I tore into the warm dough. It was rough, the best a city this far from bean and wheat fields could manage, but right then it was the most sumptuous thing I had ever tasted. I washed it down with the jaspizzik tea, which heated me down to my toes. Not until then did I realize how exhausted I was.

Menteus sat across from us. "I saw this boy standing on the street near the torch tower, looking as lost as a hadro runt dropped from his tribe." Holzir twitched at the description, which came close to what he actually was—although he had left the tribe, not the other way around. "I sometimes see good young men trapped in this town, and I always give them help. You see, I had a son myself, and he was just about your age, fifteen or so—"

"I'm seventeen," Holzir said, not rudely.

"Oh, how I wish my son had seen seventeen summers!" There

was a daub of wetness in Menteus's eyes, or perhaps it was only a reflection from the hearth. "One Month of the Moon, some men knocked at our door, and they—"

I almost opened my mouth to finish the tale for her. It was one I knew too well.

"—they took him away. The servants of the Shapers dragged him off. He didn't volunteer, like some young men do so they can get out of this sinful city. No, they took him away because he was ... different."

"Different how?" I knew how, but it would be suspicious if I didn't ask.

"He was always a happy boy. He wouldn't let this city weigh him down. The Sorrow never bothered him like others. And so ... they took him away. That's all."

Menteus rested her hand on Holzir's shoulder. He did not flinch away; he was under the bittersweet spell of the old woman' story. "You're bigger than my Rolant, but you have the same sort of eyes. And you, young lady—" She looked toward me, but her gaze darted away. "—there's something of my son in you too, although I do not know quite what it is."

My fingers gripped so tight to the mug of tea that they started to burn. I wanted to tell her the truth. Tell her what her son was. What I was. She must be testing me. The innkeeper was waiting for me to give the password that would say to her, "I am Sorrowless." Then she would open up the hidden sanctuary.

Before I spoke, I looked over the room at the wealthy men sitting in silence with their food and tea. The Sorrow hovered around them. Lighter, eased from the glow of the room, but still the Sorrow. I couldn't make up my mind if I had found safety or not. So I decided to say nothing for the moment. If this was a sanctuary, Menteus would learn soon enough on her own that I was one of those "happy" people like her son.

"Thank you for your kindness," Holzir said. "We can pay you a few coppers when we leave."

"Which will be tomorrow," I leaped in to say. I made it sound as if we were eager not to fritter away at her generosity.

With the tea warming our insides, we walked after Menteus up a narrow staircase to the room she had set aside. I followed the glow of the candle in her hand, and a distant memory flooded through me. During the Month of the Moon I used to follow Mother around the house, watching that same drifting candlelight as she checked the doors before we went to bed. Candles would burn all during that winter month, when the people around me were far down in the Sorrow. I wondered how it could hurt them so much when all I needed to make my spirits glow in the darkness was to watch a candle in my mother's hand.

But any semblance of home and help was as permanent as a candle's flame. Not until I found other Sorrowless and handed the orb in my pack into their care would I think I had found a flame that might burn forever.

The room looked as if it was once used for storage, since its only window was tiny and high on the wall. Maybe the inn's builders realized visitors wanted to see as little of greasy Iyalonda as possible. But the red rug spread on the floor, the table with two sturdy stools, and the cots made from hadro mangers and nested with blankets made it easy for a weary travel to forget what was outside the inn's walls.

Menteus lit an oil lamp hanging from the ceiling. "I'm afraid there's not much food left tonight. I can see if we have some more bread, if you like."

I nodded. The edge of my hunger was dulled, but even talking about food sharpened it again. Holzir was also glad for anything else he could get into his stomach.

Menteus left us with a cheery goodbye. Rint had already

picked out my bed and hopped into it to curl up and sleep.

"We've had some strange specks of good fortune on this trip, but this is the strangest," Holzir said as he slung down his pack and sat on a stool. "Do you think that this might be one of those sanctuaries?"

"I'm not sure," I said. "I hope so, but I think we're getting tested first. Somebody is waiting for us, watching. I can feel it. And I don't think I like it."

"Stop that, Belde. You can't be suspicious all the time over everything. Maybe this is just a sweet old woman. And now we've got walls between us and the rot out there. People like me—like everybody but you—need a quiet rest from the world sometimes."

"Is that what you found when you took care of your mother?"

It was only a curious question, but I immediately wished I hadn't reminded him of someone he had left behind.

He wasn't angered. "Most people spend their worst Sorrow days alone. Tending to my mother was the best way to soothe it when it got bad."

He ran his hand across the flat of the sword sticking from his belt. "I never would have made much of a Koltzer warrior, would I, Belde? They take their Sorrow onto battlefields and feuds and drown it in blood. I had my mother instead."

"You've shown yourself a good warrior since you've been with me."

"Not one like Dyzlin."

"Now you stop that," I said. "Dyzlin can swing a sword and batter with those meat fists of his, but he's nothing more than a wormy wretch. I'd like to hear him sing a song, or write one, like you do." I took a breath. "Do you know why I hated the tribe so much?"

It was a question I shouldn't have asked. I was afraid to give the answer.

It was too late. "Why?" Holzir asked.

"Because the others in the tribe were not like you."

I turned my back on him. I was finished, and I didn't want him to make any remarks about it.

He didn't. He sat in the quiet made by the heavy walls, fumbling in some kind of Sorrow. Then he reached down into his sack and took out the Sun-or-Moon board.

"I don't feel like playing," I said. Moments ago I would gladly have sat down and started turning over all his moons, but something had happened in the room that made me not wish to go back to old routines.

"You'd rather sleep?"

I tossed my sack down on the bed and heard the globe roll about in the layers of clothing. "You might go down to the parlor and see if anybody at the hearth knows how to play. If Menteus has food for us, eat it down there. I need to have the room alone."

He looked at my pack. "You're going to use it, aren't you?"

"Please, Holzir."

"Aren't you afraid it will do to you what it did to your father?"

"No. But I know what it will do to you. Please, go down and play your game. I'll come get you when I'm done."

He picked up his Sun-or-Moon case and slouched toward the door. He reached to take off his sword, then changed his mind. "Be careful, Belde. Maybe you think you're protected because of who you are. But the things locked inside that witch globe might bring the Sorrow to you. I'd hate to think you might have to suffer from it when it's never touched you."

"I've had my sorrows, Holzir."

"Not the constant ones. You always have a reason, Belde. Please, be careful."

He closed the door behind him. His eyes had not left mine the whole time we had talked.

FIFTEEN

The light seemed dimmer in the room when I finally gathered the courage to lift the pack from my bed and lay it on the table. I squared the stool and sat down, as if I were a merchant setting up for the first buyer of the morning, or a fortune teller preparing to spread cards to chart a seeker's destiny.

I had a hazy idea of the inside of a vision orb from the few moments when I had gazed into the one the Shapers had thrust at Father. The images struck in flashes, and my mind could hardly sort them out. Mostly, I recalled men and women dressed head to foot in orange clothing with black shields strapped over their eyes. White surrounded them, which I now thought might be from holes in the orb-memories.

Rint stirred in his sleep and clicked his beak at tasty bugs in his dreams. Watching him twist back into a comfortable position made me feel confident I could forge ahead and endure whatever the orb had to reveal to me.

I reached into the pack and pulled out the globe, wrapped in a shirt. The light peeked out, so I kept my eyes turned away. I would make the plunge only when I was ready. My eyes stayed fixed on the ceiling lamp as I unwrapped the cloth and bunched it beneath the globe to make a cradle so it wouldn't roll away.

The vision orb's surface was glassy and warm under my palms. I took a deep breath, and then lowered my eyes into its glowing center.

At first all I could see was the light of the orb. Then the glow started to take form. The beams of white light became coarse and started to drift past me like falling grains of sand. My hand was still on the curve of the globe, but as the light turned grainier, my fingers slipped through a place on the glass that crumbled into sand. Cold sand. I continued to sink into it. My arm passed through the hole, and when I reached out to stop it, my other hand and arm also passed into the globe.

I'm drowning, I thought. But I wasn't frightened. The light had turned into a river of crystal specks and swept me on its currents. The eddies tugged the rest of me inside until my head dropped below the surface.

I shut my eyes against the pressure of the grains of light, and when I reopened them I was floating on a plateau of white. What I thought was sand or crystal was actually ice with a covering of snow across it. It rolled out to meet a stark blue sky at the horizon. There was not a hint of cloud in the dome of the sky to cast shadows on the ice.

Was I seeing a vision of Aman-Sah? The strongest believers in that paradise often spoke of its whiteness and purity. But there was no comfort here. Who could find paradise among ice and a sky so bare and cheerless?

I knew for certain this was no place on Ahn-Tarqa, where only the highest peaks have snow. I turned my head to see what lay behind me, and was surprised that I could turn my head. The back wall of the inn should have been there. But the river of ice had drawn me deep enough that the memories of the globe had become all the world, and nothing except ice and snow spread in all directions.

A moment of fear gripped me: *How am I going to get out?* But then new sights got my attention, and I floated along with them.

The men and women of orange had returned. While I had turned my head to see how far away the white plain stretched, they suddenly appeared around me. The orange clothing covered every inch of their bodies except for black shields over their eyes. Tubes stretched from where their mouths should be and connected into plates on their chests.

The covered faces would have made most people believe these were Shapers of some kind. But they walked with imperfect and exhausted strides, nothing like the inhuman motion of the Shapers I had seen. They were pulling enormous sledges across the ice using straps over their shoulders. On the sledges rested blocks of metal crusted with icicles. One of the sledges did not have people pulling it, but instead a team of bizarre animals. They had the fur of rodents, but were as large as nychs. I thought of the legends of the huge rats that hunted the Acivis Wilds. But these creatures weren't rats at all. Their four legs were long, and their lean bodies from furry tails to sleek snouts were so beautiful that as one walked past I put out my hand to pet it. But I felt nothing and couldn't even see my hand as I stretched it out.

I was inside a memory the Lightborn had captured. I was allowed to see what the device of the Art had seen, but I was not truly there. I was more of a ghost than the figure of the long dead woman from the airship—I was invisible to everyone, a stranger from far ahead in time.

I moved my eyes to see the march of the orange people. I had that freedom, but my body could not move from where the memory-gatherer had once stood and captured these sights to seal in the orb.

One of the men—perhaps a woman, the clothing muffled all shape—carried a flag. The ice wind blew so hard that it was difficult to see the symbol on it. It might have been another outline of Ahn-Tarqa, like the one in the airship. On one of the metal boxes pulled on the sledge were the letters I had seen on the picture-glasses of the airship. Familiar but unreadable.

The landscape shivered from side to side. It made me dizzy, but I didn't feel actual movement. Suddenly, the world split into bars of gray, the visions snapped apart, then snapped together again.

Gaps ... I was passing through gaps in the orb-memories. Thousands of years of waiting must have damaged them. Each time the images shook and broke apart, a buzzing stung my mind. When I turned my head this time, I hoped I'd see the wall of the room, or Rint sleeping contentedly in a pile of blankets. The damage to the memories might harm me if I didn't get out soon. But everywhere I turned was the shaking and splitting world of ice and the people in orange armor.

Then the broken memories stopped. All light clicked off. Perhaps I was back in the room, and the oil in the lamp had run out. There was no sound to tell me anything.

A light stirred ahead of me. For a moment, I thought it was Mother on her nighttime rounds to keep her family safe. A second light popped up beside the first. Then another ... and many more sparkled to life until they became a starry night sky. The starlight showed the orange men and women standing around me in a tight group. Each one gripped a torch of the Art in a gloved hand. Circles of light crisscrossed the ground, which was now bare of snow. The exposed rock was dark and grooved, similar to the burned marks of the pit where the airship had crashed.

Was this a memory of that crash? No, impossible. The vision orb was already aboard the airship when it went down. This memory came from an older time.

The people scattered the light from their torches, searching every spot before they stepped. They seemed to know as little about where they were as I did. All of us were lost.

The light beams gathered together, and whoever captured the scene with the orb pushed me toward the center. The circles of light fit together in one place, adding their brightness to each other. The crossing and dancing beams hurt my eyes, and I could see little of what they were exploring. But I did catch sight of a word across the side of a larger container. The letters were blackened into a smudge and had almost turned into the recognizable "Ahn-Tarqa."

This was one of the great metal boxes the orange people had been dragging, but its shape was beaten and broken. Pieces of it lay across the ground, and a hole was burned through it.

It wasn't broken yet. As the lights explored it, one of the orange men approached. He put his hand toward the metal box, reaching for some means to make it do what it needed to do. A glow started inside the metal ruins, and even though the people surrounding me had their eyes and faces hidden, they were clearly hopeful and excited.

Then a frost-blue light rippled outward. The world teetered and flipped as the memory-gatherer went down and pulled me with it. All the others toppled as well, and their hopes with them. I felt it as strongly as if I were really among them instead of a ghost in a globe seeing it thousands of years later.

This was the Arrival. It couldn't be anything else. Here was the moment spoken of in the temples of the Lightborn when the gods first arrived on Ahn-Tarqa. The name "Lightborn" had come from this instant, when hope and fear balanced over a device that could have saved a race. A moment of the Art, the beginning of the Sorrow.

Was I seeing the start of history?

The orange people began to stand. A few did not. The others did not seem to notice the motionless ones on the ground. Their eyesight behind the black shields was directed upward, where light now streamed down on them.

I looked up as well, joining the people in curiosity. But it wasn't a magical light shining on us. It was only the moon, almost full, coming from behind the cloud that had covered it until then.

Now I could see where we were standing. The wide pit looked freshly scooped from the rocks; loose gravel was still tumbling down the sides. The people in orange glanced around, and they knew as well as I did where they were: Nowhere.

A young woman who had only known life in a city and on the plains didn't deserve to recognize every location on Ahn-Tarqa. Yet I could guess what this place was. It was the Valley of the First Scar, a lifeless gouge in the earth where the Lightborn had first appeared—or so it was told in songs and parchments. No one knew the true location of the Valley, or if there was more than one. Some tales said they were in the forbidden Land of Scars, others in a forgotten dale of the Cirrus Mountains. Down in the pit, there was no way for me to tell what part of the world I was looking at.

All around me were the Lightborn. And they were not gods. They were people lost and unable to return to their home: that white place that was maybe Aman Sah, but which was not paradise. It seemed an awful place to dream of as an escape from the trudge of life.

The people in orange started to remove their head-shrouds and eye-shields, although a few made warning signs not to try it. I wanted to hear their voices, even if I couldn't understand their language. But there was no sound. The light blast seemed to have blotted out my ability to hear what was happening.

But I could tell this—the Sorrow was growing all me. It was seeping into these people.

The man nearest me had his hood off. He turned my direction and looked through me at the world surrounding him. His light skin and hair were similar to an Idenite, but nothing about his look completely fit any race I knew. His eyes were filled with shock and incomprehension. He pulled off the gloves of his outfit, and touched the bare skin of his fingers to his face. He shouted something to the woman beside him, who had just removed her head covering. The shout started to pass among the others, and in a wave everyone started to pull off the tubes and shields over their heads.

I tried to feel what they did through the orb-memories. But it was a stew of emotions that hurt to consider. What madness this would cause in someone with the Sorrow! But they would never have gotten this deep into the memory. No wonder the Shapers needed people like me to dive into these pictures of the past and return with the knowledge.

Joy and terror surged around me. The pain of the Sorrow, the wonder of the Art. And then I knew for certain. This was the beginning. For the Lightborn had come to a new start, one that filled them with a sadness of a lost world, one that was cold and gloomy ... but it was theirs. This beginning would roll forward thousands of years to us, in a legacy of a curse and a gift.

The Lightborn had never gone back to Aman-Sah. They stayed. *We were the Lightborn.*

Now a sound reached me. My mind sharpened. I had to hear this, had to understand. But none of the orange people turned toward the noise.

The sound again. It came from outside the pit, across the distances of the blasted lands. It shouted a word I knew.

"Belde!"

I shook. The vision tilted around me.

"Belde!"

Holzir? What was he doing in the Valley of the First Scar? How had he found me?

Get out of there, you fool! a voice inside me yelled. *That's Holzir on the outside!*

At last I heard myself and ripped my eyes away from the globe. The orb gripped at me, like sticky strands pulling at every spot on my body. I grasped at the sound of my name and strained to break free. An angry clanging of metal on wood gave me the last push to crash back into the room at the inn.

THE STOOL TEETERED backwards and I hit the floor right as Holzir burst through the door.

"Belde, there are—" He reeled back, covering his face with his arm to avoid the light from the orb.

I stumbled up and doused the brightness with a blanket. Rint had leaped onto the table and was pecking at my hand. From downstairs came a commotion like an army crashing against the walls. The stairs creaked under enormous weight.

"What's going on?" I asked.

Holzir slammed the door and put his back against it. "Soldiers. Idcnites! They burst into the parlor. They're coming up here!"

I looked toward the window ... high on the wall, too small to squeeze through. The door ... no lock on the inside, no bar. The tiny room wasn't an old storage place converted for boarders. And it wasn't a sanctuary.

It was a trap.

There was still one way out. "Get back from the door, Holzir. When it opens, cover your eyes."

He nodded and stepped beside the door frame, sword at the ready.

Rint was hopping in a frenzy as the sound of boots and clattering steel reached the top of the stairs and started down the hall. I looked at my small friend and made the hand signals: *Run when I say. Don't follow.*

Rint chirped. He wasn't happy, but he'd obey.

The thundering reached the doorway. There was a pause for a shouted command, and then the door burst open as an armored shoulder slammed against it. Men in blue tunics draped over chainmail charged in.

I ripped the covering off the orb and held it over my head.

The first three soldiers through the door screamed and dropped to the ground to cover their eyes. What vision had pierced them first? What embers of the past made their Sorrow burst into searing flames?

Holzir swung his sword blindly with one hand while he covered his face. More soldiers piled in and tripped over the ones on the floor.

"Now!" I shouted to Rint, and he leaped over the heap of soldiers. There was a glint of green in the crush of blue uniforms, and then the little saurian vanished. He might make it outside, but I doubted either Holzir or I would. The soldiers poured in, falling aside as the power of the Art stabbed at their minds, but there seemed to be no end of them.

I pressed forward with the globe burning my palms. Maybe I could shred open a pathway for us.

A hand in a heavy gauntlet seized my ankle. I had gone too far forward for the orb's light to reach everyone, and one man had pulled out of the Sorrow's scorch. I tripped, and the orb slipped from my hands. As it tumbled through the air, the visions jabbed into my mind as well—ice, metal cubes, furred beasts, the Lightborn in the moment of revelation.

It all vanished when a gloved hand caught the orb and dropped it into a black velvet sack. The light snuffed out as a last wave of soldiers crashed through the door. I heard Holzir shout his battle cry, but it was snuffed out as the press of soldiers overcame us.

SIXTEEN

Astonishingly, in the madness packed into that room, neither Holzir nor I received anything worse than a few bruises. The soldiers subdued us with cold efficiency, and then bound our hands behind our backs with twine. They cleared a path from the room and marched us down the stairs to the parlor. Holzir tried to say something to me, but the nearest soldier cracked his fist across his jaw. We didn't try to talk to each other after that.

Leading the way down the stairs was the man holding the sack containing the orb. He had a bandolier across his chest and was the only soldier armed with a blackpowder weapon: a long-barreled killer of more elegant design than the blastgun I had taken from Kalzzik's tent. The other soldiers carried swords and axes of finer craftsmanship than anything forged in Iyalonda. But the rich blue of their tunics told me all I needed to know. These men served the Shapers and had come from the mystery outpost northwest of the city.

The story I had overheard in the caravansary was half right.

The Shapers were looking for Sorrowless in the area. But not a band making raids in the south. The Sorrowless they were looking for was *me*. I had walked right into an open ravager's mouth, thinking it was a warm, snug cave. It was that terrible last day in Tyrn all over again, except this time I hadn't escaped. There was no woman in disguise to pity me.

The soldiers had packed the other boarders at the inn into a corner of the parlor and held them there. All the soldiers appeared to be Idenites; the Shapers recruited from Father's people more than any other.

Standing apart from the soldiers and the guests, watching us with dead eyes, was Menteus.

"Excellent job," the rifle-carrying leader said to her. "This is certainly the two my masters want. The young woman was using a piece of sorcery when we seized her. Only someone with the sickness could do that."

A smile slithered over Menteus's lips. "I only needed to see the lost-looking young man in manure-farmer's clothing to know I'd found the ones you wanted. Don't I always pull them in for you?"

So the sanctuary was a lie. Were all the sanctuaries of the Gray Lands lies? Had I marched from the tribe across mountains and swamps and plains just to put myself into the Shapers' icy hands?

I couldn't hold back: "You lying scut! How much are you getting paid to sell us?"

My shouting did not not upset Menteus, but she wouldn't look me in the eyes. I had that small triumph. "I am paid with this inn and protection should Iyalonda's looters bother me. In return, I lure in those the Shapers find good to use."

"And your son—was that just a story, or did you sell him to those monsters too?"

The soldiers' leader stood beside Menteus and faced me. "Hardly. I volunteered, long ago."

Menteus patted the man's cheek. There was a family resemblance in his narrow face. "Rolant isn't a diseased one like you," Menteus said. "But I knew a story would soften you and convince you that you were safe."

Holzir wrenched against the men holding him and shouted insults in his own language at our faithless hostess. If the soldiers in the dim parlor understood what Holzir was saying, they would have ripped out his tongue and then probably ripped off his head after it. They settled for slugging him in the gut until he was gasping for air.

Rolant cast a hooded gaze at Holzir. To him, the Koltzer man was nothing but trash caught in the net he'd used to catch his prize. Then Rolant looked toward me. He was coy about avoiding my gaze. He held up his dominance without trying to stare me down. He had dealt with the Sorrowless before.

"You may be dressed in rags, girl, but I can see you have the proud carriage of a woman of Iden. A woman of the rich cities. I don't know how you can tolerate being with this mindless grass-chewer."

"Holzir is worth more than all of you Sorrow-bitten futches. He has honor. You haven't a drop of that for all your Idenite blood."

Rolant didn't bite back. "You should thank me. If you had stayed in Iyalonda much longer, someone of your fresh looks would have met a messier end."

"How did you even know to look for me? Your bitch mother said we were the ones you were searching for."

Rolant still wouldn't let my insults or anger rattle him. "The rumors that witch-people like you might find a safe hovel in the Gray Lands—we created those. We've snared a few by spreading around such crumbs."

"But you knew about *me*. Not just anybody. How did you know about me?"

"I'm not here to answer your questions. You'll learn soon enough." He waved his men toward the door, and they shoved us ahead of them. Holzir's moccasins dragged across the boards; after the beating to his stomach he could hardly keep himself up.

On the mud of the porch I saw a set of tiny prints. Rint had made it outside. The Shapers' servants had no care to look for a tiny saurian who was no threat to them.

"Goodbye, old friend," I whispered. No time to cry over it. I hoped Rint could find a way to live in the city or the plains outside. He had a better chance in Ahn-Tarqa than I did. Than any human ever did. It was, I understood now, the saurians' world long before we came.

To look at the street outside the inn, it would seem the whole city was deserted. The road was empty, the shutters on the windows facing it sealed. Even the sky had clouded overhead so it did not have to look at what stood in the middle of the road. No one in Iyalonda would dare approach the monstrosity of Shaper magic stopped in front of the inn, or even walk on the same street with it. The carriage resembled an enormous club-tail's shell mounted on iron wheels. No saurian team was reined to the front; this was a machine of the Art that rolled on its own power. A similar one had brought the Shapers to Father's harness shop. Anyone who lived within the reach of the Shapers feared these hideous machines, for it was the only way they traveled when they oozed out of their towered cities.

Two Idenites stood guard with blackpowder guns over a hatch on the carriage. As the soldiers marched us outside, one of the guards shouted something into the hatch. I didn't hear what he said, but the person he summoned from inside the carriage needed no announcement. Before I saw his face in the tower lights, I recognized his limp. I had given it to him.

Holzir found breath enough to shout the name. "Dyzlin!"

Rolant held my neck and shoved me forward so the man on the carriage could see better. "Is she the one you told us about?"

Dyzlin nodded. It was too dark to see his face as he turned toward me, but the sneer I imagined was worse. "Hello, pretty Beltza," he said in Koltzer. "Didn't I tell you I'd feed you to the Shapers?"

"The Sorrow will shrivel you for this," I snarled.

Rolant tugged me back and said to Dyzlin, "You've done well. Collect your payment from the sergeant and leave."

Dyzlin slid down from the carriage and limped toward me, trying his best to swagger with a lame leg. "What if I don't want to leave?" he asked in accented Idenite. "I don't want gold coins or anything else you have. Only this."

He reached toward me, but Rolant batted his hand down. "This sweetmeat isn't for you. You know that. Her capture should satisfy your anger. Our masters will do things to her your nightmares could never touch even if you lived a thousand summers."

Dyzlin recoiled to the carriage's side. "At least you can let me see what you'll do to her."

"Speak our language, you coward!" Holzir shouted. He wanted to hear Dyzlin's insults himself.

Dyzlin pointed to Holzir. "Or just let me see what you'll do to him. I know the wet-blood girl's sickness means something to you. But I want to see what will happen to this traitor. That's what I'll take in payment."

"Very well," Rolant said. "A fair bargain. We will allow you to know the Koltzer boy's fate."

Moments before I had hated Dyzlin more than I thought I could hate anyone, but now I almost pitied him. He was too dense to hear the treachery sown in Rolant's tone. Dyzlin's payment would be more than he could bear.

Dyzlin clambered back into the carriage and vanished into the hatch. The Idenites pushed Holzir after him. His fury at Dyzlin had given him back some of his energy, and he would need all his strength if he were to survive the next few hours inside a machine of the Art.

Rolant forced me up the metal steps on the side of the carriage. He didn't take me to the main hatch but drew me toward the rear section, where a large bulk housed the gears and pistons that powered the wheels.

"You will ride in the master's chamber," Rolant said. "You're not likely to try to escape if you're in the same room with him."

My muscles tightened. "Master" could mean only one thing to a servant like Rolant and his thugs.

The Idenite unscrewed the top of a smaller hatch which then hissed opened. The Sorrow boiled up from it like a stream of sulfur. I waited to see Rolant pull away—it stank with dread that even a servant the Shapers had trained couldn't handle. But he stood rigid. He put his hands on my back to shove me in.

I twisted my shoulders from his grasp. "I can take it, Captain Rolant. I'm the one with the sickness, remember?"

"You're brave and beautiful," he said. "I'm sorry it has to go this way for you, but my masters are my masters."

"Then I'm sorrier for you." I stepped onto narrow spiral steps and descended into the night of the carriage.

The hatched sealed overhead. I fell back against a corner of the stuffy chamber. Rivets pressed against my back.

Seated on a bench across from me was a shadow within the shadows. The Sorrow from the wizard who commanded Rolant and his men reached out to enfold me. But it fell away before it could touch me.

"I'm not frightened of you," I said to the shadow. "I *hate* you. That's more powerful."

The mask of the Shaper dipped in acknowledgement as the wheels started to turn. The two of us sat in our corners, glaring silently at the place where we knew the other was wrapped in blackness.

SEVENTEEN

The only marker to tell how much time had passed was my stomach. It felt as if I had grown a second one, just as empty as the first, so at least a day had gone past since our capture. I may have slept. The rolling motion of the carriage across the hills made me drowsy, but inside that stuffy carriage it might as well have been the Month of the Moon where "sleep" and "wake" were almost the same.

At last the machine quivered to a stop and sighed as the power of the Art whirred out of it. The long ride had made me understand better why this magic frightened the Sorrowful. It was filled with a sinister energy found nowhere else in nature. I had seen the clean, graceful interior of the Lightborn's airship. That was what the Art could be. The Shapers' cogs and gears were spiteful and foul copies. But the monstrous Art of the Shapers didn't make me afraid just because it existed—only because of what it might do to me.

The top hatch hissed open. Watery daylight poured down, and when I looked for the creature that had sat across from me during the journey, there was an empty bench. The Shaper had slithered out while I slept. Maybe it was never there at all, only a trick of my fogged memory.

The barrel of a gun banged against the hatch. "Time to get out, witch-girl!"

I walked up the steps, moving unsteadily with my hands tied behind my back. The hair along my neck prickled; it was a feeling I remembered from standing near the Cruncher in Tyrn. My ears tuned to the roar of new sounds the walls of the carriage had muffled. Before I got to the top and into the overcast daylight, I knew this was no simple "camp," but a base filled with men, saurians, and machines. I could hear and feel a low pounding, like the hammers of the Koltzer Sky Lords flattening the earth.

The strangest noise was a natural one: the roar of a ravager. But that was impossible. Why would the Shapers keep a huge, uncontrollable carnosaur inside their walls?

I listened for too long, and the sentry got impatient and dragged me up by the shoulder.

"You there, stop!" Rolant shouted. He strode across the top of the carriage and knocked the soldier back from me. "You know the orders: the young woman is not to be harmed. Go tell the artificer to ready the demonstration. I'll bring the prisoner along."

The soldier muttered something, and his Sorrow flickered, either because of me or mention of the "demonstration."

"Thank you," I sneered at Rolant once the sentry was gone.

My sarcasm reached part of him. "I do feel sorry for you. That was no lie."

I looked over my human captor closely for the first time. He was a handsome man, with a mop of shiny black hair and pale skin that set off gemstone-blue eyes. Their look reminded me of something that I could not recall in the tangle of everything else in my head, but nothing could make me feel anything but rage toward the man who had brought us to a Shaper lair.

"Where have you got Holzir?"

"He was taken out before you, when the master left the carriage. The other Koltzer fool was taken along with him. You won't see either again, so don't bother whining about it."

I turned away to look over the compound. The sky was sooty and matched the color of the fence of rocks welded together with girders. The closed circle towered high enough to block out any sight of the outside world that might tell me how deep into the Gray Lands I was, or how close this camp was to the Shapers' own even bleaker dominions.

Within the barrier was the same mixture of jagged power and the unnatural I had felt inside the carriage. The stone heaps and black metal bars were cobbled together without a pattern—until the eye tried to make one, and regretted it. Pits along the ground billowed smoke coils as thick and solid as snakes, a smoke no natural fire could create. Glow globes dangled on ropes that criss-crossed over the edges of the outer wall. Pylons posted at points along the barricades held lanterns that crackled with a powerful blue light.

Men wearing armor shielding only their upper bodies worked on carriages and devices that looked like titanic blackpowder guns mounted on wheels. Past these behemoths were rows of cages along the outer wall that contained saurians. A few held riding hadrosaurs and draft ceratopses, but most of the cages were packed with devil claws. The hadro mounts were restless, unhappy to find themselves so near a horde of their predators. Some devil claws snapped at their cage walls. Others stood eerily still, held in place by the gleaming helmets on their heads. All of them, even the crazed ones ripped fresh from whatever wombs the Shapers grew them in, seemed to be waiting for a sorcerous signal.

If a signal came, it would be from the ramshackle building of metal sheets in the center of the camp. The building was so foul that I knew it must be where the Shapers themselves hid. Inside the windowless walls they could play with their malignant tools while their human servants walked around in the air, fearful to breathe wrong because it might anger their masked overlords.

All this, from the stones to the machines, held the same scowling sense of purpose that poisoned everything the Shapers touched. This was the world as the Shapers wished to mold it: severe and melancholy. I had seen melancholy in sagging trees and severity in impenetrable mountains, but the Shapers crafted both with such intent that they transformed them into something hideous. It might not even be their aim to make such ugliness, but their Sorrow could not conceive of creating anything different.

There were a few wooden huts in the fortress that did not have the malignant feel. This must be where the Idenite servants ate and slept. Their masters had trained them to deal with the most hideous poisons of the Art, but the Idenites needed somewhere to dwell in their normal Sorrow.

I still couldn't untangle the meaning of what I was seeing. There was purpose to this encampment, but what?

"Did you build all this just for dangerous little Belde?" I said to Rolant, but I was poking for deeper answers.

Rolant locked his hand around my arm and moved me down the steps to the muddy ground. "You'll learn what this place is for as you go along. Soon you'll wish you knew less."

Rolant shoved me forward, but placed his grip on my arm so he didn't wrench it. I went along without struggle. Trying to escape would only get me a fast death. I might soon long for one, but I had discovered one curse of being Sorrowless is that no matter what happened, I wanted to keep living so I could learn as much as possible.

I expected Rolant to take me to the center compound. Instead, he pushed me in a circle around it. "Where are you taking me?" I asked.

"Always questions from you," he sighed. "Don't be hurried. You'll see the inside of the Hive soon. I have other instructions first. You're to watch some of what we do here in the Enhancing Grounds."

"I think you mean the 'Ruining Grounds,' " I said, with a glance toward the devil claws forced to attention through the power in their helmets.

"You have no idea what you are saying," Rolant said with a laugh. He tolerated the horror of the place with better humor than he should. It was strange. The more I saw of Captain Rolant, the more about him seemed wrong for a dedicated tool of the Shapers.

A ravager roared from the other side of the camp. There was no mistaking the sound now. I had heard ravager calls many times on the plains. They never attacked large Koltzer camps, but they sometimes lurked close to catch stray hadros from the herds. The roars got closer as we walked around the edge of the crooked building.

Then I was able to see what the Shapers were doing. What they had their slaves doing.

In the back of the building Rolant called "The Hive" was a courtyard cordoned off with a wall of stones as high as my shoulder. The only part of it I had seen over the top of the Hive was a wooden tower on stilts. Two creatures faced each other across the small arena. Neither beast was small, however. Together they filled up most of the courtyard, with only room for the crude tower between them.

The first giant was a ravager, the largest I had ever seen. The great two-legged hunters have heads the size of a small hadrosaur and jaws so massive it seems they should tip the creatures over and their stubby two-fingered arms would never allow them to get up again. I had come close to a ravager before, but it was a day-old corpse a Koltzer war party had slain in a fight that killed three of them.

This ravager had a short chain attached to its right foot. Its leg muscles could shatter the chain with a single kick, but the great beast wasn't fighting. It hardly moved. It leaned on its back tail and swooned to the left and right, like a tavern brawler who's taken too many jabs to the forehead. The ravager's lower jaw sagged open and a trail of silvery drool ran to the ground. A helmet like a devil claw's, but large enough to cap a well, was clamped on its head. Copper wires ran from the surface of the helmet to the wooden tower, where a crew of men in white outfits did work hidden behind the rails of the platform.

An insane idea came to me: *The Shapers were trying to control ravagers with the Art.* That was madness, even for them. Ravagers are nothing but unleashed hunger and savagery. Easier to rope and tie an earthquake.

I didn't grasp the full tale of what was happening until I followed the wires from the other side of the platform to the head of the opposite giant.

This was a monster I had never seen before, except in my mind when I heard old songs. I never could figure out exactly what a "colossus" looked like from the tales sung about the wars during the Hegemony. The songs described them as huge men of metal that moved with the Art's power, but the Koltzer poets weren't imaginative enough to make me envision what such a creature might look like.

I didn't need imagination now. The squat statue of bronze and steel only looked like a man in that it had arms, legs, a head, and stood upright. Everything was in the wrong proportions. The legs were stubby and wide to give it balance; the arms were so thick that three children could probably grasp hands around it in a circle. The head was a squashed oval with no eyes, only a visor of the unknown black metal the Shapers used for the most dangerous pieces of anything they made. The eyeless-ness of the thing was the fabric of nightmares. The colossus wasn't moving, and this made it seem worse: the potential coiled inside made it feel like a metal trap about to slice off the head of someone passing unsuspecting in front of it. I actually felt better when I looked back at the ravager swaying and softly growling. At least it was alive in a way I understood.

I strained to find something intelligible to say. "They can't be trying to control—? No, no, there's no way they can do it."

"You do understand, at least a little," Rolant said. "I believe your sickness gives you natural insight into the Art, even if you do not know much about it."

"They're trying to move the ravager the same way they move a colossus."

"Yes, something like that. I don't pretend to understand exactly how they send orders through wires. But my masters are trying something more ambitious than simply telling a devil claw to 'obey.' They want to control the ravager in every way, as they can command the colossus. Their will replaces its will."

Rolant pushed me through a swinging gate into the enclosure. If the ravager's mind wasn't scrambled from the wires webbed across its head, it could have taken one stride forward and gulped down both of us. The colossus could do whatever evil it was capable of even faster. But neither giant moved. Approaching us instead was a man in a white smock tied across the front with a crosshatch of black laces. It reminded me of a butcher's apron, and it had blood on it to match.

"Is this the Sorrowless one?" the man asked in an airless tone.

"If that's what you want to call her. She's yours for as long as it takes."

"Won't be long. We have the deserter ready." White Smock looked toward a group of soldiers at the base of the wooden tower. They were squeezed into a space that put them as far as possible from the two giants. Kneeling between them was a bleeding and trembling figure wearing a hood over his head, a loincloth, and nothing else.

"Offer the guest a seat, Captain Rolant," White Smock said in the mirthless tone of someone who had to use the Art every day until it drowned him in the Sorrow Sleep. He was an artificer, and I knew a few from Tyrn who worked on the glow globes and repaired the conduit channels beneath the city that ran from the Cruncher. Few artificers lived far past thirty. I guessed this one had seen at least twenty-five summers and a hundred winters. That's what life is like for someone who surrenders to the grinding mill wheels of the Sorrow.

Rolant rolled up a barrel and shoved me onto it to give me the best seat in the arena. The artificer walked toward the tower base and shouted up to his assistants, the apprentice artificers starting their own descent into madness.

He yelled orders that used terms of the Art I didn't understand, but my attention then switched to two slats in the wall of the building behind the tower. As if a cue to raise the curtain on a play, the black eyes slid open. There was only darkness there, but I knew what was happening. The Shapers were overlooking the experiment from a shadowy nook. My eyes tried to break the black veil to see the watchers, but it was still only motionless dark.

The soldiers dragged the near-naked man to the middle of the pen. He screamed for mercy through the muffling of the sack. White Smock held a metal cylinder in his hand and wrapped wires that dangled from the tower around it. He took his time fixing the cables to one end of the cylinder. To the other end, he set a knife the size of a child's toy but made of cutting steel.

Rolant narrated for me: "The hooded man is a soldier who tried to desert in Iyalonda. Sometimes even the best-trained recruits can't handle working for our masters. Usually, they are turned into olglim. This one, however, chose to commit his crime so that it fit ideally with the Shapers' plans for you."

I swallowed hard. They wouldn't show me what was about to happen if they simply planned to do it to me as well. The Shapers had grander and more barbarous ideas for the Sorrowless. This was merely the opening act of their vicious pageant.

I had no idea how vicious it would actually be.

"Open the current!" White Smock shouted. The apprentices pulled at levers from their platform, and the ravager went rigid as it awoke from its stupor. White Smock touched the small knife on the end of the cylinder, and the ravager spread its jaws and roared. The noise rattled my teeth.

"Connection complete!" White Smock shouted. He waved at the two soldiers standing beside the prisoner. They pulled the man, who was now kicking as furiously as his wounds allowed, into a spot beneath the ravager's jaws. The line of drool spilled over the prisoner's back, while the ravager stared directly ahead and didn't see the morsel at its feet. The two soldiers kicked the hooded man onto his face, then cut the rope around his arms. Finally, they ripped the sack from his head and ran to safety.

The man, whose face was beaten to the point where it was nothing but a giant bruise, looked around to see where he was. He tried to stumble to his feet, but White Smock walked behind him, gripped his shoulder, and then jammed the knife-tip of the cylinder into the base of his neck. I winced. The prisoner's scream was greater than ordinary pain. Something was throbbing in or out of him through the cylinder and the wires running up to the platform.

White Smock moved back to stand with the soldiers. He flashed a signal to the tower. "Release the upper body. Stop subject's impulses at case."

The ravager moved again. Its head tilted down and it found the cringing heap of a man in front of it.

"Move it *slowly*," White Smock called. "Remember what happened last time."

In response to whatever reached inside the ravager's mind to control it, the great jaws lowered toward the prisoner. The slow approach toward the man, who flailed from the sword-like teeth but was unable to move because of the dagger-thing jammed into his neck, put me in a waking nightmare. I couldn't close my eyes as I watched the ravager eat the man piece by piece.

It might have lasted a minute or an hour. The ravager devoured one chunk of the man at a time. First the hand, then up the arm, then it started on a leg. No saurian ate like that: the creature's movements were under the command of the artificers.

They kept the prisoner alive as long as they could, letting him shriek as the ravager reduced his body in portions. I thought it was tearing off bits of me as well. I sat in silence and struggled to remember the Lightborn, the airship, Rint, Holzir ... anything that was whole and beautiful. If I weren't Sorrowless, I'm certain I would have fallen into the Sorrow Sleep to save myself. The others were shielded with their coldness and skill—or else they looked the other way, as the soldiers did.

The ravager finally went for the prisoner's head, and as the jaws crunched down a last time, White Smock stepped forward and pulled at the cables to rip out the cylinder from the man's neck before it disappeared down the ravager's gullet.

White Smock called for a halt. The ravager, snout smeared with gore, righted itself and slipped back into a daze.

Air rushed into my lungs. Had I held my breath the whole time? "The Shapers are ... *obscene*," I whispered.

Rolant heard. "They do not torture because they enjoy it. All they do has purpose."

Purpose again. The mocking of nature and whatever good was inside the Art.

White Smock came forward with the metal cylinder, now detached from the blade and wires. He held the blood-splattered tube in front of him as if it were a venomous snake. "It's done," he said as he gave the cylinder to Rolant. He then backed up three steps, preferring the nearness of the ravager to whatever he had trapped inside the cylinder.

Rolant showed a glare of disgust as he twitched the object in his glove. He wasn't repulsed enough. The glare was nothing like the looks of Sorrow-terror on the faces of the artificers and soldiers.

I said, "Strange how it doesn't bother you much."

His blue eyes glared sideways at me. "I like you more when you ask questions, witch-girl."

So I made sure not to ask him any questions. If I asked about the cylinder, he would tell me the same thing: I would know soon enough and wished I hadn't.

ROLANT PUSHED me through the door into the Hive and sealed it behind us. Two shapes stepped from the corners of the room and into the haze of the glow globe hanging from the ceiling. They were the first Shapers I had seen clearly in the waking world in five years.

I could hardly believe they were real and not phantoms stalking my dreams. They wore robes of sickly green that brushed over the floor, and their masks had triple-points radiating from the crowns. Robe color meant rank to the Shapers, but it wasn't a hierarchy I understood, except black was one of the highest ranks: Artikons, like the one who had my parents killed in Tyrn and threatened me in my dreams. As far as I knew, Shapers had no "kings" or "chiefs," but they respected mysterious ranks. Artikons were apparently among the highest in skill, the ones who knew the most about the workings of the Art, and who also most deeply understood their own Sorrow.

Standing guard at the passages leading from the anteroom were humans swathed in stiff leather armor from their necks to their boots. Their eyes were glazed and their mouths hung open wide enough for flies to buzz in. Red scars over their foreheads showed where the Shapers' tools had opened their skulls and turned them into olglim. These servants felt no pain or fatigue, and they thought only as their creators wished them to think.

The two Shapers approached. My skin crawled to see them move over the floor as if gliding. It was hard to believe I was awake and seeing these creatures in their icy might again.

Rolant's attitude changed to subservient rigidity. "She is ready. The record in the recruder is complete." He held out the cylinder. One of the Shapers plucked it up with needle-thin fingers. The blood still staining it did not bother the Shaper. It slanted its head to stare at it, and I was reminded of the way Rint would examine a dead rat on the street, wondering how it had got that way and if he should pick it up.

The Shaper gave no response to Rolant, but drifted down a hallway with its prize. The other Shaper held out a spindly finger toward the second passageway. As Rolant passed the Shaper, it shrilled some instructions to him, but nothing I could hear.

The maze of the halls mirrored the brains of its creators. No corner was a standard angle, no straightway ran straight. The walls slanted narrow and then wide, making a series of triangles that disoriented me. Maybe the Shapers' minds didn't allow them to build in simple directions, or they wanted the confusion to keep their slaves in a daze. I certainly felt bewildered, and couldn't tell the direction we were facing or how to get back to where we had come. But Rolant knew the exact route and steered me along the bends.

Other Shapers moved through the halls, each alone. Most had green robes with three-pointed masks. Two wore storm gray, the same color the Woman had used as her disguise, and had only two prongs on the tops of their masks. They must be lower ranks, students or apprentices. I saw none in black. Olglim stood at some junctures and noticed nothing as we went past them. I watched the doors, the only landmarks I could follow. The words above them were written in Idenite, but in a bulging script that twisted like the halls, so I could make out the purpose of only a few of the rooms: storage lockers for pieces of the Art, a chamber for "Chirurgeons" that had the stink of a slaughter-yard creeping under the door, and a few rooms with hash marks over the entrances, warning anyone who wanted to come in that now was the time to change their mind.

Rolant came to a heavy iron door with no marking on it except "5." He pulled on a handle and motioned me inside. "There's food. You'll need it." Before he closed the door and turned the lock shut, he sliced apart my bonds with his knife.

I rubbed the chafing on my wrists and looked around my cell. It was less dizzying than the rest of the complex. The walls were almost straight and sensible. There was no cot, only a bench against the wall. I sat down and picked at the food left on a tin plate. Soldiers' rations: squares of dried meat that tasted like quake-foot, a few crumbly crackers, and a vial of water. It was raw nutrition, but I needed it. The moment I sat down, I thought I might never move again.

Everything in the world had beaten me. Dyzlin had taken his petty jealousy and turned it into the worst revenge he could think up. The traitorous Menteus had preyed on my memories of the deaths of my parents to trap me. The promise of a sanctuary was only a snare. The vision orb that might open up the secrets of Ahn-Tarqa was gone. I had lost my only two friends. Rint was alone somewhere in the gutters of Iyalonda, and in another room of this awful place, maybe in the hole of the Chirurgeons, Holzir was trammeled to a table awaiting the Shapers' knives. If he were lucky, fear of their devices would drive him mad before the torture began.

The worst defeat was that the other Sorrowless I had hoped were searching for me were nothing but rumors. There was no band of Sorrowless heroes waiting on the fringes of my life. There was only a helpless young woman who happened to be Sorrowless, and who for a moment thought she carried a key to save the world. But Belde, daughter of Lukan and Kryzin, was just a minor freak. Now the Shapers would devour her for their purposes as they had devoured the other Sorrowless they had caught. Like the Woman. They must have captured her long ago, the way they had captured me.

Stop it! I tried to argue with my defeat. *That's what they want you to feel, Belde. And even if it's true, don't give them that.* The Shapers wanted me to sweat waiting for them, and maybe break in fear before they came to drill into my thoughts. I wouldn't fear them. I would *hate* them. I'd fill my mind with my parent's deaths and Father screaming for me as the robed monsters poisoned him with visions his mind couldn't bear. I would not allow my failures to make it any easier for them break me.

Hate them, Belde. Hate.

Soon after I washed down the last of the water, Rolant came to fetch me. This time he tied my hands in front of me.

"Is Holzir getting the same grand treatment?" I asked.

"Don't waste your breath. Welcome to the worst day of your life."

"I had that years ago, thanks to your masters."

"This day isn't over." Again, he sounded regretful even as he tried to act like he was made of slate.

He took me to a room at the end of a long hallway that tilted so I felt like I was tipping over as I walked. There was nothing else along the walls. Everything fell toward the black portal at the end. It had that horrible *purpose* to it.

The door slid open on its own as Rolant approached. Nobody waited on the other side. It was another windowless room with colorless walls, but the walls collapsed toward a peak overhead that made the space feel cramped even though it was three times the size of my cell. The glow globes were dim, but all there was to see were two metal chairs and a pedestal of speckled stone.

Rolant pointed me into the chair facing the door. "The master of the Enhancing Ground will be with you shortly."

"The *Ruining* Grounds," I corrected.

He ignored me. He untied my hands and bound my left to one of the slats of the chair. He then tugged down the sleeve of the tunic on my right arm and pressed my bare skin onto the pedestal. He used extra lengths of twine to strap down my arm, looping it through hooks on the edge of the pedestal.

The tabletop felt chillier than stone. Then I saw what my bare skin was resting on: the blood-crusted cylinder, set into a cradle carved into the pedestal top to fit it.

"Be agreeable when my master questions you," Rolant said. "The pain from the recruder is horrible, whether you have the Sorrow or not."

Our gazes danced around each other like sword tips in a duel. "How would you know how the Sorrowless feel?"

"I know because I've seen people of your kind tortured on the recruder before. Even with my training, I can't block out the screams."

Rolant pulled a hanging cord. A bell tolled on the other side of the door. The portal slid open and he passed out of the room. The door stayed closed for only a heartbeat, time enough for me to wonder what would happen when the blood-stained device under my arm came to life.

Then the door hissed back open. A faceless figure moved in like an oozing column of tar. An Artikon. The one from my dreams. The one who killed my parents.

EIGHTEEN

It wasn't how he moved, or the spindly outline of his mask, that told me the truth. It was his Sorrow. It was like a mortuary room left unattended for years. My thoughts reeled back from this creature in inky robes so fast that I knew as clearly as I knew anything that my nightmare tormenter—"Sorrowless girl, we shall come for you"—was in the room with me.

Hate, Belde. Hate. Don't let him have any pleasure from this.

He lowered himself onto the other chair as if he were made from inflexible metal. His mask, cut and smoothed from saurian skin, had the same featureless front of all Shaper masks, but the prongs along the edges twisted like weeds growing at angles around rocks. His Sorrow billowed toward me. It might drive the most trained and toughened of his servants past the limits of their Sorrow.

But I didn't have a limit to cross. I gave him my stare. Could a Shaper stand it, would he flinch away?

Through the mask it was impossible to tell if his eyes met mine. When he moved, it was to draw a hand of mottled spider-legs out from a black sleeve. The fingers scuttled along the edge of the pedestal, found a knob, and twisted it.

Edges sliced into my fingers. The blades snapped closed so fast that I didn't realize my fingers had been bitten away until the moments after, when the pain from what had at first only been a pinch exploded through the rest of my body. I jerked against the ropes and clamped my teeth to stop the scream.

But my fingers were still there, quivering at the end of my hand. No blood gushed over the pedestal. The pain vanished the moment the Artikon released the knob. He only wanted to let me taste what the cylinder could do.

His voice echoed through the mask sound chamber. "That was the beginning. I have many questions for you. Answer them, and the beginning is all you will feel." He waved his hand near the knob. "First, tell me if you are the one we lost."

I couldn't answer. I watched the Artikon's hand close over the knob, but he was willing to wait for me to speak first. "I don't know what you mean," I finally said.

"You humans—even one such as you—cannot tell us apart, except from the color of our robes and the shapes of our masks. Perhaps you do not remember that it was I who came for you in Tyrn five years past."

I already knew that, but the admission from the faceless monster made me want to rip off my restraints, lunge across the table, and wrap my hands around the throat hidden under his mask and robes. "You killed my mother and father."

"No, I ordered the servants to do it."

"That's the same thing."

His finger tapped on the pedestal top. "I do not understand how you Sorrowless think. If I did not kill your parents, then how can you say that I did? No, do not answer. It would be gibberish."

Hate. "You murdered them."

He waved his hand. "You have answered my first question. You are Belde of Tyrn, the girl who escaped us in that city. Only one other Sorrowless we have hunted has achieved that, and to escape he took his own life."

The Shaper's mask pressed closer to me. I held myself rigid so I would not bend before him. "Do not imagine you are special, Belde of Tyrn. You are here now, and under our Art all eventually become equal. Do not imagine you were our sole priority during those years we hunted for you."

"You had other families to murder, right?"

He did not listen or care. "But when that fool of a herder brought our servants news of a woman of the right age named 'Beltza,' a woman who did not seem to have the Sorrow and who traveled in unusual company, it was a simple matter to alert our spies in Occiland to watch the roads and prepare our houses of false safety. You were easy to catch, and would serve only limited purpose. However—" The fingers scuttled into the robes, and came back with the sack that held the vision orb. "—we would have hunted for you with greater effort if we knew you possessed such a treasure."

"My father gave it to me," I offered before the Artikon could ask any questions about the orb's origin. It seemed he knew nothing of the crashed airship near Ravager Fang. He thought I had the globe in my keeping for years. I would give him nothing about the airship and what I learned from it. "He was frightened to tell me where he found it. He knew it was safe with me."

The mask did not move, nor did the wizard's fingers. He was absorbing my words, trying to place them in the web of knowledge he and his race possessed about these strange objects.

My Sorrowlessness made me harder to read, and he seemed temporarily satisfied with my lie. "The captain informed me that you have already probed into the vision orb, so there is no urgent need to force you to peer into it again. For the moment." His hand closed over the covered globe. "I will make this simple, Belde of Tyrn. All you must do is tell me what you drew from this orb. Everything you remember. Leave out nothing."

I left out everything. My mouth remained sealed.

The Artikon leaned back into the chair. The underworld echo from his mask spoke as if lecturing a misbehaving student: "It seems you do not understand what you saw in the orb, or its purpose. You have cunning, but like most humans you lack true comprehension. Otherwise you would know what these lucent globes are. They capture memories. These memories are so potent that no Sorrow can bear them.

"When we once ruled all of Ahn-Tarqa, we never encountered people without the Sorrow. This seemed natural. The Handless God teaches that no thinking creature can live without the Sorrow. It is part of the weave of life. Yet now we believe differently. It would seem that the message of the Handless God was ... misread. Humans must have brought the Sorrow with them and poisoned all that our ancestors tried to achieve with the Art. The Sorrow restrains our race, and our earlier conquests were useless expenditures of time that did nothing to lift it. The path of conquest is through knowledge, the unlocking of the secrets of the Sorrow that will take us to Aman-Sah. Then, just as we start our questing, people such as you begin to emerge. It cannot be a coincidence. You are here to serve a purpose for the Eldru."

The name "Eldru," forbidden even to the Shapers' closest servants, recalled a memory from the shrine: the word "Elder." How far back were the Lightborn and these "Elder" linked?

"The purpose becomes clearer each year as we unearth more of these orbs," the Artikon continued. "You Sorrowless are gifts to us from the Handless God. He wants us to unlock the memories contained within the orbs, and only you can look into them. This is the reason you exist: to atone for the guilt of the humans who perverted the Art we created. Accept what you are and submit to us. Only then can we end the Sorrow and open the gateway to Aman-Sah."

"Even if that means killing every Sorrowless person? And any other human in your way?"

"It may come to that. No other path has worked. We tried simple ways to cure the Sorrow. The most common is with the chemicals our Alchemists brew. In the same places we have discovered vision orbs buried in the earth, we also found stores of a kind of medicine. We have learned enough to believe our ancestors may have used this medicine to treat the Sorrow."

I could see what he was doing. He was trying to tempt me with anything familiar that might make me suddenly show I knew what he was talking about, reveal what I had seen in the vision orb. I had to hold myself as stern as the sides of Ravager Fang so I wouldn't flinch when he talked about these "chemicals." It reminded me of the silver woman and the plungers I had seen in the airship.

"But, Belde of Tyrn, you would not want to see what happened to the humans on whom we used that medicine. Their Sorrow seemed cured—at first. But in its place rushed a sort of burning madness. Fury."

I had to grit my teeth. I remembered the words in the shrine that had poured into my mind: *Not the answer. Cure. Failure. New illness.*

But the Artikon couldn't know about the silver woman's words. He was dangling knowledge in front of me, but he didn't know what it really meant. The knowledge the Lightborn kept in the shrine that they hoped to use to "to save humanity"—did it have something to do with this "cure"? And the "burning madness"?

I thought about the rage inside me after I shot Dyzlin's leg apart. And then the moment I almost dashed apart Holzir's Sun-or-Moon board and felt as if my body were burning up.

No, no, it was impossible. The failed cure was thousands of years ago. The Sorrowless were something fresh. *I wasn't the sick one.*

I had stumbled so deep into my thoughts that I missed whatever else the Artikon was trying to use to trick me. It seemed he had gotten weary of this part of the game, and finished up.

"—but all of this is meaningless for the future. No matter what humans do, we will find Aman-Sah. It is the destiny of the Eldru."

He had changed his game. Now he was also using hate as a tool, to make me fight back and tell him he was wrong, that I had glimpsed the truth in the shrine and the vision orb. His Handless God was a lie, and it was the Lightborn who brought the Art. But I couldn't tell this Shaper that I had spied the beginning of history inside an airship of the Lightborn. The Shapers denied the Lightborn entirely. In their beliefs, the Art came from them alone, woven into their minds by the Handless God. The Artikon had spoken the lie that moved their cruelties: humans had somehow created the Sorrow and therefore were fit only for experiments or slavery.

He wouldn't trick me into shouting out what I knew. I built up my hate into a shield wall. "You killed my mother and father—"

"Deaths that I now regret, since your father could have told us where he found this precious artifact."

"—so give me one reason I should I tell you anything."

The splotched fingers twisted the knob on the side of the pedestal.

The biting returned. But now it felt as if the teeth of a ravager had clamped down on my elbow and the jaws were worrying my arm from its socket. I tried not to scream, but yells of horror caromed around the skewed walls, and I recognized it was my own throat making those sounds.

The rending of my arm stopped, and the limb was still whole on the pedestal. No teeth-gouges on it anywhere. My head was pounding with a memory of pain as real as anything I had ever felt.

The Artikon spoke: "That is one reason. The recruder." He gestured to the cylinder under my arm. "An innovation from our workshops in Thulia, constructed from what we have understood of the vision orbs. We can make records of a person's sensations. Not solid memories, but primal physical feelings. This recruder houses the dying sensations of a deserter. You saw the man. His physical reactions as the saurian devoured him piecemeal are collected in the recruder. When I activate it, you feel what he did. I can turn it farther and farther, taking you along his ordeal until all his sensations ceased. A man with the Sorrow might last a minute before his mind shattered from the experience. How long, Belde of Tyrn, do you believe you will last?"

I could hardly speak. Remembering that prisoner dying in short snaps and swallows was terrible enough. Then to add to the memory the *feeling* of the jaws slicing him apart—

Hate, Belde, hate. "It ... hurts ... but it won't crack my mind. Just like the orb didn't."

Was there a flutter of admiration in the set of the Artikon's shoulders? "You may be correct. Your resilience in coming this far from your home, even daring to argue with an Artikon, is prodigious. You will serve many purposes before we dispose of you. But now—" He rolled the globe back and forth inside the sack. "—we need you to serve one purpose only."

"Try your ravager-munching memory again," I said. "I think I prefer it to hearing you talk."

This time when he turned the knob, the ravager jaws snapped

up to my shoulder. My whole arm went down its sticky gullet. The walls turned red and the food in my stomach leaped halfway up my throat. When the pain stopped, my head was against the pedestal, spittle from my lips dappled across it.

"I do not enjoy doing this to you," the Artikon said when I managed to pull up my shoulders and slump back into the chair. "But there is another reason you should consider speaking. We cannot offer you the chance to go free, but we may offer that freedom to another."

In the fog of pain and hate, I had somehow driven my friend from my thoughts. "You'll let Holzir go?"

"That is his name? It's intriguing you've come so far with someone like him. I know nothing of what the boy thinks of you. Maybe he sees you as a way to escape from tedious tribal life. But we have studied the Sorrowless long enough to know that you form attachments we do not understand. But we understand how to use them.

"Yes, we will consider releasing him. We can guarantee what will happen to him if you do not cooperate. I will show you what the Chirurgeons have planned for the young man if you refuse." The Artikon's hand reached for the bell cord.

I couldn't raise my eyes to look into the face of the person who shuffled in as the door opened. All I had to see was the pair of Koltzer breeches and the stiff, inhuman movement of the legs to realize the Shapers had already started to work dark medicine on Holzir.

But the breeches were splattered with mud from travel, not the white stains of the Lazzun Marshes. I forced myself to look the man in the face. It was a face I had hated in a time so simple and impossibly long ago.

Only a ghost of Dyzlin remained in the eyes. A speck of recognition, a glint of greed. The Shapers' Art had removed the rest of him. Across his forehead was a jagged scar, hastily stitched and showing fresh blood clots.

The Chirurgeons had "silenced" Dyzlin and made him into one of the olglim. He could at last stare me in the eyes, because his Sorrow was gone for good, along with his mind. Now I had to turn my eyes from him, because this was what waited for Holzir, somewhere in the slaughter chambers of the Hive.

"The captain who brought the man here said he desired to know what would happen to the Koltzer prisoner. We have kept our half of the bargain." The Artikon turned to look at the petrified shape of the thing that was once Dyzlin, son of Ulgitz. "A fool. Of all the human breeds, the Koltzer are the most ignorant. Even worse than the black-skinned Bavtuu brutes or the sand-lice of Najael." The Artikon held up his hand, and the olglim obeyed the unspoken control and lurched out of the room. I saw a metal casing around the leg I had shot apart, but it did not seem to bother Dyzlin. He now felt no pain, or anything else aside from the commands of his masters.

The Artikon faced me after the door closed. "The speed with which you cooperate will determine how long before the Chirurgeons begin their craft on your companion."

"You said you would let him go if I told you everything."

"If you start talking now and do not stop."

I started talking. I let the words come as fast as my dry tongue could form them. The ice, and people in orange, the metal boxes, and the strange furred animals. I held back anything I could while still sounding truthful. I said nothing about the strange words, no hints about the airship, Val-Fahr, the "cure," and no mention of the name "Lightborn." The rest rushed out as if the visions were flooding my mind once more.

The Shaper nodded when I mentioned the sled team animals, as if he knew about them already. When I started to talk about the great light from the machine and the pit in the earth, his fascination increased. He drew his hands back from the knob, where it had hovered in case he sensed a lie, and his mask almost seemed to crease with a furrowed forehead.

Then I slipped. I said the one word I shouldn't have:

"And next, the Lightborn—"

His body went rigid. "Why do you say 'Lightborn'?"

"Because, I—"

The knob turned, and the ravager started to chew my hand—

"There is no such thing as *the Lightborn!*" the voice boomed from the mask chamber.

It bit past my elbow, up to my shoulder—

"No, of course not!" I shrieked.

The ravager's teeth ripped away my arm. It hurt even more the second time.

"Say that again," the mask hissed.

"There are no Lightborn!" I screamed. Then the killing-memory released my arm. I didn't collapse in relief this time.

The Artikon's voice changed into a soothing balm. Or perhaps it was only an illusion of softness after the mind-shredding pain. "If there are no Lightborn, then why did you mention them?"

I had stumbled into a trap. If I lied to escape, the Artikon would sense it. But if I didn't say something, then the next time an olglim shambled into the room, it would have the face of—

I couldn't stand the thought. I started to sob. It was an almost forgotten feeling, something a little girl did. "I don't know ... I guessed ... only somebody like the Lightborn—"

"A human superstition." The Artikon didn't believe that, or else he wouldn't have thrown tortures at me at the mention of the name. The Shapers may have denied the Lightborn, but that denial scared them. "*We* created the Art. The Handless God made the Eldru to fashion the Art. The Sorrow is your race's malfeasance, and we will undo it. Humans lie about the 'Lightborn' to excuse their fault in the Sorrow."

I knew he was wrong. The truth in the vision orb could shatter apart his illusion. And with that thought, the strength of the Sorrowless that had bled away in the pain and threats started to pump back into my heart and through my body. A plan formed, something I could use to tempt the cold creature in front of me.

The crying stopped, but I let the sobbing sounds continue so the Artikon would believe I was only a single turn of the knob away from the end. "I'm ... not a scholar," I gasped. "I can't tell ... the meaning of anything I saw. But ... the globe is damaged. It has holes in it. I must have filled those holes in with the Lightborn."

The Artikon was unsatisfied. "How do you know it is damaged?"

I described, as detailed as anything I had yet told him, about the warping of sight, loss of sound, and skips in time. I made up a few details to bait him as I noticed tiny reactions. The Shapers must have seen similar damage in other orbs, and I followed the cues of the Artikon's twitches to make an even better tale.

Before I finished, the Artikon made his decision. He swept the sack from the table and stood up. He pulled the bell cord, and when the door opened he spoke in an inaudible voice to the guard posted outside.

A minute later, Rolant walked in. He stood so he did not have to look directly at me. I'm sure I looked as if I had been drowned and then picked over by scavengers. He had called me "beautiful," and maybe it hurt what dignity was still in him to know he had sent me into this kind of torture.

The Artikon placed the sack with the orb into Rolant's palm. "Give this to the most trustworthy courier with the speediest mount. Send him to Mount Miurn. The excavators will know what to do with the orb. I will send an ether message ahead of the courier to instruct them. The courier will remain to return with it when they are finished."

"Will you still need the girl for—"

"You have your orders."

"Yes, Master." He bowed, then left the room without looking at me.

"I've done what you asked," I said to the Artikon when we were alone. "Let my friend go."

The Artikon's mask mocked me with its nothingness. "I do not know that you have done what I asked. All you have said could be lies. The Sorrowless have vivid minds that range places most pitiful humans cannot. And your talk of the Lightborn—we must look deeper into that. The Eldru at Mount Miurn will repair the damage to the orb, and when it returns in a few days, we shall go through the standard methods of forcing you to tell us what you saw inside it."

"The way you did with my father?" I wasn't hating any more. I had moved to another place, but I needed the reminder.

"Similar. By then you will have all your strength ready for the ordeal. This may be the most powerful of the orbs we have collected from across the continent. It could lead to the secret of the Sorrow. The time when the Art became tainted." The Artikon sounded almost ecstatic about the coming possibilities. It was the most emotion his race could probably show.

"One final question before the servants take you to your cell. You escaped from us in Tyrn. You led us on a maze of a chase. But at the end there was one who saved you and sent us in the wrong direction. You remember her."

He would learn nothing about this from me. Nothing.

"Do not fear you will betray her. She did that herself a year later, when she entered Black Spires and tried to join the Historians in the Fourth Spire. We uncovered her. And that is all that remains of that hope, if you still dream of it."

"You're lying." But my heart plummeted.

"Did you believe a woman disguised as one of us could survive undiscovered within our cities? Or that even the most cunning Sorrowless could deceive the Eldru inside our own dominions?"

I was trying to come up with a taunt to distract me from the icy terror that, as I had sometimes feared, the Woman was dead. But then the door to the chamber started to slide open. No one had pulled the cord, and the person coming through moved so slowly that the Artikon did not notice as he walked up behind his chair.

I tried to hold back revulsion when I looked at the newcomer. The eyes had the glaze of the olglim, the limbs were clamped at the side of the body.

The Artikon had not kept his promise. The Chirurgeons had already gutted Holzir's mind.

NINETEEN

The Artikon sensed my surprise and turned toward the door. "What is this? I said not to start on the Koltzer boy until—"

He did not expect an olglim to move so fast. The single blow from the metal bar smashed onto the Artikon's head and knocked him backward over the pedestal. There was a weak groan, then his body stopped moving.

I had only a moment to glance at Holzir as he ran behind the chair to untie my hand. It was enough to see that he had no scar across his forehead, and his blue eyes glowed with life. The dead stare he had when he walked through the door was only a practiced one.

"Holzir, how did you escape?"

"I'll tell you in a moment." He ripped away the binding on my arm. "See if that thing on the floor will ever get up again. I don't think I could touch him. That one blow almost froze my arm."

Once I was free, I leaped up and grabbed the Artikon's dangling hand. The flesh was cool, but there was a slow pulse. "He's alive. Alive as these futches get."

I turned the Shaper's hand over and pressed it against the top of the recruder in its cradle. My other hand found the knob on the pedestal's side and wrenched it as far as it would go.

The Artikon jolted from unconsciousness as the ravager-memory started to devour him, swallowing each limb, breaking every bone, slurping off skin. The mask muffled his cry, or else the sound might have driven poor Holzir into a Sorrow fit. Even dampened, the scream pushed Holzir into the wall and forced him to cover his ears. The sound didn't hurt me at all; my body burned with vigor to see the Artikon suffer from torture that made his Sorrow grind him up.

"Belde, what are you doing?" Holzir said. "You'll bring the others."

"They'll think it's me screaming." I kept my hand on the knob, trying to turn it even farther than its last notch. The violence of the Artikon's spasms finally bucked him off the pedestal. The only motion was the shallow rise and fall of his breathing.

Holzir watched in shock from the other side of the room. "He was already down, Belde. We could've just run—"

I was breathing hard, but my moment of revenge was over. "This is the one who killed my parents."

"Then why don't you finish him? That's what—what my people would do."

"And free him from his Sorrow? No. I want him to drown in it. I gave him more Sorrow just now than in all his long sick life hiding behind masks and slaves."

Pain and exhaustion then decided to remind me what I had gone through. I slumped forward, but caught myself on the edge of the stone table before hitting the ground. Holzir held me by the shoulders and pulled me to my feet. He forced something past my lips, a piece of dry meat. "I ran through the larder to get here. It might keep us going, until we get far from this hell-camp."

"But ... I thought you were tied to a slab, ready to get your head cut open like Dyzlin."

"Dyzlin? What happened to him?"

"Uhm, I'll tell you later. How did you get away?"

"It was easy, with a bit of help. The soldiers should never have used rope to tie my hands. It was too strong for me, but it wasn't too much for a beak-nose to chomp through."

Rint hopped around Holzir's legs and hooted the way he did when we played a game where he'd leap from the shadows to scare me: *Boo!* The stinker had hidden behind the boy all the time, waiting to surprise me. He jumped up to the pedestal to come to face level. I let him nuzzle his head into my neck

I wanted to grab Rint and squeeze him to me. Instead I found I was squeezing myself into Holzir's chest. "Thank you, thank you, thank you," I whispered in his ear.

"I'll take as much thanks as you can give me once we're out of here. But I don't know how we can do it. I slipped away after they left me alone in an unlocked pen with those dead-eyed things. I'd never have found you if Rint didn't know how to follow your scent. This place is a maze worse than the mountains."

"Did anyone spot you coming in here?"

He shook his head.

"Rolant was guarding the room, but that thing—" I pointed at the heap on the ground. "—sent him off on an errand. That means if we move fast, we might find a way out before he comes back."

"But I don't know the way out. I was brought in here with a bag tied over my head. Do you think you can get through this Sorrow-bitten place?"

"If Rint got in, he'll get us out." I made a bumpy hand-sign, imitating the carriage that had brought us. Rint gave back a *yes* nod. That was the explanation: he had leaped onto the back of the carriage in Iyalonda and rode as a stowaway all the way out to the

Shapers' compound. The bravest, smartest little idiot in the world!

Get us out? I signed, emphasized with the motion for hopping a fence.

Again, Rint nodded *Yes!*

"If he can get us out of this maze," Holzir said, "can he get us through whatever is outside? It sounds horrible."

"It's worse." I told him the layout of the camp, but skipped mentioning the ravager and the colossus. "I don't know how long we've been inside here, but I would wager a game of Sun-or-Moon with you that right now the moon is face-up. If we can slink into the dark, we might find a way over the walls." Rint squeaked at me. "Or maybe under them. Rint has a nose for finding drafts."

"Then let's go before you give me time to give up."

When Holzir went for the door, I turned to look at the inky heap of my tormentor on the floor. The body still quivered. "Go on, Holzir. You're getting stronger against the Sorrow, but I don't think you could stand what I'm about to do."

Holzir understood. "I'll guard outside the door. Maybe practice my blank look." He slipped out of the room, Rint at his heels, and the door slid closed.

I turned the Artikon face-up. He weighed hardly more than a child, as if he were only a wrap of skin over bones. He seemed a pitiable thing lying there, his dark majesty broken. The twinge of sympathy I felt for this creature that had ordered my parents' death disturbed me. It must come from my Sorrowlessness. I *thought* I wanted to kill this inhuman thing. Now I did not *feel* as if I did. Thoughts and feelings split along separate paths.

I took a deep breath, and felt thankful there was no fiery rage any more. What the Artikon had said about the false cures they had tried—they had to be something long vanished, the unreachable ancient past.

I grabbed the edges of the mask and pulled. A gummy substance kept it secured, but with enough tugging it peeled away from the skin beneath.

For the first time, I saw the face of a Shaper. Faces that supposedly even they rarely show to their own kind.

I saw what looked like a young man who had aged so fast that he lost the race with his own decay. The nose flattened across the upper cheekbones, making it little more than nostrils cut into the face. The mouth was a lipless gash, but no worse than a Sorrowful crone who had wasted away in the dark for decades. The mottled skin sagged under my touch and took back its shape slowly, the blood sluggishly coursing under it, but it was like the flesh of a normal sick man.

The face wasn't hideous. Or even ugly. It was simply uncanny. But still recognizable as …

"*Human*. You're a human," I told the unconscious Shaper. "Or, you were in a time you've forgotten."

An ember smoldered in my thoughts. It told me that long ago there were no Eldru, no Shapers. Only humans: those people in orange bodysuits staring up at their new world. The Lightborn had remained trapped on Ahn-Tarqa, and some of them—the "Elder"—had gotten lost in the Sorrow that had come with them, and they turned into the ancestors of the colorless, miserable thing crumpled on the floor.

But the miserable thing was also a killer, as were all like him, and I was their target. I buried my sympathy as I tugged off the robe and set the mask over my own face. The musk of hopelessness filled my senses.

HOLZIR LEAPED BACK when I stepped out of the room, but then recognized that this figure in the Shaper mask and robe was shorter than the one whose head he had bashed with a club. She also had to step carefully so she wouldn't trip on the trailing robe.

He still was surprised. "I hadn't thought about using that kind of disguise."

"No one will question me, will they?" The mask made my voice ferocious in my ears.

"Shapers don't have hair, do they?"

"Forget I asked. Just try to look dumb and I'll act like I rule the world."

"You make both sound so easy, Belde the Sorrowless." The former insult now was tender to hear.

"Well, Holzir the Brave, you may have the Sorrow but you're standing in the middle of a Shaper lair and haven't lost your mind yet."

He shrugged. "If I can think myself somewhere else, I can keep the Sorrow away for a while. Somewhere like the sea."

"One day you'll have to sing that song of the Aman-Sah Sea for me. But not now." Rolant might return to the room any moment after taking the orb to the courier.

I took the lead. Shapers and human servants who still had their minds might move out of the way of an Artikon before they took the time to notice that he was two heads shorter than before and had a full head of dark blonde hair. But I had to move cautiously. Not only was the robe too long, but I had trouble seeing through the eye-slits because the mask didn't sit well on a rounder face.

Rint hid under the robe—we wouldn't need his guidance until Holzir got us past the hallways he knew. I almost tripped over Rint a few times, but he stayed quiet even when I tromped on his tail.

Holzir walked behind and touched my lower back to guide me. He wore his olglim blank stare and lurched on stiff legs. It would have made me laugh if I could see better through the mask or could find anything funny inside this nightmare place.

There was a strange sound behind me, a soft whisper. I realized it was Holzir, singing so low it was almost mumbling. It was his song from the tunnel, but with different words:

> *Two striders through a metal maze,*
> *Laugh at monsters in the rust.*
> *We walk blind toward the Art,*
> *But the Sky Lords we trust.*
> *Sorrowful and Sorrowless*
> *Fear neither Moon nor Sun...*

I remembered the last part, and finished for him:

> *Side by side, we flip the stones...*
> *Until both can claim we've won.*

We met no one for the first few turns along the skewed corridors. Holzir stopped us at a door with a red circle in its middle.

"This is it," he whispered. "They kept me inside, but the door isn't secure. They don't expect these mindless things to move on their own." He tapped at the door and it swung on its hinges. "Rint must've pushed right through."

"Are there any weapons inside?"

"I don't know. I got out fast, and just had time to tear off the locking bar on another cage." He held up the club he had used against the Artikon. "I couldn't see much in the dark, but I heard other people breathing inside the pens. I can check to see if there's anything we can use."

"No, wait—"

But he had already started to push his way in. I pulled him

back, but it was too late. The door swung all the way open. The room beyond was doused in darkness, but anything looking out into the light from the ceiling glow globes would see us standing in the hall.

Someone did. There was movement in the oily black of a figure rising up like a smoke plume from a volcano.

Holzir pulled the door shut. "Something in there spotted us. But it's probably locked in a pen."

The door flew open, swinging out. It slammed into Holzir's chest, and he nearly toppled over. He rammed his shoulder back against the door to shut it, but the force on the other side hammered back.

"That's *not* in a pen!" I said.

"I know!" He bashed against the door, and it gave back enough that he was able to force the club between the gap of the door and the frame. The thing on the other side continued to pound, but Holzir's crude bolt had the door wedged closed for a few moments.

I lifted the edge of the robe and Rint dashed from underneath. *"Get us out!"* I didn't need to make hand motions for him to understand. He picked a direction from the three crooked passages branching away from the olglim room. Holzir left the unseen attacker bashing at the door and ran after us.

Rint drew us through the maze, and the feeling of nearly falling over because of the weird tilts was nauseating. I needed to pick up the edges of the robe so I could run, and even in the middle of danger I felt a touch foolish, like a prissy noblewoman holding her skirt over mud holes.

We passed two Idenites with blackpowder weapons swinging from their belts, but we went by so quickly that they didn't stop to question us. The sight of an Artikon running would bewilder them for a few moments.

A couple sharp turns later, Holzir said: "Somebody's coming up behind us. I heard those guards we passed yelling at him."

Whatever was in the olglim room was on our trail. But it hadn't sounded an alarm. If it was an olglim, it was somehow chasing us without orders.

Rint led us into what looked like a dead end. Had he lost his way, or made a mistake about the scent of outside air?

I shouldn't have doubted my oldest friend. There was a hole in the corner of the outside wall, large enough for Rint to squeeze through. It must be the spot where he had slipped into the Hive. Holzir and I pushed it and discovered it was a weaker piece of metal than most of the patchwork on the outside of the compound. Holzir reached down to the hole and grabbed the edge. When he flexed his muscles, it peeled away just enough for us to duck down and creep through the opening to follow Rint.

We stood in the open of the Shapers' wicked fortress. The sky was dark, but a watery red bled over the outer wall. My directions were bent, and I couldn't tell if it was sunrise or sunset. I had almost no side vision through the eyeholes of the mask, so I pulled it off. The heated air from the energies pulsing through the camp washed over my skin. The place had changed for the worse in the darkness: it hummed and glowed with lamps, and fire and crackling blue arcs of lightning flashed over the workbenches and stations. Sickly orange lights burned from beneath the smoking pits. Powerful beams glared down from the guard towers, meaning the dark would only protect us so far.

Holzir was frozen in stupefaction at my side. The monstrosity around us was a gathering of the Art unlike anything he had witnessed before. Then he stared behind us, and his face changed from bewilderment to horror. He had discovered the ravager and its metal partner.

"Don't look at them," I said when he tapped my shoulder.

"Is that a coloss—"

"Don't look!" It was a warning to myself as well. I wanted no reminder of the Artikon's cylinder and the man I saw—and felt—die one piece at a time.

We had already stopped too long.

"You there! What are you doing?"

It was too late to slip the Artikon's mask back on. Guards in blue tunics near the devil claw pens had already spotted me without it. A light beam on a swivel passed over us long enough for anyone watching to know we didn't belong.

I threw the mask aside and tore off the robe. Holzir had already found a spot to hide between two of the wheeled war machines. He pulled me into the gap between them.

"We got this far, at least," I said. "I hope Rint has another escape path in mind. We aren't getting out the front gate, that's certain."

Boots stomped toward us. It sounded like only a few men, but if they had blackpowder weapons, their numbers wouldn't matter. We didn't even have Holzir's improvised club left to us.

I gave a signal to Rint to get us over or through the outside wall any way he could. He was smart enough to have scouted the camp before coming inside the building to find Holzir—or at least I hoped so. Either way, his nose and eyes were keener than ours, which made the difference in the dark.

A thin beam of light flashed onto us. "Stay where you are!" a guard shouted. Two of them stood about twenty spans away, holding glow globes that focused the light toward us. Their other hands held blackpowder pistols.

"Get ready to run out the back, and then split two different directions," Holzir whispered.

"We tried that once before"

"It worked, didn't it?"

"Not the way we expected."

"Maybe we'll have the same dumb luck," he said. "Wherever Rint bolts, you go that direction."

I was ready to argue against splitting up, but then the guards started to move for us. If we had any chance to escape, we had to run now.

"Don't argue, just do it." Holzir's body tensed for the run.

But before either of us could move, one of the guards pitched forward, and his lamp cracked apart on the ground. The other guard swung around and reached for his weapon, but a hand came from the dark and seized his wrist. The surprise attacker's other hand pinched around the guard's neck and yanked him from the ground with one motion. Holzir and I watched in amazement as the guard went flying toward the tall wheel of the war-machine, smashed against it, then slid to the ground. Like the first guard, he wouldn't be getting up again.

The second guard's lantern spun around where it had fallen. It flashed in our faces and then flickered toward the man lurching toward us. Dyzlin had the mindless olglim look, but the dull fury I had spotted when I first saw him still smoldered in his face. He had recognized me in the burst of light from the hallway.

"It's Dyzlin," Holzir wheezed.

"It was."

The olglim hulk stopped when he heard my voice. His jaw worked sideways as he groaned: "Bel-tza!"

Too much of Dyzlin was still left. If any memories survived in his mind, they must be of a metal shard of the Art ripping through his leg bones and the bright eyes of a girl named "Beltza" behind the weapon that fired it. He would never let go until "Beltza" was dead. He grunted the name once more, then charged.

"Rint, go!" I hollered. I seized Holzir's arm. No more arguments about splitting up. We ran together after the green glint of Rint's tail.

We were fortunate to have the dark hiding us most of the way; the lights from the towers were aiming in cross directions, and none came near us. Dyzlin had battered a path between us and the rest of the camp, and perhaps the Shapers' servants thought it was the loose olglim who had caused the turmoil in the first place. They didn't know yet what had happened to the Artikon.

Rint sprinted toward the wall circuit near the sun side. The shadows cast from the light in the sky gave us an extra blanket of dark to disguise us from the guards. But Dyzlin stuck on our trail like a barnacle on a rock. There were no limits to his adrenaline now that he was an olglim. He seemed to move *faster* with the steel cast reinforcing his broken leg.

My foot struck the post of a hadro enclosure and I tripped. Holzir was still holding my arm and kept me from falling, but he had to stop to get me back on my feet. Dyzlin closed in. He had no taunts to shout, not even the grunt of my false name. I missed that; I wanted something human from him. The silent beast the Shapers' knives had carved was more loathsome than the bully from a distant earlier life.

Rint's excited chirping rang clear through all the other noises: *Here, here, here!*

"Rint's found a way out," Holzir said close to my ear as we got moving again. We stumbled toward Rint's call and away from the stomp of Dyzlin's legs.

"Wait, I think we're at the wall," Holzir said. I put my hands out and felt the rough points of piled stone.

Wood splintered apart behind us. Dyzlin had taken a shortcut, smashing through a hadro pen to reach us. Even hadros twice his size hopped back from the olglim as he broke through the weak planks.

I had lost sight of Rint and shouted for him. If we had gone the wrong direction along his trail, we'd be trapped against the wall. For a moment I had the mad idea of trying to climb up the surface of the rocks, putting us exposed above the camp with guards along the top. But then Rint's squeak came from right under my feet.

I stepped back to find him. Cold water splashed over my ankle. We were standing in a kind of drainage ditch.

The circle of light from the towers that found us answered my questions, even as it revealed us to the wall lookouts. Rint had sniffed out a stream of fresh water running through a culvert into the hadro pens. The hole through the wall was just large enough for a person to wriggle through.

The sentries behind the lights that framed us sounded alarms throughout the camp. Bells clanged, and the devil claws let loose with hunting shrieks. The towers came alive with powerful lamps. The burst of light silhouetted Dyzlin but also surprised his dim mind and slowed him.

"Rint's got the way out, Holzir," I shouted over the din of the awakening camp. I bent down toward the crawl space and tugged at his hand. "Dyzlin might not fit—let's go!"

Holzir wouldn't look at me. He stared at the lurching thing coming for us. "It's too late. Dyzlin will get one of us. It's going to be me."

"But—"

He shoved my hand away. "Go! You said it was all about you, and you're right. Go!"

Rint's tail vanished into the watery tunnel. I couldn't follow. My eyes were locked on Holzir, who pulled away a stone from the wall and walked toward the backlit brute stomping toward him.

It was the ravine of the Fencer Mountains again. But this time I had no weapon, and I wasn't saving Holzir's life as he cringed in Sorrow-fear in front of Dyzlin.

The thing that had been Dyzlin moved straight for the man standing in the way of him and the only thing his ruined mind wanted. Holzir brought the stone down as the two shadows collided.

I was gone before I could see or hear anything else. Cold water and choking dark sloshed around me. I dragged myself through the tunnel, scraping my head and back, wondering if there was enough space at the end for even Rint to squeeze through.

Water flooded my mouth and I gagged. I prayed to the Lightborn not to let me die here. I prayed that Holzir had enough strength to stop the olglim wearing Dyzlin's face, and that he would not die here either.

But who would hear those prayers? The Lightborn were gone long ago, diminished into a sad race and smoldering ends that barely knew what life felt like when it had hope.

But it was the thought of hope, and the memories in the vision orb of the Lightborn struggling for the future, that made me force the water from my lungs, keep my eyes on the beacon of the green tail ahead of me, and grate myself over the gravel toward the end. I *had* to survive to carry away the knowledge of the Lightborn I had discovered. The vision orb was now lost to the Shapers, but I still had what was in my head. Those memories would have to be enough for whomever could use them … "To save humanity."

I spilled into bright light, gasping and spitting out water. I stumbled up, listening to Rint's calls as he ran from the walls, and then staggered toward the light of day. The light of sunrise. The sun had turned over the moon, but it did not feel like victory.

TWENTY

I didn't run. I stayed for a moment to watch the culvert's opening, waiting for Holzir to emerge. But the water flowed from it evenly. There was no sign of another body blocking it.

Rint dashed back when he saw I wasn't following. He bit at my leg. "I know, we have to go," I said. "Please, let's wait a minute more."

Then the first blackpowder shot sounded, and dirt kicked up near my feet. The guards on the wall had spotted me.

I ran toward boulders silhouetted in the sunrise, and Rint stayed at my side. He had as little an idea of where to go as I did. He must have ridden the carriage all the way into the walls of the encampment before he jumped off, so the only place he would know was the main road in. I could only make out shadows as my eyes struggled to adjust to the sunlight burning into my face. There were jagged boulders all around that stuck up from the barren soil like an enormous spindle-backed saurian had burrowed under the ground and gone to sleep. At least they'd give me some shelter from a blackpowder slug in the back.

We dashed for the nearest rock. Gunshots zinged into the ground behind us. The guards weren't trying to kill me, only explain that running away wasn't a good choice. I made it anyway.

Rint and I got behind a narrow boulder that was only wide enough for my shoulders. The land around the Shapers' base became clearer as my eyes adjusted. It was a place as broken as their Art, filled with gravel piled in curious cones and bare hills that the wind had gnawed to the bone. The encampment was closer to the Shapers' lands than I had imagined. Nothing grew here except rocks, as if all living things recoiled from the presence of the Shapers' sorceries.

Distance was difficult to tell in the flattening of the sunlight, but one wide rock looked near enough that a sprint would put us behind it before the sentries could act. With enough dodges and zigzags, we might lose our lookouts.

I dashed for the rock, slid around it—and almost toppled into a pit gouged out on the other side. I slammed myself against the boulder and watched loose pebbles slide over the edge. A minute passed before I heard the *plink* of the stones hitting bottom.

That explained the gravel pyramids and the haphazard rock cairns: the Shapers had quarried the stones from around the compound to build their fortress walls. If Rint and I had run any faster, we would have shot over the ledge and shattered at the bottom of a pit the Shapers' machine had ripped from the hills.

The flat space between the boulder and the quarry was safe for the moment as long as I didn't look down. The sunrise shone straight onto me, so it was also glaring into the eyes of the shooters scanning for something to hit. I took a chance and moved along the edge of the pit to the next boulder. No shots echoed as we passed between the gaps, but I heard shouts and the continuing blare of alarms. I wished I could hear what the voices were yelling. They might even tell me what had happened to Holzir. Had they captured him before the olglim killed him? Or had Holzir triumphed over Dyzlin, only to end up in guards' clutches?

A clanking of chains began to drown the shouts and alarms. For a quiet moment I thought they were releasing the ravager. But that fear came from the memory of watching the monster under the metal helm. The clanking chains were the front gates to the enclosure opening. The hunting parties were marching out.

"*Cave*," I told Rint. Finding one in the rubble was our one chance of staying unseen and making it through a search. A straight run over the low hills on the other side of the quarry would never work; we had to outlast the hunt here and find a way to slip out after dark. But the hunt could last forever. I was a prize the Shapers needed as much as the vision orb. A quick glance through the rocks and then a shrug to go back to the fires for breakfast would never satisfy them.

Rint sniffed the air to check for the direction of our pursuers. We would go the opposite way and hunt out a cranny in which to blockade ourselves. But the soldiers had sharp-nosed trackers of their own: devil claws, or one of the special breeds of beak-noses like Rint. One of those had chased us in Tyrn, and it never lost the scent or let up until it died. We also didn't have city streets we knew better than our hunters. Our only advantages were Rint's heightened senses and my determination—my "sickness" that made me believe I might come through when there was no reason to think I could.

The black boots of the Idenites crunched through the gravel; I didn't need Rint's ears to tell where they were. We slunk to another boulder, but the men were spreading out. Rint jerked his head around, tracking smaller noises and scents. Our options were soon to get cut down to nothing.

We dashed to another ledge, where the slope of the quarry was shallower. There was a chance the guards wouldn't think to look into the pits, and down lower might be pockets where we could hide. I took a chance and held onto the lip of the pit and started to ease myself down. Rint cocked his head at me, thinking I was crazy.

I was. On my second step, the worn bottom of my moccasin slipped, and I lost my tenuous hold on the lip. I started sliding down a slope that wasn't so shallow after all. The rocks under my flailing hands were no larger than pebbles and started to tumble with me as the grade steepened into a cliff. Frantic kicks did nothing but rip away more shale, clearing an easier path to plunge down.

I yelled "help!" from instinct. There was nobody to hear. Rint could only watch helplessly from above as I dropped down to break apart on the pit floor.

A loop of leather whipped around my wrist and tightened. It almost ripped my arm out as I snapped to a stop, and the rough hide cut into my skin, but it was a wonderful feeling not to be falling.

It also meant I was caught.

"Don't yell. They're close by," said a voice that seemed to come from the sky.

I had expected the mocking voice of an Idenite. Maybe even Rolant, leading the chase himself. But the voice was conspiratorial. Almost ... friendly.

When I dared to crane my head back to look at who had snared me, I saw a man in serge colors holding the grip of a lasso. The tumble of sandy hair that fell past his shoulders marked him as Idenite, but he didn't have the hateful glare of one of the Shapers' soldiers. His long dusty coat and worn leather trousers were those of a hadro-trapper, people who spent their lives wandering the steppes. The lasso holding me was one of their essential tools. But the weapon strapped over the man's back, a blackpowder gun of such slick lethality that the Shapers would never entrust it even to a high-ranking servant like Rolant, told me he was more than a hadro-roper who had wandered too close to a Shaper camp.

"Don't move, you'll kick away more shale," he hissed. He pulled on the lasso hand over hand until I was close enough that he could grab for my wrist. I had to fight the instinct to help by pushing with my legs, but I obeyed his instructions. Rint stood beside the man and watched him draw me up to safety. He understood this stranger was a friend, for the moment at least.

The man lugged me back onto the ledge. I started asking questions before I could get back on my feet. He put a finger to his lips to tell me politely to shut up.

"My name is Rouss. I'm a friend. The rest can wait until later."

He crouched down and slunk behind the next rock. Rint hopped up to hold onto the back of my tunic and we followed.

I still had to know the bones of what was going on. "Lucky you came along," I whispered.

He glanced around the far edge of the boulder. "Luck had nothing to do with it. I expected you. But I thought you would come up the road, not come out of that Sorrow-bitten place. What happened? They lure you into a snare-house in a city?"

"Yes. An inn in Iyalonda."

"That's a clever trap. I should've checked that one. But I can't keep watch over every snare-house."

My mind was whirling. "How did you know I'd be here?"

"Rumors of a Sorrowless woman travel faster than rumors of fake sanctuaries," he said. "We hoped to grab you before those masked leeches did."

"*We?* There are more with you?"

He waved away more questions. The tread of the boots of our pursuers was fanning out around the quarry, but none moved straight for our hiding spot. Rint's claws kneaded at my back, but it wasn't a panic-pawing as if someone were right on top of us.

Rouss patted my shoulder and pointed toward a niche in the rocks down a short incline. It looked steep, but I nodded to him. We made the sprint down, half-sliding at the end until we ducked into the new hiding spot. A tumble of rocks rolled in our wake, and one large chunk ripped away and rolled past us after we reached safety. It fell to the right and made an enormous crash when it shattered on the stones below. Rouss winced at the sound.

We stayed silent and listened for the movement of the hunters. The rock crevice dampened the noise so we heard nothing other than the last dribble of gravel going down the slope. The Idenites may have missed the crash of the breaking boulder, but it seemed unlikely.

Rint poked his beak into my shoulder. Someone was approaching. I tapped Rouss's arm and pointed toward the ridge we had just left. Rouss unslung his gun and trained it on the spot.

"A gunshot will bring all of them," I said as low as my voice could drop.

"We might not have a choice. We'll have to sprint to reach my mount." He thumbed back the hammer on the gun.

"Hold off," I said. "I have an idea."

He looked away from the sights on the blastgun and into my eyes. He decided that this young woman might know what she was talking about. She'd found a way to escape from a Shaper compound, after all. He eased his thumb off the hammer and lowered the weapon.

I leaned out from the alcove until I could see the head of the man walking toward the edge of the incline. It was Rolant, no longer dressed in his blue captain's tunic but in a brown heavy shirt and trousers covered with rusty splotches to camouflage him among the rocks. It was a hunter's outfit, much like Rouss's. It made sense he would be the first man out of the gates, since he showed the least Sorrow of all the soldiers in the encampment, and he knew how to keep the others together on a chase.

He also appeared to have come this far alone. Was he trying to act the hero? Or did he not enjoy having the others around? There was even more to this man than I had guessed, and if Rouss fired a chunk of metal through his head I might never find out what it was.

I stepped out from the alcove, pretending not to see Rolant on the ridge. He reacted with the speed of a pouncing nych.

"Hold it, Belde!" He had his weapon held at his hip. A twitch of his finger would splatter my head. I locked my muscles and acted surprised. But I didn't act frightened. I didn't have to.

"Turn around slowly and come up here."

I followed the first part of his instructions, but made no move toward him. "I—I can't. I tripped down the slope, and I don't think I can climb back up it."

Rolant's eyes swept the area. He decided I couldn't lay a trap for him, and the missing beak-nose wasn't a danger. He started to move down to me. He made the walk easily without any rocks giving way.

"You want to believe you still have some power," he taunted. "You escaped from the compound. I'll admit that is impressive. My masters will keep you around even longer to find out what fuels that witch-brain in your head."

His path would take him past the alcove where Rouss was coiled. I didn't dare flick my eyes that direction to see if he was ready. Rolant had his caution up and he would figure out the trick in a moment if I made a wrong move. So I tried to hold the Idenite captain with my stare. I now knew he would not shy away from it, and I was beginning to understand why.

"What happened to Holzir?" I asked. That was another reason

I didn't want Rouss to blast out Rolant's brains. I had to find out if Holzir was alive.

"That boy is a remarkable one. He killed the renegade olglim with only a few stones. Crushed its head in. I've never seen a grass-chewer fight so desperately. He'll make a useful olglim when the time comes. But he's back in his pen now, and there's no chance he'll rescue you this time."

Rolant took one more step closer to me, and Rouss struck. With the speed of a devil claw, he whipped from the shadows and jammed the barrel of his gun against Rolant's head.

"I guess she'll have to depend on someone else." Rouss wiggled his thumb on the hammer. "Make a noise, and I'll take out both your ears and all the gunk in between. Now, put the weapon down."

Rolant let his gun dangle at his side, and then let it drop to the gravel. "Whoever you are, hunter, you're dead. This girl belongs to my masters, the Shapers of the City of Thulia."

"We'll talk ownership when you wake up." In a move so fast it was only a blur to me, Rouss spun his gun around and cracked the stock against the back of Rolant's head. The man fell like a piece of fruit chopped down with a hatchet.

"I've roped a second prize," Rouss said when he looked at the captain's patch on Rolant's tunic. "This one will end up skinned and pegged over a hearth fire."

"You aren't going to kill him, are you? Can't you just leave him tied up behind?"

"What do you care what happens to him? But no, I'm not going to kill him. Not right now. We can't leave him behind to tell the chiefs what happened, and his head has secrets of those monsters he serves that we can use."

"I think he might be Sorrowless," I said.

Rouss looked at me in disbelief. "A Sorrowless man working for the Shapers? Impossible."

"A gut feeling. You're Sorrowless too, right?"

"You need to ask?" He glanced at the discarded gun on the ground. "Can you handle the rifle he's got?"

"The what?"

Rouss pointed to the blackpowder weapon. "That's called a 'rifle.' A slide bolt pulls up the next shot. Usually holds about six bullets."

"I've used a blackpowder blastgun before," I said.

"Oh, a 'shotgun.' Good practice, although these do a cleaner job. Take this one off him. I don't think we'll meet anyone else. We took him down without much noise. But just in case, I might need your finger on the trigger."

I tugged the rifle from under Rolant. Rouss then seized the captain by the armpits and lugged him over his shoulder. Under his loose hunter's garb, Rouss must have muscles more tempered than Vatruslan steel.

And he was Sorrowless. In the fear and surprise of the last few minutes, that part hadn't yet had a chance to strike deep into my mind. This was the first person like me I had met since the Woman saved my life. I loved the Woman as much as I could ever love anyone, even though I only had moments near her with a mask between us. I didn't feel such warmth for this swaggering man, even though he had also saved my life. He spoke and acted as if he wanted to be harder than the rock canyons around him, and even though he knew I was important, he didn't act like it.

I was about to follow Rolant when a powerful feeling of absence hit me.

"Wait!" I said, letting my voice get as loud as I dared. "I can't leave yet. Holzir's still alive behind those walls. I have to go back for him."

"Who in the Sorrow's Hells is Holzir?"

"My friend. He helped me escape. I have to go back for him."

Rouss flashed the strangest smile at me. It double-marked him as Sorrowless, since I could never imagine such a teasing smirk on anyone else's face. "You're an astounding one. I can see why we've gone so far to grab you. I've done crazy things, even gone swimming in Lake Mustok where there are more mosasaurs than water, but 'Sorrowless' doesn't mean 'stupid.' That whole compound is turning inside out—men, devil claws, gun-wagons, and worse—to get you. Step a foot closer and they'll snap you back up and drop you into a holding pit you'll never claw out of."

I was about to argue, but Rouss held up his hand and turned his back to me. There wasn't any choice. I knew that, but I had to at least say something.

As I walked behind Rouss through a ravine, I felt the reassuring weight of Rint clinging onto my back. I still had one friend. How could I have expected to run so far without losing someone else important to me? It was selfish to imagine it could go any other way. Holzir had told me to go. He wouldn't ask me to come rescue him, not if he knew it would end with me in the Shapers' pale hands once more. But still ... *selfish, selfish, Belde* ... the words beat in my head.

Wherever Rouss was taking me was toward other Sorrowless. The ones I had thought were only a rumor were real after all. This moment should be one of the highest points of the short tale of my life so far. So why was I letting thoughts of Holzir, a Sorrowful boy who was no longer a part of the tale, whittle it down? Why did it hurt to think I would never hear his song of the Aman-Sah Sea?

Maybe in some small way I did have the Sorrow. It made no sense that I should feel anything but joy now. Instead, the sun rising in the sky made me feel as if black clouds circled my head.

This must be the Sorrow, or the closest I could come to it: a feeling that nothing would ever bring me back up no matter what I did.

It was only a short weaving path through the stones until we came to Rouss's mount: the most graceful hadrosaur on Ahn-Tarqa. No nobleman of Tyrn or even the capital city of Rolt could own a creature so stately. It had an elegant sail head-crest and shimmering blue and gold-striped skin. The sleek muscles warned any rider to hold onto the saddle with a nych's death grip when the animal started to gallop, or else he'd be thrown and eat dirt.

"A gift from the Shapers," Rouss said. "An unwilling gift, of course. His name is Kilvot. He understands it too."

The hadrosaur turned his head at Rouss's voice to prove it. Rint peeked over my shoulder to fix fascinated eyes on the beast. He recognized the same breeding for intelligence in this creature. He made a greeting call, his way of saying "hello" to a friendly stranger. Kilvot answered with a low honking sound, which made Rint leap off my back and run over to the large hadrosaur. He had never had one of these creatures pay attention to him. Rint stretched up his neck and Kilvot lowered his crested head, and the two saurians from species that usually ignored each other touched snouts like nest-mates.

Rouss slung Rolant's body over the hadrosaur's haunch. "We're ahead of the hunt, but they'll come on fast. They have no idea you've got a mount, so they won't turn out riding their own hadros until we're far gone." He reached into the saddle pack and tossed a few strands of hemp rope to me. "Get his hands and feet, quick."

I bound up Rolant as instructed, thankful for some of what I had learned from helping pitch tents in Kalzzik's camp. "Where are we going?"

"Our roaming home," Rouss said. "You'll have plenty more

questions and too many answers, even for you, when we get there."

He noticed I had my arms clasped tight around my body. "Are you cold?"

"No," I lied. It was a chilly morning, but with the clear sky I knew it would warm up as the sun mounted higher. I didn't want Rouss to offer his dirt-clogged coat for me to wrap around myself. The Koltzer tunic I'd worn for more than a week was all I wanted.

Rouss leaped onto the front of the saddle, and I made the last cinch on the ropes around Rolant's wrists, and then crawled up the hadro's tail to sit on the rear of the two-person seat. I held onto the hand-straps, and Rint crawled up my breeches leg and gripped the front of my tunic.

Kilvot's start was snap-quick. One tug on the rein coaxed the magnificent hadro into motion, and if I had gripped the straps a bit looser I might have tumbled over Rolant's body behind me and onto the rocks.

We dashed through the canyons of the quarry. The sun broke away from the horizon and splashed its light over the low hills. Beneath Kilvot's running feet, I saw lush grass, croaker-bugs, and the love-invitation of pink tanzen flowers. After an eternity among metal and stone, gazing down at something alive and growing felt better than sleep to my exhausted mind.

I remembered little about the ride. My head was pressed behind Rouss's torso to shield my eyes and help hold Rint in place. The wind against us was strong, but soon turned warm and made me sleepy. We might have galloped to the other end of Ahn-Tarqa for all I knew. My mind whirled with the speed, exhaustion, pain, terror, and victory that had crowded the longest day of my life. And the actual day was only starting.

TWENTY-ONE

The shadow Kilvot cast across the ground was almost down to a stub when I had my first sight of the caravan of wagons. It was gathered into the shelter of a tall bluff where rain had washed away half of a hill. It made an ideal hiding spot: even in the midday sun, the steep sides pushed out enough shadow for the carriages to disguise themselves when seen from a distance, which was just how they wanted it.

There were six wagons in the chain, laid out in a straight line to take advantage of the sliver of shade from the broken hill. A team of drowsing ceratopses lay on the grass in front of the first wagon. The other carriages looked like nothing more noteworthy than the transports of the wealthy merchants who rolled from one town to another peddling tools and baubles. But if this was our destination, something more astonishing than ploughs, wood axes, and glass beads hid behind those caravan doors.

A man seated on the driver's bench of the front wagon saw us approaching and waved. Rouss pointed at me sitting behind him, and the man suddenly leapt down from the wagon and ran toward us. He had on the same loose serge clothing as Rouss, although the coat that came down to his ankles was much cleaner. When I saw the fall of his straw-colored hair and the blue of his eyes I thought he might be Rouss's twin brother.

Rouss slowed down Kilvot's gallop. The hadro seemed as strong as when he first started his dash, which made me wonder how far away we could have gotten from the Shapers' compound. We must still be somewhere in the hills of Occiland, although this lush place did not fit my image of the Gray Lands. But now that I was away from the Shapers, anything looked radiant.

The man from the front carriage patted Kilvot's snout as the animal came to a stop. Now that he was closer, I saw that the creases at the edge of his eyes and the touch of gray on his temples put him at least ten years older than Rouss. He looked to have blood closer to the people of the Gray Lands than Iden.

"So while Ketandu and Eiichi are still out choking on the dust of an empty road, you amble back before lunch carrying this gleaming gem." He looked up at me with a smile, and I understood he was Sorrowless as well. Meeting him in other circumstances might have made it harder to tell, but I would have figured it out soon. My sense for people like me was growing.

"So you're the young woman who has caused such a mess of hunting and yelling in these peaceful hills?"

Rouss answered for me: "This is the prize, all right."

It was the second time Rouss had called me a "prize." The third time I'd tell him what I thought about it. I slid off Kilvot's saddle so I would look less like baggage. "My name is Belde." I decided I wanted to sound grander than I felt. "Belde of Tyrn, daughter of Lukan and Kryzin."

"Thank you for telling me, Belde. Rouss never feels like making introductions. And my name is Locke. Locke of Gaspuh, son of nobody you'd know." He gave me what looked like a salute. I didn't return it. I wasn't sure if I deserved to yet.

Rouss patted the still unconscious man bound over Kilvot's hump. "I also hooked a captain of the guard. The girl thinks he might be Sorrowless."

Locke walked over to Rolant's limp body and pulled up his head by the hair. "Sort of hard to tell if he's Sorrowless when he's out cold. Sweet nych's breath, Rouss, won't you ever learn to hit these people a bit softer? You know Hallett hates waiting a full day for them to wake up so she can question them."

"You'd hit them just as hard if you still had the muscles for it, grandfather." Rouss pushed Locke's hand away so Rolant's head crashed back onto the saddle.

I broke back in: "I'm sure he's Sorrowless. Nothing about the Shapers or the Art bothers him at all. He tried to pretend it does, but I could see it was an act."

"You sound awfully friendly with him."

I knew Locke was joking, but I scowled. "He's scum from Iyalonda who traps people for the Shapers. His name's Rolant."

Both men suddenly jerked their heads toward me. Locke went back to the saddle and dragged up Rolant's head again. There was slight movement in the man's eyelids. "Ravager piss, she's right! This must be Rolant the Sell-Soul."

Rouss looked at me in astonishment. "Rolant runs half the snare-houses in the Gray Lands. If that is him, you lured the worst traitor in Ahn-Tarqa right into our grasp."

"Is he a finer prize than me?"

Rouss didn't take the bait. I had earned a bit more respect from him, so I probably wouldn't be called a "prize" a third time.

"I'll take Belde to see Hallett," Locke said. "You want to get Sell-Soul here strapped down and uncomfortable in the iron wagon?"

"Best chore I've had all day," Rouss answered. "This means I won't have to waste more time hunting for him in Iyalonda. I bloody hate that dung pile. And their ale is bitter as burning rain."

"The red-paint ladies there aren't worth the money either," Locke added.

Rouss's glare was sharp. "I don't have to worry about finding pleasures that way, Locke."

"Oh, I know you don't. And I'm glad she doesn't let you flaunt it more."

This seemed to be an old argument between them. But since I knew so little about the other Sorrowless, I had a hard time understanding if they were sharing a joke or if a genuine anger brewed under their words.

Rouss tugged Rolant from the saddle and used his knife to cut the bonds around the captain's feet. Rolant was starting to come around; he managed to stay upright against Rouss and even slur out some insults.

"Maybe your muscles are already wasting away, Rouss," Locke said. "The Sell-Soul has almost recovered from your blow. We could wait to see Hallett until after you've gotten him stored. Maybe you want to tell her about the exploit yourself."

Rouss was already walking away from us, dragging Rolant along. "I prefer Hallett's company at night."

"I know you do, you lucky futch," Locke muttered so only I could hear. "Come on, Belde. I'll get you to our striking leader. Pardon an old plainsman acting as bitter as Iyalonda's ale. There are never enough Sorrowless beauties to go around. That's no offense to you. You're a bit young for me, you understand."

I didn't understand much of anything he was saying, but I nodded.

I kept Rint in my arms, although he was squirming to get down into the warm grass and dash around. We passed the sleeping ceratopses at the front of the wagon and then a team of hadros tied to the rails along the side of the caravan. Each of the mounts was as wonderful a specimen as Kilvot. They were probably stolen from the same stock of Shaper breedings.

The rumors of a band of "strange folk" to the south of Iyalonda were false only because they underestimated the boldness of these people. They were Sorrowless and hiding a few hours' ride from a Shaper force large enough to overrun a small city, yet they acted almost thrilled and taunting about it. I still was unsure what this band would want with me, aside from another member to add to their company.

Locke led me down the line of the wagons toward the last car. "I'm sorry our lady isn't out here to greet you in person and you had to get a leathery campaigner like me. But Hallett likes to seal herself in the dark with the scholars while she's plotting to save the world. Don't worry. You'll get to like her."

"Is she anything like Rouss?" I asked.

His laugh was what you should always hear at the end of a good joke. "A rough boy, that one. I'll bet he mentioned he went swimming in Lake Mustok, right?"

I nodded. "I don't even know where that is."

"The far eastern side of the Fencer Mountains, right before you have to decide if you want to sweat your skin off to the north in Lakkad's jungles or starve to the south in the Land of Scars. Yeah, Rouss never passes up the chance to talk about dipping into those waters. It wasn't anything heroic, though. He was drunk and trying to impress Hallett. She didn't think it was funny when she had to drag him out by the legs before a mosa snapped off his handsome head. Still, Rouss is the best at what he does, which is firing a rifle and riding a hadro like his mother nursed him on the back of one. But then I couldn't imagine he had parents at all. He just sort of grew up from the street stones in Rolt."

I don't recall showing any reaction, but Locke sensed a change in me. "You lost your parents too, I imagine?"

I nodded.

"I'm sorry," he said. "If it makes you feel you're in good company, mine are long dead too."

"Did—did the Shapers kill them?"

"No, nothing so worthy of a tragic poem. Mother got taken with the ash pox when I was a boy. Frightful way to go, but it happens all the time in Gashpuh. Most people think somehow it's the *right* way to die. I guess that was the first time I realized I was thinking a bit, well, differently than other people. Father got flattened by a runaway ceratops at a Month of the Sun festival when I was your age. I was already living on my own by that time, and I knew that *I* wasn't wrong, it was the rest of the world. If you're Sorrowless, it always seems you end up alone sooner than most."

I thought about Holzir. "People seem to drift away all the time."

"Now that is the truth of the Lightborn. You're smart about what you are for someone so young. But we are not going away. That's the amazing thing I realized about 'us' when I pledged on. Finding out that I could have an 'us,' that was something special. Like the first day the sun comes back up after winter."

I wanted to feel that joy. I wanted nothing more than the cleansing sense I had fought my way at last to the only people who might understand me. But the thought echoed emptily when I rattled it around my brain, or tried to make it glow to life like the machinery of the shrine. I still hadn't found the mystery woman who had saved my life, and along the way I had lost someone who perhaps did understand me, or had started to make the journey toward understanding.

We reached the last wagon, which was as wide as some of the cramped houses of Iyalonda. It was built of thick wood and painted forest green. As Locke passed by, he rapped on the side and yelled so his voice carried between the boards. "Hallett, your new charge is here!"

I stood at the bottom of the short staircase leading to the caravan's door. When it opened, the most beautiful woman I had ever seen stepped into the midday sun. Hair red as a late sunset cascaded over her shoulders and down to her waist. She wore a simple dress of the same sky blue the servants of the Shapers wear, as if she wanted to turn the color against the evils committed in it. A belt of silver fibers drew in at her waist. She stood like a fire-topped mountain above me, and even from how low I stood at the bottom of the steps, I knew her height was no illusion.

Locke said: "Hallett, this is Belde of Tyrn. Daughter of Lukan and Kryzin."

Her eyes, a more vibrant blue than the dress, sparked when she saw me. When she *recognized* me.

"Belde. So that is your name. The Artikon never told me the name of the girl who had escaped from him in Tyrn."

My knees wobbled and the breath in my throat stopped. My body knew the truth before my mind did.

The woman of fire and sky walked down the step to me and laid her hand on my shoulder. "You don't look much different from five years ago. Except that you've grown into a young woman. So beautiful in your Sorrowlessness."

"Y-you said you would come for me—" I stuttered.

"I did. I am sorry. Sorry that it took so long that finally you had to come for me first. Can you forgive me?"

I fell down at her feet and started to cry. It was the only "yes" I could manage.

TWENTY-TWO

After the inky interior of a carriage, dim cells, mind-drowning torture, and a wind-blown gallop across the hills, my body's clock was a bramble of snapped springs. But it knew it was starving. I attacked the plate of dark bread and the bowl of cinnamon-spiced porridge as if I were sacking a city. Even the astonishment that "The Woman" was sitting across from me couldn't stop me for a heartbeat from filling my stomach with real food for the first time since Iyalonda.

Hallett—how amazing to be able to give a name to that mystery of five years!—had escorted me into the largest of the caravans. There was someone else inside when we first entered, the person she was in conference with when Locke had called to her. Hallett didn't introduce me to the figure who seemed to have more in common with the shadows, and before I could sit down he had slipped out the door to vanish with the other shadows in the high sun.

Hallett called this place "the synod wagon," and it was here that her band of Sorrowless followers met to make plans under the smolder of a single oil-lamp. I expected to see a glow globe, but Hallett explained to me between spoonfuls of porridge that the generator stored in the "iron wagon" was only to power their experiments, and they used it sparingly. A lamp of oil or butter served their needs for light.

Even in the clear day, the windowless synod wagon was an ominous, musty place. I could see few details aside from Hallett sitting across the table. My eyes picked out maps drawn on wrinkled parchments nailed to the walls, a metal box with wire webs sprouting from its top, and broken half-glass globes mounted on shelves that might once have been vision orbs like the one taken from me.

The table was a marvel of woodcraft: the round top sliced from a giant oak trunk had a map of Ahn-Tarqa carved into it. It was the most detailed map I had seen, with mountain ranges, deserts, and thatches of forest making a rough relief under my fingers. A few spots, such as the farthest east were still flat and undecorated. Only the word "Najael" was carved across the eastern coast. The word "Tyrn" at a bend of the Glosser River lay beside where I had set my bowl. My eyes glanced at it a few times, and I wiped away a spot of food from the dot marking my birthplace.

My finger traced along the river while my other hand scooped bread into the bottom of the bowl to soak up the remaining porridge. My nail scratched at the name of a smaller city along the river, "Lodev."

Hallett broke her silence. "That's where I was born."

"Lodev is your home?" I asked through a full mouth.

"No. This place is my home, as much as I can have one. The Sorrowless have no true home. Not yet."

I wanted to say I thought the Sorrowful didn't have one either, from what I had seen in the vision orb. The Lightborn themselves were adrift. But I was too tired to talk about the orb. It was exhausting even to remember it.

"You might say that the map under your hands is our home. We've crossed much of the lands in our search, spent almost half a year in the rainforest city of Khoromel, scouted the Jalask Plains, and dug in the northern forests trying to find Lightborn treasure. For each place we explore or merchant's map we discover, a new spot is chiseled. Alkjanz, a Sorrowless wood-carver from a Vatruslan town, did most of that magnificent work."

"Will I meet him as well?"

Hallett shook her head. "We gain people, and we lose them. There are more dangers in Ahn-Tarqa than the Shapers and their tools."

My head was bent over the bowl, looking for the last dollops of porridge, when Hallett spoke again. "You must be tired. I will take you to the barracks wagon and let you sleep as long as you like. We'll probably be underway again by the time you wake up."

Holzir. I needed to tell her about Holzir, and that we had to go back to rescue him. And retrieve the vision orb. But my mind had almost turned to porridge itself, and Hallett's voice was so soothing. She wove a spell over me that the years of waiting made too potent to resist. All I had managed to tell her was about my torture at the hands of the same Artikon who had ordered my parents' deaths. I had forgotten that this was the same Artikon who had once commanded her. She found it interesting that her "old master" was now so close to her, but if she had the same deep hatred of him that I did, she masked it. I was too tired and amazed to understand much about the fiery woman who had just stepped out of hazy memories and into my life.

"The Shapers who want you so desperately will soon expand their search. Their servants still have the Sorrow to rein them, but the Shapers are relentless masters who can push them harder and farther, and they don't care if they break them. The soldiers will reach this spot in a day at the earliest. Once the rest of our band returns, we'll strike to the east."

"How many of you are there?"

"Across Ahn-Tarqa, we don't know. We've heard tales of a tribe in the deserts of Najael serving someone called 'The Summoner' who claims to lift the Sorrow from people. For our little group, there were six of us. Until today. Now we are seven." Hallett smiled, which warmed me as much as the porridge. Here was the "us" that Locke had told me about. Now I could feel a bit of the joy.

"Are you trying to save humanity?" I asked using the words from the shrine.

"That's exactly it. Will you help?"

This was the "great us." I hadn't expected to meet it so soon. "Yes. To the end of the Sorrow."

Hallett nodded. "We like to call the end of the Sorrow 'The Rising.' Locke came up with it, of course. He's the most up-looking of all of us."

"Are all of—us—Sorrowless?"

"All but one." She did not offer to tell me who, but it could be no one else except the shadow that had flitted out the door of the synod wagon. "Even our prisoner in the iron wagon is Sorrowless. It seems you discovered that."

I nodded. "You know about Rolant?"

"He is the only of the Sorrowless I've met who chose willingly to ally with the Shapers. He kept what he is hidden from them, something that takes skill but can be done. I did it for two years."

She sighed, remembering a long deception among masked monsters. "I first encountered Rolant when I was disguised as a student in the city of Black Spires. I had supervised some of Rolant's training to work in the human guards, and I recognized immediately what he was. I thought he had also come to spy on the Shapers like me, and I almost revealed to him who I was beneath my mask. I found out in time that he cared only for himself, and his disguise was his way to keep alive. I cannot expect that everyone with our gift will want to use it to help Ahn-Tarqa.

"After I was discovered and had to escape from Black Spires, the Hierarkons assigned Rolant to lead the hunt to catch me. He also devised the 'snare-houses,' which you unfortunately found have an attraction to people with nowhere else to go. I'm not sure what we'll do with Rolant now. Killing him seems simple—but there are so few of us that it feels like a crime to make one less."

The food was gone, but even though my heavy eyes made the inside of the caravan swim, I didn't want to go to sleep yet.

"How did you find me?" I asked.

"That man who left the tribe to betray you—"

"Dyzlin."

"He must have a powerful hatred for you to do what he did. I've never heard of a Koltzer tribesman going to the Shapers directly. Once he abandoned his tribe, he asked anyone he could on his travels the fastest way to find the Shapers' agents. He spoke too much. Word reached the Shapers, but we also keep a close eye and ear on their activities. We can even pull down the ether messages the Shapers send through the Art." Hallett pointed toward the box with the wires weaving out of it. "We learned that patrols from the peninsula and spies in the towns were watching for a 'witch-girl' named 'Beltza' who was wandering the hills with a pet beak-nose. I knew immediately who they were hunting. We seek out any Sorrowless person we hear rumors about, but this time I moved us even faster—because of a promise I had almost broken.

"We found out too late that the Shapers had set up an artificer compound near Iyalonda, and they were sending patrols out to seize you. I sent Rouss and two others to watch the roads into the Shapers' camp, but I did not imagine they had already caught you and had you inside. We might have given up if we had known. But escape! That we *never* would have imagined possible. You are remarkable, Belde, even for the Sorrowless. No wonder the Shapers put up such a great search for you."

She pulled the bowl and dish away from me. "I'm wearing you out. Even the Sorrowless must sleep."

"No, not yet. Please, can we walk outside for a bit? Show me your camp. And I—I want to ask you something."

Hallett nodded. "Only a short walk. Then you must rest." She was already setting herself up as a mother, and I wasn't certain if that was how I wanted us to be. For the moment there was no choice.

My head cleared in the sun and warm air. Rint, who had been sleeping in the shade under the wagon, ran up and tried to leap into my arms. I made him stay down and walk at my knees as Hallett led me up the line of the wagons, pointing to each one and explaining its function: food storage, clothing, weapons. The second to last wagon had a wooden exterior, but I could see iron between the planks. The "iron wagon," Hallett explained, where the Art generator and a workshop for their creations were stored. Along with, for the moment, Rolant.

When Hallett finished the tour, she said, "Now for your question, Belde. I warn you, you will only get one. There's all the time for the rest of your life to ask more."

I had considered asking to go after Holzir, but I was thinking about the refusal I would certainly get. And he was already turning into one of the many lost people that the Sorrowless seem to collect. So I asked an older question:

"What happened to my parents?"

"The Artikon had them executed."

"I know that. You told me in the alley. But you were there. You saw it happen. Tell me what it was."

"It was fast, Belde. You don't want to know any more."

She was right. But I had to ask, and against my best judgment I wanted more. I wanted an explanation.

"You stood there and watched it happen, under one of their masks."

Hallett turned so I could see only the fall of her red hair and not the beauty of her stern face. "That day in Tyrn was the second hardest of my life, Belde. I had disguised myself as a Shaper for a year by then, but what they did to your parents after they saw you escape—it took all my strength to keep from showing my false masters what I really was. There is nothing to be done about it now."

"And what was your hardest day?"

"That's two questions, Belde." Her response was like a sword slash, and I saw the commanding woman underneath the mothering guise. I suddenly felt frightened of her. And because she had stood there and watched my parents die, there was a coal of anger burning in me that I didn't want to turn into a blaze. Sleep would douse it, so I was grateful when Hallett said, "Let's go to the barracks wagon. When you wake up, I'll have more questions for you about your escape."

I nodded. "I couldn't tell you much about the vision orb now, anyway," I mumbled.

Hallett's hand dropped onto my shoulder like a blacksmith's hammer. "*What?* What did you say?"

"The vision orb. The one I found in the airship and the Shapers took from me."

Hallett was suddenly standing in front of me, partially bent over so our faces were even. "What vision orb? What are you talking about?"

I blurted out as much as my fuzzy mind could about the airship and looking into the vision orb I found there, but it couldn't have made much sense. Enough of it did so that Hallett was suddenly alive with all the commanding power she possessed.

"Why didn't you tell us this immediately, Belde? This could be the most important news we've gotten in years."

"I—I thought you knew about it. If you were after me, then—" But not even the Shapers had known I had found the orb. I had forgotten all about it when I arrived at the caravans. What I had left behind was Holzir, not some piece of the Art.

Hallett asked me what had happened to the orb, and I mentioned all I could recall about a courier, and a place called Mount Miurn, and—

"Rouss! Rouss!" Hallett shouted. "Get over here!"

I leaned against the iron wagon, my mind feeling like a battering ram had tried to smash it open. Rouss came around the side of the wagon to answer Hallett's call, a rifle ready in his hands. "What's wrong?"

"Ride out and find Ketandu and Eiichi. They're probably making their way back now that they haven't spied anyone on the road, but we need them here immediately."

"What's the panic?"

"A vision orb, Rouss. From a Lightborn airship. The Shapers have one. That's why they had Belde locked up. She discovered it."

Rouss looked toward me, mystified that I kept becoming more important. "I'll ride out immediately on Kilvot."

Before Rouss turned away, Hallett reached her hand toward him. She pulled him in and their lips met for a deep kiss. I understood why Locke had grumbled about Rouss being a "lucky futch."

The next thing I remember was Hallett's hands guiding me toward the last wagon. My eyelids dropped shut, popped open for a second, then drifted shut again. Time was slipping into a Month of the Moon where it passed in unreal ways. I stumbled into a dark wagon, and felt the net of a hammock against my back, and then a soft blanket tucking me in. The moist breath of Rint fogged my cheek as he curled by my head. There was a soft meeping of insects in the grass, the day-warblers imitating the night-croakers to sing me to sleep.

TWENTY-THREE

When I stirred awake, Hallett was seated on the hammock across from me. A night breeze through the open caravan door had woken me.

"The Sorrowless are light sleepers," Hallett said once I was fully aware. "The others have returned and they're all gathered in the synod wagon. Come and tell them your full story, and then we'll decide the next move. Our time is getting tight."

The whole band, numbering seven with their newest member, crowded into the murk of the wagon. It was a place designed for conspiracy, stuffy and furtive against the outside chill of night. The mood under the lamp glow was urgent; my news had brought fresh fear among the group. But they were Sorrowless, so instead of fear grinding them to a stop, it ignited a fire in each one.

Hallett introduced the three I hadn't met before as Eiichi, Ketandu, and Quarl, but told me nothing else about them. They were seated at the map table between Hallett on one side and me on the other. "Of course, you've already met our two brave battlers," Hallett said. Rouss and Locke waved from where they sat on a bench behind the table. They had their rifles balanced across their knees.

The person closest to me was the woman named Ketandu. She had spoken to me as I sat down at her side, before Hallett made her terse introductions. She pointed to a spot on the north edge of the map along a coast on the other side of the world from Iden, and told me she was a princess of a Bavtuu tribe from the Cloudytop Forests. She did not need to say "former princess." That she was here meant her Sorrowlessness had either forced her to abandon her people or terrified them into exiling her. She had smooth skin as dark as any I had seen, and it was as beautiful as a cloudless night sky. She would strike envy in others for her youthful sheen all of her life, regardless of her true age. Yes, Ketandu had once been a princess. She had become something greater here.

The man named Eiichi looked like the oldest of the band, and the crevices over his face and the thick mustache that drooped below his chin made it hard for me to know his race. But his name sounded like one from the island of Atami in the Vedil Sea north of us. The saffron color of his skin and the slight slant of his eyes were similar to the Atami traders I had seen in Tyrn. He had a thick mane of hair, still a healthy black despite the creases of his face, which he had laced into an intricate weave across the back of his neck. His hands resting on the table looked supple and quick, the tools of a jeweler. I guessed he might be an expert in the manufacture and repair of the Art and spent most of his time in the iron wagon.

I knew the frail man named Quarl as the shadow that had seeped from the wagon when Hallett brought me in earlier. He had on a traveler's cloak that looked as if it was sewn for a person

237

three times his girth. The way the burnt brown hood fell around his face completely hid his features. Even when he was seated I could tell he was a head taller than Hallett. His bony white hands rested on the table as if they were part of the map relief.

Hallett didn't need to tell me that Quarl was the member of the band who still possessed the Sorrow. His contrast to the others was like the moon to the sun. In the past the Shapers must have scarred him in a hideous way that forced him to hide his face from the world. I couldn't imagine why the Sorrow Sleep hadn't consumed him if he had suffered so. Why would he have come to the Sorrowless, and what role could he play among this band of the bright-eyed and hopeful?

Hallett had barely let me settle among the others before she started speaking and pointing to places on the map. She was younger than most of the people in the wagon, but her command and vitality overmastered everyone. She had dared to hide herself among humanity's worst enemies and lived for months inside their vilest city. She was Sorrowlessness itself in a beautiful shape.

Hallett quickly ran through the story of how they had tracked and found me. Some of them knew part of it, but none had heard the whole of it, all the way back to how Hallett had rescued me in Tyrn five years ago. The audience listened in silence until Hallett came to the part about my escape. Eiichi looked toward me in wonder. "You mean, before Rouss reached you that—"

"The little witch-girl had already smashed her way out," Locke laughed from behind. He reached forward and patted me on the shoulder.

"Amazing," Eiichi said. "How in the Sorrow's hells did you manage it?"

Hallett sat down and pointed at me. "Tell everyone your part in this, Belde. From the start. Be quick, but don't leave anything out.

Let all of us know why the Shapers are so desperate to recapture you."

I started. It was like when I had spoken with the Artikon, but this time I told everything about the fallen airship and the memories in the vision orb. I put in a few details that perhaps the others did not need to know, most of it about Holzir. My audience listened to each part in amazement.

Ketandu asked about the fur-covered creatures pulling the Lightborn's sleds. "I think I saw one of those when I was a girl. My father took me on a royal hunting trip to the Acivis Wilds. A flash of silver shot across the brush ahead of our train, and then was gone. Father told me they are called 'dogs,' and they were once the loyal companions of the Lightborn."

Eiichi interrupted the most. He stopped me to ask for details about the Lightborn airship, and then for more specifics when I mentioned the ravager and the colossus in the camp.

"You said the Ravager didn't try to escape at all?" He took out a piece of parchment and started scribbling on it with a charcoal pen.

"No, it just swayed back and forth, but never moved its feet."

Eiichi was about to ask more, but Hallett broke in and told him to stop slowing me down.

I told the rest: meeting the Artikon, his sending away the vision orb, my escape. When I finished, a rustle went through the room. Eiichi looked the most astounded, and was the first to speak. "A memory of the Arrival. An actual record of the Lightborn about themselves, possibly for their own analysis or to send as a message to another group of them. And one of their ships, almost intact."

"Do you think she is right?" Ketandu asked. "That the Lightborn survived and we are their descendants?"

Hallett shrugged. "I don't know. It's almost too much to think about."

"If Belde is right," Ketandu continued, "this could lead us to the true point of the Arrival. The place where the Sorrow and the Art started, and why."

"I'm curious about those 'plungers' you saw, Belde," Eiichi continued, his mind hopping from notion to notion as he scribbled on his paper. "Syringes, probably. Some sort of cure the Lightborn were trying for the Sorrow. And that the Shapers tried it as well—that's frightening. But did—"

Hallett interrupted: "Philosophy and machinery I'll entrust to you two and Quarl. We'll find out what the memories mean later. What is important now is that the orb is in the possession of the Shapers." Her words brought down a grim curtain upon the wonder in the room. "Belde, tell us again the name of where the Artikon was sending the orb."

"Mount Miurn. I don't know what that is."

"I do."

The voice was a wisp, but every head swiveled toward the hooded figure. It was the first time Quarl had spoken.

"Mount Miurn is the Eldru name for what lore-masters call the Mountain of Masks." He placed his finger on a spot on the map across the border in the Shaper peninsula. "The Eldru have excavated parts of what may be a Lightborn base in the roots of the mountain. They sent the results to the Scholiasts in Thulia and Black Spires, but there is not much they understand. I don't believe they have discovered any vision orbs in the ruins, but they have uncovered a device of the Art there that can apparently extract the memories from the vision orbs. The Eldru still cannot see the memories: no matter where they come from, the memories hold too much Sorrow to endure. If this orb is damaged as Belde says, that is where the Artikons will take it to attempt to repair it.

They will record its memories, and then find a Sorrowless person they can force to interpret them. If they can, they will get Belde. She obviously understands better than anyone else what is inside the orb, and her resistance for one so young is formidable. Even you, Hallett, might not have such strength of mind."

Something passed between Hallett and the hooded man. A sharp break, like a stick of wood snapped in a child's fist. For a second, the beautiful leader was weak and unsure.

Then it passed just as swiftly. "There's no more time to talk," Hallett said. "Rouss, Locke, and I will take the three fastest mounts and ride the north roads toward the peninsula. We're a day behind their courier, but we might be able to overtake him before he crosses into the Shapers' dominions. The rest of you move south toward Iden on the Featherstone Road and stay ahead of the hunters. We'll rendezvous with you after we get back the orb."

"Wait, what about Holzir?" I blurted out when everyone started to stand up to follow orders. "My friend, they've still got him captured there."

"No doubt they've already turned him into an olglim," Eiichi said. "The Chirurgeons can do the procedure fast now."

"Maybe not," Hallett answered. "If they want to lure Belde back, they may keep this man intact to use as bait. We can't walk into a trap like that."

"But he saved my life," I said. "I wouldn't have escaped without him. I owe him. *We* owe him."

Hallett leaned forward onto the table so she could look directly at me. I was about to ask again, but suddenly found I could not speak. The stare I had used on others before was now turned on me.

"Belde, I know it hurts to lose someone who helped you. But all of us have made sacrifices because of what we are. Right now, we are the most important people in the land. This orb you found, and the Lightborn's airship, may offer the key to understanding the Sorrow and saving humanity before the Shapers' methods destroy us."

"But—"

"Trying to enter that compound is suicide. Bravery is one gift we have for being Sorrowless, but if we confuse that bravery with foolhardiness, it will kill us."

Rouss cut in. "Actually, from what Belde remembers about the Shapers' compound, we could get around inside once we can trick our way through the gates."

"My knowledge will help," came Quarl's voice from beneath the hood.

"Mine as well," Eiichi said. "If they're experimenting with controlling a ravager using a colossus, then I have this idea—something I've wanted to try with their control helms—that could smash the place apart. Just get me to the tower, and I can do it."

"That's enough!" Hallett shouted. "The Koltzer man is only another sufferer from the Sorrow. What help does he bring us? We have to retrieve the orb. If the Shapers can unlock it and find the location of the Arrival, the knowledge it will give them will put them ahead of every effort we make from now on."

I weakened, because she was right. It was so simple. The silver woman of the shrine had told me "to save humanity." That was a burden I carried, and the keys to achieve it ended up in the hands of the Lightborn's enemies. Nothing was more important now than finding that orb. Nothing, except...

That word rattled in my mind: *except.*

Hallett swept through the door of the synod wagon and called Locke and Rouss to follow and prepare the hadros for their ride. Locke's hand fell on my shoulder as he walked past. "Sorry, girl. It hurts to lose them. But this is a sort of Sorrow we've all got to carry. Though, to be honest, I wouldn't mind a crack at busting up one of those Shaper piss-pots."

Rouss said nothing, but he met my eyes. He was sorry as well, probably more because he also wanted the thrill of torching the Shapers' camp. It was a condolence anyway.

After the door shut, I looked over the three still seated at the table. I waited for more empty sympathy, more "sorry, girl." But Eiichi, Ketandu, and Quarl sat quietly. Quarl was a blank to me, while there was eagerness in Ketandu and Eiichi, whose eyes continued to glance down at his notes. But they had nothing to say to me, and I had nothing to say to them. This was how it would be from now on: me and these people who were also born free from darkness. Free. But there was no joy. I jumped up from the table and walked out into the night.

Rint sprinted over to me. He had gotten friendly with the hadros and enjoyed playing teasing nip-and-hide games with them. I picked him up and held him. "Why does it seem like it'll always be just the two of us, even after we find something like a family?" I asked him.

Rint's rough tongue lapped out and wiped a drop of moisture from under my eye. He then looked over my shoulder and gave his *hello* chirp to someone behind me.

I swished around. Quarl stood a few spans away. The hood still draped his face in shadow, but I felt his eyes peering out. His voice was stronger than in the wagon. "May I speak with you, Belde?"

I wiped away the dampness from my face and nodded. He gestured with a lanky arm toward the barracks wagon. When he reached the end of the carriage, he did not open the door, but instead motioned for me to sit on the steps. He remained standing.

I asked the question before Quarl could start. "I know you're Sorrowful. How can you stand to be around the others?"

"Have you ever wondered something similar about this young man you wish to rescue? How he can tolerate being around you?"

"Sometimes. But I've known him—we've known each other—for half a decade."

"How long have you traveled with him?"

"Over a week, maybe two. Just him and me. And Rint."

"Does his Sorrow affect you?"

"A bit. When we started out, I worried that he'd slow me down because his Sorrow would force him to stop, and he'd be like a stone chained to my leg. And it was like that at first. But now—"

"Now you would rather have him around you. More so than anyone else you know."

"Yes. The Sorrow doesn't seem so bad for him any more either. He can look me in the eyes without turning away at times, although I don't think he realizes it."

Quarl's body was unnaturally still. "Every day, I fight against my Sorrow. I fight to lose it. The fight goes so slowly that it pains me each morning to wake up and know I still have so far to go to survive. And I started with a greater burden than most."

His hands reached up and drew back his hood. Beneath was slate-colored skin, a hairless pate, and slits for a nose and mouth —similar to only one other face I had ever seen.

"You're—a Shaper!" Even with the early signs, I had still never imagined the truth.

Quarl said, "I still think of myself as 'Eldru,' although I am barely of my own race any more. In the history of the Eldru, I may be the first to have willingly abandoned my melancholy and murderous people."

"The other side of Rolant," I said. "But how can you be here? How can you even have a name?"

Quarl's tongue clicked against the roof of his mouth. Perhaps it was as close as he could come to a laugh.

"Everyone thinks the Eldru have no names. It is almost true. We never use our birth-names among ourselves. We tell each other apart with our titles, robes, and masks." He looked down at his coarse, hemp-woven traveler's cloak. "Once I had a robe of indigo and a plain mask, the marks of a Scholiast. I lived in a chamber in the Fourth Spire where I was an Historian. That was how others knew me: 'Historian of the Fourth Spire.' But I had a name. Like all the Eldru, when I was born the Artikon present at the birth wrote a name on a scrap of paper, slipped it into a bone cylinder, and hung it around my neck before he took me from my —mother, as you call them—to the other infants in the wards, where the provosts raised me. When I was old enough to read, I looked at the name, then burnt the paper. That name is not to be revealed until the point of my death."

The tall shape folded in the middle and sat on the step beside me. "But, my name is Quarl. And I am still alive."

"How did you come among people like—us?" It still felt strange saying "us" and meaning it.

He drew a long breath through his lipless mouth. The Sorrow around him was thick, but nothing like what I felt billow from the Artikon when he tortured me. Quarl's Sorrow was no worse than Holzir's Sorrow in his darker moments.

"The same person who saved you also saved me. Hallett ended her time as a spy when she smuggled me out of the city of Black Spires, where I worked cataloging time-stained manuscripts the Eldru think may help in their quest to excavate artifacts. It was not a terrible life. I did not think anything greater was in my reach. I even had a pet, such as yours. A jehol, one of the rodents. He is dead now." Quarl let out a long sigh, and I saw a normal sadness come over him. The sort I would feel. The sort I felt then.

"How did Hallett convince you to leave? I never imagined that

Shapers cared what humans did or said. You only seem to want to use and destroy us."

"Hallett spied for years in her guise as a student of the Academy with one goal in mind. She worked in the cities of Iden, pretending to seek the Sorrowless, but in truth what she sought was a weakness in one of her masters. A weakness she could use to lure him away to recruit as a weapon in her cause. The most audacious theft: to steal a Shaper. When she returned to Black Spires and the Artikons assigned her as an Acolyte to the Scholiasts in the Inner Core, she came to apprentice under me. I had the weakness she was seeking. I am the weapon she still uses to understand the Eldru mind."

"How did she steal you away? She didn't kidnap you, did she?"

"No, because that would have broken the mind of any Eldru. She needed one who would go willingly."

"So why did you go with her?"

"Because I had the weakness she could exploit. Hallett forced out of me an emotion I did not know I had."

I thought about what Hallett's "hardest day" must have been, and then I understood. She gave her body to Quarl, and then she took all of him with her in return. What might shatter the cold mind of a Shaper? The warm touch of skin on skin, bodies linked, the most intense intimacy life can have. I couldn't envision it between Hallett and this almost-human creature beside me. But what did I know about lovemaking? I was a woman in most ways, but not that way.

Both of us sat in silence for a minute. Another thought began to pester me, and I felt it move through all my body.

"I cannot have her," Quarl finally said. "Hallett belongs to nobody, of course, and her lure was only a lure for that one moment, not a promise for the future. She has her own desires."

I remembered the passionate way she had kissed Rouss. Quarl must have seen it many times.

"I am sorry." It was the best I could manage.

"I sometimes say to myself, 'thank you for a sadness that is not the Sorrow.' Maybe it is a blessing. But you, Belde, do not have the Sorrow. You do not need a special pain in your life to distract you from it. Your mind must have something different for its blessing, even if that something—that someone—has the Sorrow. Do you understand what I mean?"

I nodded.

"Then let us go." He stood, and my hand guided him, for he did not have the strength in his pale muscles to balance himself. "We will go together to Hallett and explain why you must return to rescue this young man."

We walked toward the iron wagon and the sound of clinking hadrosaur bridles. Hallett, Rouss, and Locke were working in a splash of moonlight saddling the speediest hadros for the ride north. They did not hear us approach until Quarl spoke.

"Hallett, I would speak with you," he said.

Hallett looked surprised that Quarl had removed his hood. "Be brief. We're almost ready to move."

"You must go to the encampment and fulfill Belde's request."

"Leave it alone, Quarl. I've explained—"

I interrupted. "I'll go back myself if nobody else does. I don't care how important you think I am, I have to go back for Holzir."

"And you know why she does, Hallett," Quarl added.

Hallett held up her hand to signal Rouss and Locke to stop their preparations. In her voice was a devil claw's snarl: "Maybe I don't know, Shaper. Explain it to me."

"I have not forgotten the one night you spent with me. That final bait you used to bring me among you. I carry the hurt. I do not regret it. I steer by it the way sailors steer by the stars. But this young one—" He put his hand on my shoulder. "—she does not need any more pain to guide her. She already has enough from you."

Hallett's eyes weren't staring at Quarl, but at me. "You ungrateful ... I would have come to take you from that tribe. I always meant that. You think whining to this—"

"This *what*, Hallett?" Quarl said. "Am I still only that Shaper you need as a tool to outwit your enemies? But you are accusing the wrong person. I approached Belde. She did not come to me. And there is a different pain you caused her aside from your lateness in finding her."

I caught what Quarl meant. I fixed my eyes on Hallett's. I used my stare. I never thought I could turn it on someone who was like me. But it grabbed her, and our eyes pushed against each other like ceratopses with their horns locked in a duel.

Then I struck: "My parents."

Hallett's body froze. Her eyes dodged mine. "There was nothing I could have done to save them."

"You watched them die. You stood with the Artikon and watched him order their deaths."

"I helped you escape."

"Yet it disturbs you. It has to. How many innocent people died while you were disguised among those killers?"

Hallett turned a crimson face toward Quarl. He flinched away from her eyes but stood his ground. "Damn you to the Sorrow Sleep for this, Quarl. This is the lowest and shadiest manipulation. You do your race proud."

"Some of it I learned from you."

I thought Hallett might strike him. She could do it.

But Quarl said: "You owe her no more Sorrow, Hallett."

Hallett spun away from us. She spoke to Locke. "Get the traitor out of the wagon. Bring him to me."

Locke jumped to follow the order. Hallett then told Rouss to fetch Eiichi from the synod wagon. Rouss looked confused. "What's this all about?"

"Eiichi said he has a plan on how to destroy that Shaper compound. We'll need to know it, since we're making a stop along our north route to smash the place apart. And rescue someone."

My heart jumped, but I kept still. Quarl's hand stayed on my shoulder, and I sensed his Sorrow fade as my joy rose.

Rouss tugged Rolant from the back of the iron wagon by the chain looped around his wrist shackles. Rolant looked groggy, but he was Sorrowless and resilient. Hallett stood in front of him, and Rolant pulled himself upright to look her in the eyes. "Rolant the Sell-Soul," she said.

"Hallett the Impostor. I had heard you were a beauty. It seems good looks are something we Sorrowless share."

Locke laughed, and Rouss elbowed him in the gut to make him stop.

Hallett continued: "You have a chance to make up for your crimes, traitor. Or at least stop us from killing you here and leaving your bones for a fang-bird feast. We must ride fast to the north, but we are going to make a stop along our route at your wicked base. You will help us get inside it."

Rolant laughed. "You think you can win. There's no hope for you. You're all nothing but a few gnats buzzing around a ravager's head."

"Soon we will be a swarm." Hallett grabbed Rolant's chain and pulled him in so her breath steamed up his irises. "I will kill you, Rolant. Death is more frightening for people like us because we have hope. It's beautiful how that works." A knife in Hallett's hand gleamed in the moonlight. She pressed it against the Rolant's ribs. "Don't you wish you had the Sorrow to protect you now?"

Rolant managed a seductive smile, the kind he had to repress around his masters. "Do you act like this with all the men you seduce to your cause?"

There was a spurt of red across the grass, and Rolant crumpled over, screaming and clutching his stomach. Hallett stood over him holding the bloodied knife. "Want to join the swarm, little gnat? Or should I cut below your belly next time?"

Rolant yelled slurs at Hallett that the whores of Iyalonda wouldn't tolerate. But she kicked him once, and then he shouted, "Yes, dammit, yes! I'll help!"

Hallett wiped off the knife on the grass, then told Rouss to bandage Rolant and keep him close by on his chain. "I'll bring him to my wagon later and get what I need from him."

"Why do you need him alone?"

"Be quiet and do it, Rouss," she said and turned her back to him.

The plans moved fast. When Eiichi arrived, Hallett asked him about the ideas he had to wreck the camp. Eiichi started a flood of an explanation, one I could hardly understand, and immediately Rouss and Locke leaped in with their own plans. Locke had ached for a chance at an assault on the compound, and now that Quarl had wedged an opening with Hallett, Rouss was also roused to take steel and blackpowder to the Shapers. Ingenuity intrigued Locke. Battle drew Rouss.

"If Belde and Rolant have accurate information, and if we pull this off the way Eiichi says we can, I promise we can make that whole compound go down in flames," Locke said.

"I can do it," Eiichi said. "Quarl can help with manipulating the Art."

Quarl, who had put his hood back on, nodded. "I'm only an Historian, but if my kinsmen have put a special lock allowing only our blood to start their machines, I can help you get past it."

"No point in hiding our firepower on this one. Get the best burning guns, Rouss," Hallett said.

I think Rouss was ready to lunge forward and kiss her; the excitement at the mention of these ghastly sounding weapons animated his whole body. He ducked into the iron wagon.

"Ketandu will bring the outfits we need," Hallett said to Locke. "She can pass as a Shaper almost as well as Quarl when masked and robed, and her Sorrow imitation is often superior to mine."

"Our princess is good with a gun and spear also," Locke answered.

"We move before the moon reaches its peak. We may lose the orb by doing this, but the strike will make the Shapers think twice about putting any more slave-churning fortress outside their own dominions."

Hallett started to walk toward the front caravan, and I ran up beside her. "Don't thank me yet," she said. "This is an insane plan, maybe a ruinous one. But Quarl has a stronger grip on me than I realized."

"He loves you," I said.

"I know. I wish I didn't. Is there anything else you have to say to me?"

"I'm coming with you, right?"

"You want to return to that cesspool after you escaped it?"

"Holzir is my friend. I have to go along. And you need all the people you can for this."

Hallett was about to argue, but I had given her enough of a moment of doubt to drive my argument home. I ran in front of her and stood my ground. "I know where they've imprisoned Holzir, and I'm the only person who's gone inside that place other than Rolant. How far can you trust him? I can catch him if he tries to lie. And I can pose as your prisoner to help get us through the gates."

"Curse you, Belde," Hallett said. "You are the hardest conniving Sorrowless person I've met. You'll lead us all someday. All right, go to Locke and get yourself ready." She swept around me toward the front wagon.

A tiny beak nibbled at my ankle. I looked down at Rint, and he clicked: *We go?*

"*I* go. You stay with your new hadro friends. This is one time I can't have you underfoot." Besides, if I asked for one more favor from Hallett, the entire deal might fall apart. It was mad enough as it was.

TWENTY-FOUR

After a final meeting under a dim lamp, a band of seven Sorrowless people and one Eldru rode on hadros and a single wagon along the road that wound between the stones to eventually reach the gates of the place I had named the Ruining Grounds.

Once I had insisted on coming along, Hallett decided to make the rescue an everything-or-nothing assault. She bet every coin on Eiichi's plan and what Rolant and I knew about the world inside the compound walls. We would either get back in time to keep raiders away from the hidden wagons, or we would not be back at all. It was something only a collection of Sorrowless would imagine attempting with any dream of success.

The single wagon we took was the bottom section of one of the caravans. Locke and Rouss had unbolted the top, then hoisted a simple wooden frame with a linen canvas across it to hide the devices Eiichi needed for his plan to work.

I sat on the bench in the back of the wagon. Eiichi and Quarl sat close to the curtain that divided us from the driving board, where Hallett was coaxing the two ceratopses pulling us along the serpent road. Ketandu was smearing a pack of red-colored mud onto my face, adding the right touch to make it look as if I had been seriously injured when I was "re-captured."

"I can feel your heart beating all the way up into your cheeks," Ketandu said as she finished. "That's a good sign. The Sorrowless should always feel nervous and excited near danger."

"I'm not nervous," I said. "I'm terrified."

"Even better," Ketandu said, and smiled. In the little we had talked, I had learned Ketandu was a philosopher of both the Sorrow and its absence.

"No need for anyone to be terrified," Eiichi said and patted the piece of machinery at his feet. It resembled a bloated honey melon with wires wriggling from it like worms bursting from its center. "I know my child here will work. I've seen a colossus before. Not one of these new ones either. One of the originals, from the Hegemony."

"You've never mentioned that," Ketandu said.

"It was before I met Hallett. I was a wanderer even then. Well, weren't all of us?" He grinned, and I did too under the mudpack. "I was on the Jalask Plains, dressed like one of the nomads so they would leave me alone. I saw what I thought was a strange, thin rock in the middle of the grass. But it wasn't a rock: it was a colossus, rusted and dead, alone where it had run out of power some time beyond even the memory of Jalask songs. I camped for days in the shadows under its legs, because I knew no one would pester me there. The Sorrow of the thing would drive everyone off."

I searched my memories of the table-map. "That must have been very close to Vatrusla. Have you been in its cities?"

"A few times. Durvill, mostly. Once in Bljana."

"Do you know about Belische, the city that was destroyed?"

Quarl stirred in his corner. Eiichi answered: "I know of it. But I can't say if it's real. There are many ruins at the edges of Vatrusla from the wars. Dangerous places. Some Shaper machines and creatures they twisted still lurk there. One of those dead places might be Belishce, if there was such a city."

"Belische was real." The deep, hollow voice came from Quarl's mask, which he had already put over his face to match the robes of his people. "But even the Eldru seldom speak of it. In the histories I worked on, the city is rarely mentioned."

"What happened to it?" I asked.

"I do not know. The Eldru have smudged out the records. Whether my people destroyed the city, or another force did, is known only to the highest of my race."

Hallett leaned her head inside the flap. "We're going to come into view of the spotters on the towers soon. Get into position."

We moved fast. Eiichi shifted to the driving board to take the team reins from Hallett, and I leaped down from the back of the wagon. Locke rode up on his hadro, pulling another mount beside him. I climbed onto the empty saddle.

Locke handed a blackpowder pistol to me. "This little lovely is one of the best in the armory. Don't lose her, young lady. I like her too much. Now, start looking beat up and pathetic."

I couldn't see the Shapers' compound on the road ahead, even though it was a clear night with an almost full moon. The blackness of the Shapers seemed like a living shroud set against us. "Can the spotters see this far in the dark?" I asked.

"They have spyglasses of the Art," Locke said. "Eiichi has wanted to get hold of a few for some time. There's a special Art needed to ground the glass that he can't copy yet."

The ceratops team trundled around a bend. The gate to the encampment was only a few wagon lengths away. Five sentries armed with rifles stood before the closed iron portal inside a circle of light from the overhead glow globes. I knew many unseen sentries were stationed on the palisade and towers flanking the gate. I could feel weapons of the Art aimed toward me, and maybe even a few simple crossbows.

Those of us the guards could see as we moved into reach of the lights had on blue tunics identical to theirs. The outfits came from the store of uniforms the band had seized over the years. Ketandu even supplied everyone with a proper patch of rank. Eiichi had put on a helmet to disguise his skin and eyes, while Locke and Rouss riding on the backs of fine hadros looked like pure Idenite soldiers. Finally there was Rolant, wearing his hunter's outfit and looking only a bit roughened up for the time he was gone.

When our small party was about twenty spans from the gate, a man wearing the insignia of a lieutenant held up his hand and shouted. "Hold! Identify yourselves!"

Rolant spurred his mount forward. "It's me, Burnell, you futch! Are your eyes so dulled that you can't tell your own captain?"

"Rolant! Where have you been? The Artikon and the other masters thought you had fallen into a pit during the search."

Rouss rode his hadro, loyal Kilvot, behind Rolant. He had a blackpowder pistol aimed at Rolant's spine to keep the captain from getting any rebellious ideas. But Rolant played his part perfectly. "I imagine that you've tired yourself out looking for me all day? Or was the escaped girl taking up your time?"

"No, sir. We had orders to—"

"Never mind, the girl is found. I had to get outside help, but I've brought her back."

Rouss pulled at my mount's lead to bring me around the wagon and into the glare of the lights. Locke had wrapped my wrists in twine, but he made a false knot I could slip off whenever I needed to. I thought of what the Koltzer looked like in their worst Sorrow, and tried to copy it in my face using some of Ketandu's coaching. The fear our trick would fail and we'd get punched full of more holes than a fisherman's net helped my act.

The lieutenant Rolant called Burnell snorted when he saw me. "I can't believe you let her get so far. Well, the Artikon won't turn you into an olglim now. But he's furious. This runny-nosed scut even *unmasked* him. If she weren't so valuable for whatever the masters need, I think the Artikon would feed her limbs one at a time to the ravager."

He already did that, I thought with a crimson flush in my cheeks. The red dye hid it.

Lt. Burnell took in the rest of us. "Who are these others? And what's the wagon carrying?"

"Your masters."

The front flap of the canvas opened, and Quarl made the riskiest move so far in our game of Sun-or-Moon. He stepped onto the wooden beam behind Eiichi, and after him came Hallett on the right and Ketandu on the left. The three had on the robes and masks of Shapers the band had looted on their previous adventures. It wasn't a disguise for Quarl, although he wore the gold robe and many-spiked mask of a Hierarkon, a rank far above the humble Scholiast he once was. Hallett and Ketandu wore smooth masks and gray student robes. I had first seen Hallett in this disguise when I watched her from the rafters of my childhood home in Tyrn.

"I am a Hierarkon of Black Spires on mission in Gaspuh," Quarl said in as loud a voice as the Shapers allowed themselves to use. He spoke in Idenite and then repeated it in the guttural racial tongue of the Eldru.

The bluff worked. The gate guards trembled and bowed, and the tower lights dimmed in respect. As Quarl had explained to me, Hierarkons ruled and administered the Eldru cities, while the

Artikons concerned themselves with machinery and the quest into the Sorrow. Both ranks were equally feared and obeyed.

"What brings a Hierarkon to our camp?" Lt. Burnell asked.

"That is not your concern." Quarl sounded less imperious than the Artikon, the edge gone from years of shunning the cruelties of his people. The sentries didn't notice. "We encountered your captain on the road, and provided our knowledge and Art to help him track down this pitiful fugitive."

I hunched over to look more pitiful, but Lt. Burnell and the others blocking the gate weren't looking my direction. "Our masters did not mention there was a mission in Gaspuh," Burnell said.

"For what reason would they tell you? It is not your affair. Do the Artikons of your Enhancing Grounds wish to have their prisoner back or not?"

Burnell was trapped in a confusion between masters, and it took Rolant to kick him into action: "Just open the Sorrow-bitten gate, Burnell! I'm getting cold." I noticed Hallett's composure shiver. Rolant losing his temper might unbalance our delicate act.

Lt. Burnell backed up and called to the wardens on the other side of the gate. Chains clanked, and the steel doors to the compound groaned open. The guards backed away to let our procession pass inside.

I had seen the grounds of the encampment squirming at night before, but this was the first time I had walked through the proper way of the front door. Glow globes lit up the devil claw pens and showed bright red and green plumage and piercing yellow eyes. The creatures were less restive than when the camp was up in alarm, but the men walking around us as we rattled inside were obviously agitated since the events of that morning. I looked toward the weak part of the circuit where I had escaped. A freshly piled stone cairn now blocked the culvert. I had suggested one of us try to sneak under the palisade this way, but Hallett and Quarl knew the Shapers would have blockaded it already.

The weird lights from the towers made the Hive look like a bloated swamp tick sucking the blood from the ground. It waited patiently for us as its invited supper guests. A crackle of blue energy from behind lit up the ravager and the wires that linked it to the colossus.

"Lightborn, watch over us," Ketandu whispered from the wagon.

Rouss was also stunned by what he saw. "You described it perfectly, Belde." He looked over to Eiichi on the wagon. The tinkerer had the same look of wonderment. He caught Rouss's glance, nodded, and mouthed the words: "We can do this."

Locke slipped off the back of his hadro and went behind the caravan. Eiichi handed the reins to Ketandu. It was undignified for a Shaper to drive a wagon team, but the soldiers were doing a proper job of avoiding looking at their masters. Eiichi slipped around the back with Locke, and I didn't see them when they moved off again before we reached the circle of glow globes that lit the front of the building. They had their own task, and the rest of us would have to wait to see if they could execute it.

Lt. Burnell walked beside the wagon, uncomfortably close to Rolant and Hallett. Rouss still had his gun aimed at Rolant, but Hallett had gotten nervous. From where I sat, still a pretend prisoner, I saw the outline of Hallett's weapon, what she had called a "burning gun," pushing from inside her robe and also aimed at Rolant. If Rolant tried anything, she couldn't miss.

"Masters, you will need to stop here," Burnell said. Quarl's mask swiveled down to hit the lieutenant with an invisible stare to show that he did not appreciate receiving orders from a human. But nonetheless Quarl waved his hand, Ketandu pulled on the reins, and the ceratops team halted the wagon.

A half-circle of guards spread out around us. But they did not have their weapons raised and ready. The ravager growled, and I looked up to see if anything had happened yet. It was impossible to think that Rouss and Eiichi had gotten up into the towers so fast to work with the devices hooked to the ravager and the colossus. They still required Quarl's help, and at the moment we needed his presence to convince the guards.

"I will take the prisoner now," Rolant said, continuing to play his part. "The two Students will come with us and bring their respects to your master."

Burnell stepped across the path of Rolant's hadro. "My apologies, Captain, but the witch-girl is the business of the Artikon. I will send a messenger and we will wait for him."

Rolant slung himself down from the saddle and approached Burnell. "I am the captain here, or have you forgotten?"

The smaller man nervously touched the barrel of his gun. "Yes, sir. But the Artikon is the Artikon."

"Will you follow *my* orders then, Lieutenant?" Quarl asked.

"Master," he gulped, "pardon me speaking my mind, but we are under the orders of the masters from Thulia, not Black Spires. And I don't know you. I know my own master."

"You are an impertinent human." This came from Ketandu. Her height made her a convincing Shaper, but she had to give her powerful voice a rasp and hide her hands inside the robes so not to reveal their dark color. "The Hierarkon is one of the most respected in Black Spires. You would argue with him?"

My hands itched against the twine. This wasn't going right. I was supposed to walk through the front door of the Hive with Rolant, Ketandu, and Hallett, while Quarl went to join Eiichi and Locke. But the Idenite guards were uneasy. They might have sensed the lack of the Sorrow from two of the supposed Shapers and didn't realize why they felt unsure.

Then it got worse.

A black shape limped into the light from the door of the Hive. Although it moved like it was dying from a slow bleed and seemed barely able to hold up its head, it demanded the attention of everyone within sight.

The Artikon had recovered the mask I had peeled off his Sorrow-eaten face. The cracks from Holzir's club made it hang skewed, which was appropriate on him. His robes rippled with a deeper black, or perhaps I was putting dark thoughts onto them.

I wanted to look to Hallett to see if she had reacted. She must know that this was the same Shaper who commanded her during her years as a spy. The one who ordered her to stand silent as people died under the experiments and guns and blades of their servants. But I didn't dare draw attention to her.

The Artikon gestured Lt. Burnell toward him. He should have summoned Rolant. Suspicions were growing. I moved my fake bindings so I could feel the handle of the pistol hidden under my belt. If a fight broke out before Locke and Eiichi had a chance to start their operation, we would have only a meager chance of getting out alive. I might get a shot at the Artikon, but I didn't like the thought of killing him. I held back once before, and even in this moment when our lives teetered on a precipice, the idea of killing was one I wanted to stay far from.

The Artikon remained in the doorway, and Burnell came back to the wagon. "The Artikon asks to see you alone."

"Very well," Quarl said, and moved to step down from the wagon.

"Not you, Hierarkon. The Artikon wishes to see this Student." He pointed to Hallett.

It was finished. The Artikon knew we were disguised. Quarl tried to bluff his way through it. "The Student cannot speak. She has—injured her throat—and—"

It was a terrible lie, and Quarl was so terrible at stuttering it that it was a relief when Hallett cut him off.

"That's enough. If that slug in a mask wants me to speak to him, I'll speak to him. But only without the foul mark of his sickness touching me." Hallett pulled off her mask and flipped it away like she was flinging out rubbish.

Neither side could move. Hope dropped out of me, and the others as well. We were exposed in the open—impostors. But the Idenite guards looked up at where they had expected to see the shriveled and broken features of one of their masters, and they were stunned to see a beauty in burning red with eyes that spoke of a life beyond the sadness that ground away at them each day.

The moment of amazement broke, and then every gun was aimed at us, fingers on triggers.

"Spies!" Lt. Burnell shouted, a bit late for credit.

"Of course, gnat-brain," Rolant said. He walked toward the guns without fear. "They were holding me prisoner. If you'd listened to me instead of trying to act like a preening pack leader, I could have signaled you earlier."

"You're a traitor twice-cooked, Rolant," Hallett said. But she seemed unconcerned with him. Her eyes were on the Artikon's shadow in the door.

"You think I'd roll over and drool because of your big eyes?" Rolant said to her. "All of you are insane. And now you'll get your reward." Rolant reached over to one of the other guards and pulled the gun from his hands. "Master, for the humiliation I have suffered at their hands, I would like the honor of killing the spies."

The blue tunics parted as the Artikon passed through the guard ranks. The Shaper leader had lost the glide to his steps. Under the robe, his feet swayed unsteadily, and his body quivered with aches shooting through every part of him. This gave me a small victory: the pain of the ravager memory I had poured into the Artikon had scorched his mind, turning his Sorrow heavier. It may have even carved a few years off his life.

"You do not understand the importance of these people," the Artikon said as he walked beside Rolant. "We will not let them die. Not yet. Not until all that is in their heads is wrung from them."

Hallett spat a strung of syllables in the hateful Eldru language. It must have been a taboo insult, because even Quarl recoiled to hear it. But her outburst did not fluster the Artikon. He answered Hallett in cool Idenite. "So, Hallett the Impostor. Now that I hear your voice I know for certain it is you. And this one—" He gestured toward Quarl. "—is the Scholiast who let a human body overcome his wisdom."

Hallett said, "His name is Quarl."

"To hear his name means the moment of his death is at hand. For you know, Impostor, that our race only reveals our birth names at the point of death."

"I—I am not one of you anymore," Quarl struggled to say.

Hallett put her hand on Quarl's shoulder and forced him to sit down. "Don't dignify the futch with arguing." She pointed toward Rolant. "You know you have one of the Sorrowless among you, right now."

"She's lying, master!" Rolant shouted. "Let me kill the scut for this insult."

"If he were Sorrowless, we would have sensed him out long ago," the Artikon said. "It took only the simplest glance to know you were false."

"And yet I fooled you for two years. You only know me now because you knew me before. You sensed nothing in those times I stood beside you as you ordered people murdered."

I couldn't help myself now. The scene before me, like a stage play, seemed only there for me to watch. But it was my play as well. I shouted: "You made her stand there while you killed my parents!"

That was how I forgave Hallett for everything—right at the moment when I thought nothing would matter any more.

The Artikon didn't care at all that I had spoken. "These accusations and arguments are stale to me. Humans are all stale, whether slaves or rebels. But we will still make good use of you." He motioned toward Lt. Burnell. "Bring the Impostor to me first."

Burnell walked forward, his hands trembling on his weapon even as he approached Hallett. She did not bend.

Rolant interrupted. "Master, I know you do not wish me to kill them. But may I ask that you grant me a humble favor? I wish to confront the Impostor for what she made me do."

The Artikon nodded, almost exhausted with the effort. "But if you injure her, you will suffer her fate as well."

"I understand. I swear on the wrath of the Handless God I will not harm her." Rolant walked up behind Burnell. He looked into Hallett's face without a trace of fear. Hallett lowered her head, and her eyes glimmered.

"I will suffer your fate as well, Hallett Sea-Eyes," Rolant said.

Then I realized what was happening. It made sense to me, even before Rolant raised his rifle and fired a shot that tore open Lt. Burnell's chest.

TWENTY-FIVE

Before the body of Burnell hit the ground, Hallett snapped to life. She pulled the great burning gun from beneath her Shaper robes, squeezed the trigger, and hurled a fire blast from the muzzle. The lance of flame hit the front line of guards and spewed across them in an arc. The first man's uniform went up like an oil torch, and the others retreated, firing shots in a panic.

"Everyone, go to ground!" Hallett shouted.

I was already moving. I rolled off the saddle and slipped off my bonds. I landed between the carriage and the hadro, where I hoped nobody would have a clear shot at me.

The double shock of Rolant's betrayal and seeing a wicked weapon of the Art vomiting flames toward them scattered most of the guards. The rest were held down in a momentary lock. If they had managed straight shots, all of us would be dead. But Hallett moved fast, and the heat and fire from her gun spread out and sent the remaining line of enemies scurrying away.

My hadro started to buck without a rider. I rolled under the wagon and wiped the mud from my face with my tunic sleeve so I could see better. I spotted a shape like an oil blot moving against the red light. The Artikon had survived the first blast, as Eiichi's plan required. I looked to see where he had run, but he disappeared into the chaos exploding in front of the doorway into the Hive. Rouss, Rolant, and Ketandu had started to fire their guns, and now some of the guards managed to return fire. Rolant was blasting away more enthusiastically than anyone.

Alarm bells rang from the towers as they had when I had escaped. The rest of the soldiers of the camp would fall on us soon. Hallett's gun couldn't torch everyone. Rolant's distraction had only bought us enough time to fight back and die with our weapons out.

Quarl had also taken refuge under the carriage. "I guess this is where it ends," I said.

"In such a place as this, to die Sorrowless or Sorrowful seems equal. Perhaps I will see you in Aman-Sah, young one."

But his goodbye was premature. An enraged roar suddenly fell from above and paralyzed all of the compound. Even Hallett stopped firing her flame weapon for a moment. Eyes turned toward the sound that had come from the other side of the Hive.

A blue bolt ripped into the sky. Then came the noise of metal links snapping apart. Another roar shivered the ground of the camp. It was nothing like the occasional growls from the ravager as it swayed in captivity. The great saurian was furious—and free.

Quarl swore through his mask: "By the Handless God, they did it." In his shock he had lapsed back to his old religion. "Even without me, they did it. Eiichi's skill with the Art is formidable."

It was a part of the plan, but I didn't mention that a loose and enraged ravager wasn't the most wonderful thing to happen to us so far.

Shouts announcing what everyone already knew—"It's loose! The ravager is loose!"—echoed around the encampment. Over the confused yells, lieutenants tried to rally the soldiers into action against the freed saurian. The remaining Idenites guarding the front of the Hive fled. Some dashed toward the ravager to pump bullets into it, overcoming their Sorrow to follow desperate orders. The rest gave in and ran for the front gate in panic.

I crawled from under the wagon, and Ketandu had her hand out to pull me up. As I stood, the ravager's enormous head rose over the roof of the Hive. The remains of its helmet clung to its skull, but most of it had burned off and was still smoking. Eiichi had explained during our last gathering before we rode out what he planned to do. He called it a "mind-fry," a way of disrupting the control of devil claws by sending a single order into their heads with such force that they went into a frenzy and would listen to no other command. He had never tried it on something as large as a ravager; it required too much power. But the colossus had given him an idea: reverse the orders to the colossus and hurl them straight into the helm of the ravager, using all power from the metal man to drive the signal.

It had worked. The helm cracked and exploded under the force, and the ravager was as crazed as if it were dying of bleeding-mouth fever.

The rest of the plan depended on the Shapers doing what Quarl guessed they would. It was why the Artikon needed to survive to give the commands to stop the mad saurian in the middle of the camp.

I was lost in amazement at the rampaging ravager. It was flinching and snapping at the men I couldn't see who were firing at it from below. I was so enrapt I didn't hear Hallett yelling at me until Ketandu pushed at me from behind.

"Go, Belde! Run!" Hallett's weapon was almost extinguished, but she had burnt a clear path to the door of the Hive. Pistol gripped in my damp palm, I sprinted for the light of the doorway. I almost tripped over a roasted corpse of a guard. As I got back on my feet, I took his sword with me. I had no skill with a blade, but I had another use planned for it.

Shots fired behind me, but none nicked the ground or the walls. The others were taking down the last of soldiers around the front of the Hive to keep my way open. The rest of the camp was in a rush to either fight or flee. The blackpowder guns of the braver of the Shapers' servants boomed in a constant rumble.

As I crossed the threshold, I heard a new alarm shouted outside: "The colossus! It's moving!"

The Artikon had done as Quarl had predicted. He went inside the Hive and sent orders to the metal behemoth. The Art came alive inside its joints, and the colossus would now carry out the command to kill the loosened ravager. The Ruining Grounds were about to turn into an arena for giants, a sight that would push the Sorrowful Shapers, servants, and slaves toward madness. Enough madness that maybe a girl running into the middle of their wasp nest wouldn't get anyone's attention.

I moved through the Hive's passageways, picturing Rint sprinting along them and backtracking him. But as I turned down a familiar corridor, the Hive shook and the walls rattled as if ready to tear apart. Outside, metal screeched against metal. The colossus had made its first blow against the ravager, and the saurian must have struck back and hurled the colossus into the side of the building. I was now less worried that someone might find me running through the Hive's corridors and more worried that the "distraction" outside would crumple the Hive onto my head.

I aimed my gun low to fire at the knees of anything that tried to stop me. But I only saw olglim, and without any orders to follow they were witless shells terrified of the noise outside. Any guards who still had their minds in one piece must have fled out other exits to join the fight or run for the gate. The Shapers would be shivering inside their hovels, their Sorrow and superiority telling them to stay in place.

The walls shuddered again. The ravager's battle roar sounded as if it were right over me. A second later, I found out that it was. A taloned foot that could have flattened me into Sorrowless paste smashed through the roof. I dodged down another hallway as the patchwork walls collapsed behind me.

I found my way around from another direction, and in front of me was the door with the familiar red circle on it. It hung from a single hinge.

I should have been running for it to grab Holzir. But I stopped for a moment, and made my ears dampen out the chaos until I was in a bubble of quiet. A hand reached into my head and pulled out a song. My voice, no singer's but the best I had, rang out:

> *The Sorrowless are mightier than you!*
> *The Sorrowless are mightier than life!*

It was Holzir's changes to a sad song, his fight of hope against the hopeless tale of Belische. Maybe he would hear the words beyond that door.

I pushed inside, gun ready. There was plenty of light inside. Too much. The glow globes had shattered from the blows against the Hive, and sparks had set fires in the wooden pens and beddings of hay. Shapers were inside the room, Chirurgeons with four-pronged masks and brown robes. They were trying to quench the blazes exploding from the corners of the room. Olglim were screaming as they burned, fists pounding uselessly against the walls as they tried to escape without any orders from their masters to guide them.

I only cared about the man strapped to a stone table in the center of the room. Holzir's open eyes had a dead look. A red slash cut across his forehead. I had come too late. The Shapers' scalpels had already silenced him.

I wanted to start firing my pistol at the Chirurgeons stumbling around the inferno, blasting metal through each of their awful masks. If I couldn't have Holzir back, at least I'd have the burn of vengeance.

"Belde—"

Holzir lifted his head from the slab. The glaze was gone from his eyes. It was only a reflection from the fire. "I thought I heard you singing."

I ran to him. A Shaper stumbled into my way, getting enough wits to wonder who this stranger was. I shouldered her out of my path, and she fell back among the burning debris.

"Holzir—are you still you?"

"I'm all here. They wouldn't work on me until they could force you to watch. It's all about you, right? Well, this time I'm glad it is."

I hugged him where he lay. In that embrace I could forget about the fire and the sounds of giants battling outside. But Holzir couldn't. "Did you bring the end of the world with you, Belde the Sorrowless?"

"No, only the end of this horrible place, Holzir the Brave," I said.

"If Belische is falling, isn't it time we left?"

I now saw the slash on his forehead wasn't from a Chirurgeon's scalpel, but a crude cut from a fight. A legacy from his stand against Dyzlin. One day, he would tell me the whole tale and brag all he wanted. He could craft a pompous song from it and I'd let myself believe every rhyme was true.

The edges of the Hive were collapsing around us. A clang of bronze rocked the room, and the beams of the ceiling shook and bent. Holzir's restraints were simple leather belts I was able to unlatch and loosen in moments. I grabbed under his armpits and pulled him off the slab. "Can you walk?" I asked.

"Maybe. Can Rint find a way out?"

"Rint stayed behind for this one. I have new friends helping."

"The ones tearing the place apart?"

"You'll like them. Now shut up, grass-chewer, and get walking."

Before he could move, the ceiling ripped open. I looked up to see a metal giant gripping the jaws of a ravager. I dragged Holzir as fast as I could toward the door, but a beam fell across the back of his body. He was so weak that his shout of pain was almost a sigh.

I threw aside the pistol—fighting hardly mattered now—and used both hands to pull him from under the beam. The strength in my body was something I never thought I had. Even so, I wouldn't have gotten Holzir clear if the beam wasn't made from a light metal.

Holzir's legs weren't underneath him, but he was conscious. "I can't make it," he muttered.

The Sorrowlessness had given me the rush to make this final dash. But Holzir needed more. I grabbed his right hand and pressed the handle of the sword I had snatched from the dead guard into them. His fingers felt it and wrapped around it. "Holzir the Brave," I said. "You will cut a path to safety for the rescued maiden, won't you?"

He couldn't fight. If he could stand on his own, it would be a miracle from his Sky Lords. The weapon might give him confidence, the way it could give a Koltzer warrior a suicidal Sorrow. But the sword dropped out from his fingers. The ceiling moaned above, ready to crush us.

Holzir needed something else to push him on. I grabbed the only idea I had left. I started my poor, scratchy singing again, remembering those words he once sung in a tunnel beneath the mountains:

Sorrowful and Sorrowless
Fear neither Moon nor Sun,
Side by side, we flip the stones...

He finished:

...Until both can claim we've won.

His feet pushed beneath him and started to rise. That let me hurl us through the door and into the hallway before the room smashed down on us. But Holzir started to limp again, and I had no more songs I could use.

"Holzir, your song of the sea. The one you told me about in the marshes. Now is the time. I want to hear the Song of the Aman-Sah Sea."

Even before he opened his mouth and let the melody of the song flow out, his strength began to return.

At first I thought the waves a dream,
The clean winds and white foam a lie,
The sails that fluttered,
The mosas that leaped,
Were nothing but tricks in my eye.
Yet so lovely was Aman-Sah,
That sea of Iden's golden shore,
That if I were drowned in sleep,
Still I would cry, "Now I can die..."

"That's lovely Holzir. Keep singing." An outside breeze blew through my hair, and that gave me an idea where to move. Holzir pushed with his feet to move us along, and the two of us,

Sorrowful and Sorrowless, groped down a dying hall to the music of a sea poem:

> *But if these are a mere boy's dreams,*
> *These waves as blue as summer skies,*
> *Then each bright vision sailed from you,*
> *From the sea-blue shine of your eyes.*

The direction I picked put us right into a fiery barrier. Wind gusting from a hole torn in the ceiling—the perfect size for the colossus's fist—had tricked me that it was a way out. My eyes flashed around, frantic for another path. Nothing. The flames were rolling toward us.

I held tight to Holzir. At least he could finish his song before the fire took us.

> *The sea, the eternal*
> *Stealer of the Sorrow!*
> *Yet not such a fair thief,*
> *Not such a lovely thief,*
> *As you, my—*

"Belde!"

The sudden voice, no part of a poem, tore me away from Holzir's singing.

"Belde, over here!"

I followed the sound to a hole in one of the walls. The edges were dripping from the heat blast that had melted it open. Beyond was a woman in a blue tabard. Hallett had tossed away her Shaper robes. She waved to me through the opening in the wall. "There's a way out this direction, come on!"

I pushed through the smoke toward Hallett, my eyes stinging and sweat dripping over my forehead. Holzir's song was done, but his slow breath was like a mountain zephyr against my cheek. It kept me moving ahead of the flames licking at our feet. The bottom of my breeches caught fire, but when I got through the melted hole, Hallett moved fast to smother the flames with the edge of her cloak.

When I was no longer on fire, Hallett tossed aside the drained burning gun. "That's the last for this thing. At least it got me to you. But we're going to have trouble getting out. I didn't imagine the colossus and the ravager would have smashed the Hive this fiercely."

"Is the front door blocked?"

"Sealed. It went down soon after I got in. Even if that gun had any fuel left, it couldn't burn through that."

"What about the others?"

"I don't know. I left them running for the main gate. And we've got to get out fast ourselves." She reached down to string Holzir's arm over her shoulders so we could carry him between us.

Even in the madness, something bothered me. "Hallett, why did you come after me? You should be outside leading the others."

"I thought you might not find your way back out again."

She wasn't telling the truth. The way she had found us was too convenient. She wasn't looking for me; she only happened to stumble on us. But I said nothing. If she could lead us out, it wouldn't matter why she had run into the Hive.

Hallett pulled us down a hallway that still held its shape. It drew us toward the center of the Hive. Perhaps she thought we would be in less danger of the outer walls collapsing, but it was a strange direction to choose.

I was going to ask her what she was planning when Holzir found his voice again. "Who—who are you?" he muttered when he glanced at Hallett on his left side. "One of Belde's new friends?"

"Holzir," I whispered to him, "she's *The Woman*."

"Good for *The Woman*," he mumbled. Then he dropped back unconscious.

Fire burst behind us, and Hallett yanked us through a gap in the corridor made from the buckling. It took us even deeper into the Hive. Hallett stopped and looked around at the intersection we had reached. Smoke hissed through gaps in the ceiling, and down one hallway echoed the noise of the two giants shredding the encampment apart. "This way," I shouted, pointing toward the hallway. Hallett was staring at the roof and not listening to me. Some argument was going on in her head, and the wrong side of it looked ready to win.

Holzir's weight was starting to crush me from having to stand still. "Come on, Hallett, there has to be a way out this direction!"

"No," she said to herself more than me. "It's this way." And she started off down a short hall that looked like it was going into a dead end. I wasn't strong enough to resist her and went along.

It wasn't a dead end: it stopped at a narrow stairway with a waterfall of smoke rolling down it. Hallett pulled us up the stairs, but I fought against her. "What are you doing?" I screamed. But she had a strong grip on Holzir, and if I tugged too hard, we'd all crash down. I relented and let her drag us into the wall of smoke.

I coughed and my head swam from lack of air. Hallett didn't notice the smoke at all. Then the air cleared as we reached the top, and the smoke roiled around near our feet.

The staircase ended inside a conical dome. The top of the Hive. The smoke poured from a wall of machines that reminded me of those in the airship, except these were the ugly devices of the Shapers. The machines had burnt out, and sparks still flew from some as they died. Half of the cone chamber had collapsed, and through the hole I could see the head of the ravager snapping at the relentless colossus fighting it.

Hallett paid no attention to the spectacle outside. She was focused on the heap of toppled machines across the floor. She expected to find something there, and in moments she had her answer.

"Help..." The sound was faint, almost a whimper. I recognized the voice. Hallett did as well.

A figure was caught under the tangle of machinery. He was so still that at first he looked like a piece of the wreckage. The Artikon still had on his mask, but his head tilted at an angle as obscene as the dying Hive.

"Help..."

Hallett took Holzir's arm off her shoulder. "Can you carry him yourself?"

"Yes, but—"

She pointed to the stairs. "Go down and take the hallway you wanted. It should get you out. I'll catch up." She unhooked the blackpowder pistol from her belt.

The Artikon was unable to see what was happening above him. "Help..."

Hallett walked toward him. She raised the pistol.

"What are you doing?" I asked.

"This monster killed your parents. He made me do things I'll never be allowed to forget." She aimed the barrel of the pistol at the Artikon's skewed mask.

"You can't do this, Hallett."

"Go, Belde. I told you, go."

Now I understood. "This is why you came into the Hive. This was why you agreed to do any of this. You wanted to kill him. From the moment I told you who had captured and tortured me, it was in your head to come here and kill him."

"Yes. And thank you for pushing me to do it. For reminding me there are goals other than ending the Sorrow."

My throat was coarse from the smoke, and I was about to tumble down from Holzir's weight, but I shrieked at her: "It won't do any good! I wanted to do it, but I know it won't do any good!"

Hallett was ice. "Good or bad do not matter. This is *justice*. Something the Shapers have never given anyone."

She paused, waiting for me to leave. I didn't.

"I let you rescue your friend," she said. "I gave in on that. I won't give in on this. If you won't leave, fine. Turn your head."

The pitiful thing under the beams stirred. A few sinews still worked to move the head. The spiny-edge mask tilted toward Hallett. The Artikon was no longer a fearsome servitor of the Sorrow. He was just Sorrow.

"Help..." he pleaded again, as if he did not see the mouth of the pistol aimed at him.

"Turn your head, Belde."

I did.

Hallett spoke to the figure under the ruins: "Shaper, do you recognize me?"

"The ... Impostor. Why ... did you ... come back?"

"Shaper, tell me your birth-name."

He said nothing.

"You know what this moment is, Shaper. The Sorrow demands that you tell me your birth-name."

The voice that spoke now came strong through the chambers of the mask. They were the clearest words the person behind it had ever said:

"My name is ... Valmeyr."

"I free you from the Sorrow, Valmeyr."

The shot exploded through the peak of the Hive. A light redder than fire lit the wall I was facing, Hallett's shadow blazed across it. The light subsided, but the woman's shadow lingered in my eyes.

Hallett turned me around and grabbed Holzir's loose arm. A splotch of blood from her face smeared onto his hand.

"You should have gone ahead," she said.

"I needed to know."

She hooked the gun back on her belt. "You have much to learn yet, Belde."

For the first time in my life, I envied those with the Sorrow. Our band struggled against death, fought it to the end. The Shaper—Valmeyr—had surrendered his life easily at the end, with only his name. To slip into the dark without a fight ... maybe that was Aman-Sah for the Sorrowful.

And for the Sorrowless ... was there a "burning madness"? What I had felt before, and had just seen in Hallett—

But no, that couldn't be possible. No, we weren't the sick ones.

TWENTY-SIX

The Ruining Grounds was now a dueling pit for two wrestlers, one of flesh and one of metal. The torches that lit the arena for the battle were the burning barracks and the remains of towers that had toppled over and ignited the Art generators. But there was no mob of breathless spectators watching the death match. The crowds were either dead or fleeing.

The mass flight Eiichi expected when the colossus awakened was greater than he could have imagined. It wasn't only men, but the animals whose pens were shattered apart that were rushing the gates. Devil claws without commands in their helms were leaping through the flames, snapping at men and each other, but mostly trying to get away from the madness. Hadrosaurs trumpeted as they stampeded away from the middle of the compound where the stamping iron feet of the colossus and clamping jaws of the ravager destroyed everything as they sought to destroy each other.

The three of us burst out of the Hive through a door that opened onto where the ravager and the colossus were grappling.

The duel, once evenly balanced, was now tilting toward the colossus and its tireless body. The ravager looked wearied and dazed, while the blue glow from the joints of the bronze and steel creation still crackled with power. The ravager threw its body at the colossus, and the metal man grabbed the saurian around the neck and shoved it back against the outside circuit wall. A section of the stones collapsed in a landslide, and another tower tilted over and smashed onto a barracks building below. The ravager yanked its feet up and kicked the colossus backwards, but the creation of the Art didn't fall. It rushed back to tear at its warm-blooded foe.

The spectacle of the battle was enough to make even Hallett stop for a moment and watch. But when the colossus hurled the ravager back toward the middle of the camp, we both realized we should be moving as fast as possible away from them.

"Hold onto him," Hallett said, and laid both of Holzir's arms around my neck. It should have made me crumple to carry the extra weight, but my muscles had stopped caring about fatigue.

A hadrosaur with an empty saddle on its back ran past. Hallett grabbed the reins and whistled at it to stop. The saddle wasn't entirely empty: the stirrup still had a boot in it, and a half-gnawed soldier was attached to the boot. Hallett pushed the boot out, and when she heard my warning shout, she raised her pistol and fired three shots through a devil claw lunging toward her. The devil claw had been eating the soldier and wanted to finish its meal.

"Even in the world's ending, there are still gluttons," Hallett said as she hoisted Holzir and then me onto the saddle. We pressed the unconscious man between us. Hallett snapped the harness to urge the hadrosaur into a gallop. She didn't need to guide it toward the gateway. It knew to follow the stampede.

As we rode through the front gates, leaping over bodies of men and devil claws and losing ourselves in the mad current of refugees, I turned around to watch the last act of the duel. The colossus had wrapped both its arms around the ravager's neck. The ravager wobbled with exhaustion. Blood poured down from wounds across its neck and torso. One of its tiny front arms was ripped off. The colossus used all the power in its metal body to flip the ravager onto its back. It slammed the saurian into the center of the Hive, bringing down the last of the building's teetering remains.

The generators of the Hive exploded into columns of fire. The colossus ignored the explosions and stepped into the flames. The heat made its body glow white and changed it into a demon from a bonfire story. The ravager twitched at its feet. The saurian was scorched black and probably dead already, but the colossus had orders it must follow to the end. It seized the ravager's jaws and twisted until the head faced the opposite direction. Even over the howling fires, I heard the *snap* of bones and muscles.

I lost sight of the colossus when Hallett coaxed the hadrosaur off the main road and out of the stampede of men and beasts, tormentors and tormented, fleeing the death of their tiny world. The hadro took us down a gravel chute that wound through a maze of boulders.

Holzir's body rolled back against mine as Hallett pushed the hadro up a short hill that would take us to the gulch where the wagon was hidden. I could feel Holzir breathing, but his eyes were closed. I was thankful for that. He was falling fast into the blackest broth of the Sorrow, and watching the last of the fight might have shoved him so deep into it that he'd never return to the surface. Maybe the strength he had shown would let him come back once we were away from the compound.

I looked back toward the crimson sky. For a moment, as we moved past a crack between boulders, I saw the colossus again. It stood unmoving in the fires. Flames spread across its metal skin.

Limbs sagged and dripped like meat coming off an animal roasted on a spit. The colossus' task was done, and now it would stay until it melted into a pile of slag, a grave marker for the Shapers' vile fortress.

KETANDU MET US FIRST, riding the wagon beside us on the path. I passed Holzir into the wagon's back so he could lie flat. The rest of the band was waiting for us in a narrow dell. Dead devil claws and a few Idenite corpses surrounded them, and Rouss, Locke, and Rolant all had burn marks and slashes over their skin—but everyone was alive and able to ride.

"All accounted for?" Locke said with a laugh as we rode up. The whole venture might have been a drunken tavern brawl to him. His ruffian humor lifted my spirits, even as the thought of Holzir lying injured in the wagon tried to pull them down.

"We took care of the worst of the leftovers," Rouss said to Hallett and pointed to the bodies of soldiers on the ground. "But we shouldn't trust to staying safe for too long. The loose devil claws will get hungry soon enough and stop panicking."

I imagined that a new "rebel tribe," like the bleached-white Marsh Phantoms, would sprout in the trenches of the quarry. The place where the Ruining Grounds had stood would become a ghost land of fright-tales for years to come.

Rouss wasn't finished talking to Hallett. "Oh, and dear leader, thank you so much for telling us you had a back-up plan if the Shapers suspected anything." He gave Rolant an angry look. "I almost shot this canker in the face when I thought he had sold us out."

"I don't trust your acting skills, Rouss," Hallett answered. "It was better if all of you believed Rolant had truly turned against us." She got off the hadro and walked between Rolant and Rouss.

"I took Rolant aside to my wagon before the last planning meeting and we arranged his false betrayal to distract the Idenites if things went sour. He also told me where to search inside the Hive for— what I needed to find."

Rouss shot suspicious looks at both of them. He ended on the self-satisfied Rolant. "So, you're already certain you want to ride with us? Ready to embrace the Rising, done with coddling the enemy?"

"Your leader is a convincing woman. She got a Shaper out of Black Spires, didn't she?"

For a second, I thought Rouss would break Rolant's jaw with his fist. He was so furious that he didn't notice the way Hallett and Rolant were looking at each other. I did, however, and hoped it didn't mean trouble down the road. Hallett had interesting tastes, and few men could refuse her.

Rolant tried to get Rouss to back down: "My old masters are dead. The other Shapers will kill me when they find me. Who else am I to join? Besides, you seem to know how to have your fun."

Locke, who had placed himself outside the argument, had a chuckle at that. "We do, we do."

Hallett stopped the potential fight. "Less talk and more riding. Rolant, you'll come north with Rouss, Locke, and me to catch up to the courier riding to Mount Miurn. We'll take the vision orb back from him."

"That'll be a hard ride," Rolant said. "I picked that courier myself. He has a fast mount and he won't rest."

Hallett had the grin of a predator. "After what just happened, do you not believe I can do what I claim? Saddle up and let's ride."

While they picked out the speediest mounts and started preparations, I ran to the open wagon to see if anything had changed. Holzir was asleep and eerily still.

Locke came beside me, pulling out his guns from the wagon. "So is this the grass-chewer we went to all the trouble for?"

"The Koltzer don't like being called grass-chewers," I said. "His name is Holzir."

"Didn't mean anything by it. Looks like he could make a strong warrior. Too bad he has to have the Sorrow."

The riders were ready to go when I returned. Hallett rode past me, seated on lovely, lean Kilvot. She caught the question in my eyes. "No, Belde. You aren't coming with us. I know you feel responsible for the orb, and when we return with it, we will need your help to unlock it. Right now, you have another responsibility."

I glanced at the wagon bed. "I know."

"You are angry with me for what happened in the Hive."

I wish she hadn't mentioned that. The execution of the Artikon was almost buried beneath my concern over Holzir. I nodded, but would not meet Hallett's eyes. It wasn't time for a stare-against-stare duel.

"I hope you can find a way to understand, Belde. I had to do it as much as you had to do this." She pointed at Holzir.

I had forgiven her once, but for another crime. That had vanished now that a new family was around me. But Hallett scared me even as she drew me in. Another time I would have to face it.

Hallett accepted my silence as an answer. "Guard him. Guard yourself."

She turned from me and faced Ketandu on the driver's seat. "Return to fetch the caravans, then go south with the rest to our rendezvous place. We'll return as fast as we can with the orb." There was no question of failure, not the way Hallett spoke.

She gave no more instructions but kicked her hadrosaur into a gallop. Locke and Rouss hollered cries of victory and rode after her. Rolant was silent, but rode even faster. By the time the haze and darkness of the northern road toward the Shapers' dominions swallowed them, Rolant was riding side-by-side with Hallett.

Quarl and Eiichi came up to the wagon, and the four of the band who remained behind stood together. Quarl and Ketandu had their Shaper robes on, and Quarl's mask remained on his face. We must have looked like the oddest collection of people on Ahn-Tarqa.

"Hallett is glad you brought her to this, Belde," Quarl said. "She may not say it, but this ruin wrought upon the enemies of the Sorrowless is a significant victory."

"It was a *beautiful* victory." Eiichi said. "I wish I could've stayed to watch the end of it."

Ketandu shook her head. She was the most cautious of the band, except for Quarl. "I worry. Perhaps the Shapers are getting tired of their 'questing,' this continuous spying and hunting, and wish to conquer again. Earlier we spoke of Belische. What if the Shapers did destroy that city in only moments? They could still have that kind of power. What if what we just did pushes them to move against the southern cities, and make a second Ever-Sorrow of Belische in Iden?"

Quarl said, "It's a war that will come one day, no matter what. And if Hallett returns with the orb, she'll have the greatest weapon against my old race."

"But will she get it back?" I asked. A dash into the unknown north lands where the Shapers still ruled seemed far more dangerous than even the raid we had pulled off.

"I do not know," Quarl said. "Forgive me, the doubt is my Sorrow speaking."

Ketandu whipped the team and started the wagon on the road back to the caravans. "Hallett was right: less talk and more riding. The Sorrow will overwhelm the soldiers who escaped, at least for a few hours, but we should have the wagons gathered and be on our way south on the Featherstone Road to the rendezvous long before then."

"Where is the rendezvous?" I asked.

"The city where we often hide between expeditions. At the northernmost bend of the Glosser River."

Tyrn. I was going home.

TWENTY-SEVEN

The last time I had looked at the city of my birth was through a slit in the canvas over a Koltzer wagon. The short grass of the plains before the walls of Tyrn were now greening in the spring and a few puffs of clouds moved over the sky, but otherwise the sight of the city as we approached it looked no different than five years ago. The sandstone walls with limestone tips, free of any gawking fang-birds. The black-wood steeples of the temples of the Lightborn. The slow wafting of trade ships down the Glosser River. It was as if nothing had changed.

But my parents no longer lived here. I had no home except this caravan of wagons pulled over the grass by a team of ceratopses. I was no longer little Belde, daughter of Lukan and Kryzin, but Belde the Sorrowless, who had seen the Lightborn and come through fire and ravagers' teeth with a band that had the charge to save humanity.

I rode beside Ketandu on the front wagon when she guided the team through the Gate of Foam, the main entrance for overland traders to Tyrn. The gate opened onto a broad avenue beside the churning river. I had lived far from here, but on the hottest summer days my friends and I would get a ride in a wagon carrying sailors to the docks and take dips in the cool water.

What had happened to my friends? Junius and Collett—had they married? I had teased Junius that he was sweet on Collett, and he'd tried to beat me up when I did, but Rint wouldn't let him.

I watched the waves lapping against the wharves and pylons. The river wasn't warm enough yet for children to play in it, but I stared at the shallow surf to see if I might catch sight of my friends and me splashing and laughing at a time before "Sorrowful" and "Sorrowless" meant anything to us. The city was so unchanged that I could almost physically summon young Belde from the breakers and stones.

But *I* had changed so much that it felt as if I were riding through a sculptor's toy of Tyrn populated with painted figurines that moved by some machinery hidden under its cabinet. The city looked similar, but it was not real. Any young Belde of Tyrn would not be real either.

I recognized no one; no one recognized me. People only gave us brief glances as we passed. Ketandu got attention for her dark skin, but Bavtuus often worked crews on galleys that sailed along the Glosser, so she drew no deeper suspicion. She explained that in places in Iden she was even a useful diversion. "When you look different, no one notices that you feel different as well. Flesh is an excellent disguise for the Sorrowless. It's only bad in Vatrusla, where some of their cities still enslave my race."

As we turned from the market square and moved into the quieter quarter of the city, I slipped from the front seat and down onto the paving stones. Ketandu was giving the ceratops team a rest with a slow amble, so I was able to keep pace as I walked to the second caravan and leaped onto its backboard.

We had laid Holzir on a comfortable bed in the spacious and clean wagon. This was where Hallett stayed. Quarl called it her "fortress," although he warned me never to let her know that name. She slept most nights here, and Rouss usually stayed with her as well. There were two wide beds, and one looked as if it did not get much use. Holzir was stretched out on this bed, and I had spent most of the week's journey south sitting on Hallett's bed, keeping a vigil over him. Sometimes his body shifted with the jostling of the wheels over the paving, giving me the unfair illusion he was waking up.

Rint had decided that watching over Holzir was his responsibility too, since I seemed out of danger for the time and not needing his protection. When I came in, the green beak-nose had his head tucked under his back leg and was sleeping in the blankets between the mounds of Holzir's feet.

I took my turn on the other bed, sitting on its edge and watching the two sleepers sway with the rocking of the caravan. The smoke and the scents of the city drifted inside. Soon it took on the unmistakable feel of night. I drew it into my lungs, drawing in childhood as well. For twelve years I had lived happily here. Like any child of Ahn-Tarqa, the Sorrow didn't touch my life for many years except in the ways of the adults around me. But as childhood ended and youth woke, the Sorrow crept into the children. The Shapers had forced me to leave the city, but how long would I have lasted here when I continued on without the hopelessness bred into the blood and bones of all those around me?

At some point I fell asleep, because suddenly my eyes opened and I felt that the caravan had stopped moving. I listened for the noises of Tyrn, but everything was muffled. Eiichi and Ketandu had told me about the sanctuary of an old granary where they could fit all the wagons. We must have reached it.

Eiichi was in the caravan with me, looking over Holzir. During the crossing of the Gloss Grass Plains, he had spent many hours in the iron wagon, working with his tools and writing down what he had learned from the experiment with the colossus and the ravager, as well as his guesses about the meaning of what I had seen in the vision orb. The other hours he sat with me, helping to watch Holzir. Sometimes he entertained me and kept my mind off Holzir's illness with the story of what had happened out of my sight in the Ruining Grounds.

Locke had silently stabbed the soldiers posted at the foot of the tower between the ravager and colossus, and he and Eiichi had climbed to the top, where Locke disposed of another man. The board where the Shapers had connected the wires to the ravager and the colossus were simpler than Eiichi expected, making the disruption a quick matter. Trickier was getting down from the tower before the thirty-foot ravager battered it over.

"It was magic to see the colossus move for the first time, Belde," Eiichi told me. "I've dreamed of how to build one. I'm sure if I had the factories of the Shapers and their foundries and laborers I could fashion a colossus just as magnificent yet more lovely. But still, when their colossus lived, and flew at the ravager, it was—it was the only time I think I *loved* the Shapers."

When he said that I dropped my gaze. He decided I had heard enough of his story.

I now rubbed the sleep out of my eyes and looked at Eiichi. He was crouched over Holzir and feeling the pulse along his neck.

"Is he any better?" I asked.

Eiichi shook his head. "Alive. But no change."

I had the bravery to ask it now that we were in Tyrn. "Do you think it's—it's the Sorrow Sleep?" Holzir's stillness, the slow rise and fall of his chest, looked too much like his mother's illness.

"My medical skill isn't the equal of my skill with the Art," Eiichi answered. "He's gone through a terrible shock, pushed into a den of the Sorrow that would kill most herders or farmers. But I don't know what exactly is wrong. There are some apothecaries in the city who might help us." It didn't sound as if he thought pursuing them was worthwhile.

A piece of parchment lay beside Eiichi with some of his designs sketched on it. I suddenly reached out and plucked up the paper, and then took up the charcoal pen he used to write. "What are you doing?" he asked, although he didn't try to stop me from using his beloved writing tools.

"Something jostling around in my head. I never told anyone else about it because it seemed so trivial. It's a name. I saw it in the airship, and in the vision orb. It looks like the word 'Ahn-Tarqa.' Almost but not quite." I scribbled down the letters I had seared into my mind. I didn't know how they would help now, but I had to have them out and spread before my eyes again.

I turned around the paper scrap and showed it to Eiichi. "Strange," he said. "It seems close—perhaps the same word. Or perhaps something else. The place the Lightborn came from originally."

I looked down at the word ANTARCTIQUE and wondered what mysteries it concealed.

EIICHI LEFT SOON AFTER, but I decided I couldn't stay and hide with the sleeping Holzir forever. I opened the caravan door and went out to see if anything else of Tyrn remained for me aside from memories.

The granary was a rectangular vault of green stones quarried from the riverbank. It was large enough to fit the caravan wagons, as well as the pens for the ceratopses and hadros. Three tall arches looked onto the street, but wooden doors closed them up so the city knew nothing about the strange people laired inside.

From a loft over the wagons came a sizzle of blue and green light. Eiichi had set up a workbench where he had more space to practice blacksmithing with the Art. A low hum from a corner told me that a small version of the Cruncher was sending power up to him.

One of the arched doors was open a crack, wide enough for me to see a few lights from the city's windows and the silhouette of Quarl standing in the archway. He had again put on his plain brown cloak and its disguising hood. He heard me walk up behind him, but did not turn around.

My eyes strained through the night. I could see a few details about the street in front of the granary. The old storage building was in the Tumbledowns, a rough part of Tyrn filled with storehouses like this one. But a few vendors set up stalls, especially those whose wares couldn't compete in the busier marketplaces.

After we stood beside each other in silence for a minute, Quarl spoke. "Is Holzir the same?"

"Yes."

"I am sorry. Maybe all I did to help convince Hallett was a mistake."

"That's your Sorrow talking. If you apologize again, I'll kick your stupid Shaper knees."

His shoulders rose. "How can I help it? I still have the Sorrow. And I am worried that Hallett is far from us and might never return."

"Do you still love her?"

Quarl backed away from the door, as if afraid someone on the street might manage to pierce every layer of darkness and see what he was. "I do. That I will never have her again, that she never desires me in that way, is the best defense I have against the Sorrow. It is a true sadness to bury the false one."

I remembered the Artikon, the man named Valmeyr, dying

calmly with only his name to go with him into the dark. "Some-times I wish I had false hope," I said.

"No, you do not. I would rather have real hope. And so would you."

There was something else I wanted to ask, a pestering problem even Holzir's sickness couldn't hold down. "Quarl, do you think something can remain hidden deep inside a race, unseen for thou-sands of years, and then one day reappear without warning?"

"It happens. My people have studied the rodents of Ahn-Tarqa, the ways they have started to develop—"

"I mean with people. What if the Lightborn tried to cure the Sorrow once, but they failed? And the sickness from the false cure lay hidden for ten thousand years, and now it's coming out again in the Sorrowless?"

Quarl turned his hood toward me. "You are thinking of what you heard in the airship."

"And something I saw in Hallett. This 'Rising'—if the cure was a failure, then maybe Sorrowlessness is really a false recovery."

Quarl's voice was sharp, a strange sound from him. "You have hope, Belde. Keep it. Whatever you think may be buried in you, you will defeat it. The Sorrowful have so much farther to go." He looked back toward the caravan. "And some of them have only a short way."

I didn't think about what he meant, because I then noticed a peddler at the corner of the street. Two tin braziers glowed in front of a folding table piled with trinkets that the stout man was sweeping into a sack. Specks of gold paint in a familiar pattern twinkled among the cheap baubles.

I tugged at Quarl's sleeve. "Do we have any silver coins in the caravan?"

"Of course. In Hallett's fortress, in a trapdoor under her bed. Why?"

"Like you said: hope. A small one, but hope."

I ran back to the second wagon. Rint was awake and nipped at me as I came inside. He was worried about my vanishing from the wagon during the watch at Holzir's side. I quieted him with a fresh fern bud that Ketandu had purchased from a grocer's stand when we trundled through the city.

I searched under Hallett's bed and found the trapdoor. I pulled it open and dragged out the first sack I touched. I drew a few tarnished silver coins from the sack and shook them in my palm. Plenty.

I looked at the clothing spilling out of trunks at the rear of the caravan. Some were disguises collected from the corners of Ahn-Tarqa: silk of Vatrusla, turbans and sandals from Najael. One stack had folded dresses, neatly piled in anticipation of something other than spying and adventure. It was Hallett's own clothes. I still had on a dreary gray Koltzer tunic and breeches, and decided Hallett wouldn't mind if I borrowed one of her outfits. I also found a comb of bone on the floor near the scattered clothing. I now had enough to make the change I wanted.

I started to strip off my tunic and pants. Maybe Holzir's eyes would open to peek, I thought with my first smile of the day.

Minutes later, I swept past Quarl, my dark blonde hair straightened out, and wearing the honeydew dress of an Idenite woman. It wasn't until I walked onto the street under the haze of a few torches that I remembered I *was* an Idenite woman. That little girl had vanished long ago. I was someone new. Seventeen summers old, the age for marriage—and almost given into one— and a child no longer.

I flattened down the fabric and walked across the street, feeling the float of warm night air around my legs in the unfamiliar clothing. I didn't feel elegant, especially since I had to pin up the edges of the dress so I didn't trip on them. I had never worn a dress before, and the feeling was as if I had changed my own skin and now declared my Sorrowlessness on the outside as well as inside.

What I wanted was still on the folding table, but the peddler was about to put it away. His hand stopped when my shadow fell over his stand.

"Sorry, I'm closed for today," he said. "You wouldn't want what I have, only bitty trifles for the lifters and grunts. Nothing a lady would want."

The dress must have looked more refined than I thought. The peddler seemed anxious that a woman in finery had walked up to him in the dark in a shady part of the city, and he wondered if there wasn't some trickery involved.

I pointed to the last item on the table. "I only want that."

"That's for children. You look young to have children, if you don't mind my saying so, lady."

A merchant who didn't want a sale must be scared. Maybe my Sorrowlessness would always make this kind of trouble. But the gleam of silver solved the problem. When he saw the coins in my palm, he flicked his tongue across his lips.

"I haven't named a price—"

"This is the price." I dropped all the coins into his palm, and then took the board.

I walked back under the granary arch. Quarl closed the wooden doors behind me and lowered the bar to secure it. He walked in my train as I returned to the wagon where Holzir lay. Quarl stayed outside as I went in. He felt his Sorrow was not welcome.

Rint jolted up as I entered. It wasn't anything to do with Holzir, however, who was still unmoving. Rint was excited to see a new outfit on me, which looked even easier to climb up than my old tunic and breeches. He immediately ran across the floor and started to play with the fall of the fabric over the wooden slats.

I kneeled beside the cot and opened up the painted birch case. The silver and gold-flecked stones fell onto the floor. I plucked up one of the pieces. The sun and moon painted on each side were done with less artistry than the set Holzir's mother had made, but the designs were identical: frowning moon, beaming sun.

I laid the board flat and put the game pieces around it. I positioned the first four stones on the board. Sun would move first, and I always played that part. But this time I picked up the next stone for play, and reached over to Holzir's hand. Gently, I rolled open his warm fingers and wrapped the stone in his palm.

Eyelids fluttered. Fingers moved, stroking the painted surface of the stone. One eyelid rose like a shuttered window opening to the morning. I saw myself in the pupil, and it saw me.

"Your move first, Holzir. Turn over the moon."

The other eye opened.

"Belde—"

"It's your turn, Holzir," I said so my breath crossed his cheek. "You turn over the moon. You push back the Sorrow—however you need to. I'm giving you the first move."

He kissed me.

ABOUT THE AUTHOR

Ryan Harvey is a science fiction and fantasy author who lives in Costa Mesa, California. He's a recipient of the Writers of the Future Award, and his fiction has appeared in *Every Day Fiction*, *Stupefying Stories*, *Beyond Centauri*, *Plasma Frequency*, *Tales From the Magician's Skull*, and the anthology *Candle in the Attic Window*. He has written extensive nonfiction articles for *Black Gate* and other magazines.

Ryan graduated from Carleton College in Minnesota with a BA in history. He worked as a Hollywood story editor, speed-reading instructor, and copyeditor before becoming a professional writer. He writes marketing content by day, and during the nights and weekends creates works of science fiction, fantasy, and horror. His ongoing science-fantasy series on the continent of Ahn-Tarqa explores the many different nooks of genre in a gumbo of dinosaurs, weird tech, and fantastic adventure.

His influences include Leigh Brackett, Clark Ashton Smith, Robert E. Howard, Cornell Woolrich, Raymond Chandler, J. R. R. Tolkien, Ian Fleming, Algernon Blackwood, and Michael Moorcock. He is a leading authority on the works of Edgar Rice Burroughs, and loves movies, history, and numerous oddball topics. In the world outside his apartment fortress, he's an improv comedian who performs as part of the Improv Collective in Costa Mesa. He lives with a sinister black cat, and his spirit animal is Godzilla.

Made in the USA
Las Vegas, NV
03 November 2020